A Murder of Hate

ALSO BY YASIN KAKANDE

The Ambitious Struggle
(2013)

Slave States
(2015)

Why We Are Coming
(2020)

Green Card Brides
(2024)

A Murder of Hate

The General's Project Series 1 of 3

Yasin Kakande

BLACK WRITERS INK LLC
Boxborough, MA, 2024

BLACK WRITERS INK LLC
318 Codman Hill Road
Boxborough, Massachusetts

www.blackwritersink.com

First Edition 2024

This book is a work of fiction. Names, characters, places, and incidents are either products of the author's imagination or used fictitiously. Any resemblance to actual events or persons, living or dead, is purely coincidental.

Book design: Pablo Capra

ISBN
Paperback 979-8-9909844-2-4
Ebook 979-8-9909844-3-1

Printed in the United States of America

Contents

Dedication

To all Africans and their enduring struggle to break free from imperialism and its puppet leaders.

Warning

A Murder of Hate contains depictions of murder, sexual violence, kidnappings, torture, racism, and graphic language. Reader discretion is advised.

Prologue

THE sight of a red late-model RAV 4 parked on School Street next to a cornfield in the early morning hours captured Samuel Mugyenyi's attention. For the last seven years, his morning commute to the nursing home where he worked curved around the cornfield and connected to State Route 2. In the peak of the growing season, summer shadows on the road would be darker and denser in the pre-dawn hours, but it was in the middle of February, where the fields stood stark in their nakedness, freshly blanketed in a slick layer of snow. The red RAV 4 would have caught anyone's attention.

Samuel quickly considered explanations for the abandoned vehicle. Had the owner run out of gas or were they stranded by a flat tire? Where was the driver now? Had they walked for help or called for assistance? Samuel knew that if he'd been stranded in a quiet, isolated spot, he'd have called Triple A. The morning commute traffic was picking up quickly as Samuel waited to merge onto the highway, but then he pulled a fast U-turn and returned to the spot of the abandoned RAV 4.

Traffic was sparse on School Street, so Samuel had enough time to get out and inspect the SUV. It was such an odd, inexplicable setting to leave a car in such excellent condition. First, he checked the tires, partly buried in the pristine snow. Then the windows, completely frosted, the contours of the vehicle obscured. Only then did he wonder if someone was sleeping in the thing. Perhaps they had dozed off while waiting for roadside assistance. Or perhaps it was just a horny young couple looking for the thrill of public sex. Young people literally wanted to have sex everywhere—the bedroom, bathroom, kitchen, dining room, sofa, on the beach, in airplanes. The edge of a cornfield wasn't so farfetched, but the engine wasn't running. And there was silence.

It was still dark. He returned to his car and angled it so his high beam lights would illuminate the interior of the SUV. It was too cold to sit in the car with the engine off. Temperatures were hovering in the middle teens before sunrise.

Convinced that no one was inside, Samuel was about to leave when he stopped abruptly. He retrieved a flashlight from the floorboard, returned to the abandoned vehicle, and began scratching at the frost, carving out a small peephole into the car's interior. He squinted to get a better view, and his heart skipped a beat as he saw the outline of a figure. His breath hitched in his throat, and fear gripped him as he scraped away more frost, revealing the inside.

A woman lay sprawled across the passenger seat, half-naked. A quick scan revealed no other bodies inside. He rapped on the window, but the woman remained unresponsive. Samuel hurried back to his car and dialed 911 on his cellphone.

"Hello, I'm reporting a suspicious vehicle parked on the roadside of this cornfield. Yes, but there is no corn, because it's winter, okay? There is a woman inside. Inside the car. She's not responding."

Ashley, the operator, calmly asked him to identify himself.

"I'm Samuel Mugyenyi—I'm a resident on Parker Street, not far from here."

"Okay, Sam, calm down, please. Do you know how to do CPR?"

"I know but the car is locked," Sam said.

"Okay, what do you see?"

He scanned the inside of the car with his flashlight. "A woman half-naked. She's… in the… the passenger seat. She isn't moving."

"Can you give me the address? Any landmarks?"

"This is School Street in Acton, just barely twenty feet away from the town highway. You know, State Route 2. I think she's passed out or… worse. I can't tell. It's practically freezing here, she's—" He sounded almost breathless, as if the shock were about to trigger a panic attack.

"Sir, are you safe to stay out there with the car until we dispatch an ambulance?"

"Yes, ma'am."

Samuel returned to his car and repositioned it again so that his high beams would illuminate the front of the SUV.

A few motorists slowed down as they passed by, glancing through their vehicle windows before continuing onward in their commute. Perhaps no one wanted to be late to work. And it was very cold for anyone to stop for long.

Samuel could see houses in the neighborhood close by. Some had lights on now. The air was still and quiet but whatever birds were around started making noise once the sirens of police cars and ambulances approached.

They had arrived in just under five minutes. One officer stepped out of his vehicle and ordered Sam to put his arms up. Sam, though a Licensed Nursing Practitioner in the US, had earlier served in an army in both Uganda and Congo—dealing with those in command was second-nature to him. He was not carrying firearms. He did not pose a threat. They searched him and an officer escorted him to the police patrol cruiser. The officer explained the protocol that Sam already knew—he would have to give a statement.

"How long will it take?" Sam asked.

"We're not sure yet, but you might want to cancel your plans for the day," the officer replied.

Now he had to call his boss to find a replacement. The officer allowed him to make the call from his cellphone while he sat in the back of the cruiser.

CHAPTER 1

Lisa

ON the morning detectives went to make the arrest, the campus air was tense. The police cruisers screeched to a halt at the entrance of the Union Hall Building. The sirens wailed, announcing arrival. No time for subtlety in a case like this; they had to move fast. It was around eight AM, and the day was already in full swing.

The prime suspect lived in the Essex University dorm, Tremont Street, Downtown Boston. Students moved in and out, chattering with excitement about the day's classes and campus activities. Detectives believed he was the boyfriend of the victim, Sheila, and had gathered enough evidence to bring him in for questioning. Given the nature of the crime—rape and death by strangulation—it was customary to have a female detective present for the victims.

As detectives approached the entrance to the dorm, a stern-faced university police officer blocked their path.

His black uniform was crisply pressed, and he wore a look of overblown authority that came with the job.

"Can I help you?"

The lead detective flashed her badge, hoping it would speed up the process. "Detective Lisa Garcia," she said firmly. "We need access to the dorms immediately."

"We have procedures here, Detective. You can't just waltz in without prior notification."

"Look, Officer," Lisa said, lowering her badge slightly. "We have reason to believe Shawn Wayles, a student here, is connected to a *murder* investigation. We need to bring him in for questioning. Now."

The officer still hesitated, torn between his duty and the hard urgency in her voice. The internal struggle played out on his face.

"Listen, I get it," Lisa went on. "Procedures are important, but we're dealing with something much bigger here. Life and death stakes. If you don't let us in, we might lose our chance to catch the person responsible for a murder. You don't want that on your conscience, do you?"

His expression softened, and he stepped aside, reluctantly granting access. "Please make it quick."

Detectives reached Shawn's dorm room, and Lisa raised her hand to knock, her knuckles hovering just above the door. This was it—the moment that could break any case wide open. She hoped he was in there and that he hadn't fled. Two policemen flanked her, hands on guns.

She knocked loudly, demanded that he open up.

By the time Shawn stumbled to the door and opened it, she was no longer knocking politely. With adrenaline surging, she barged in with guns drawn. Shawn's eyes widened as he found himself face to face with the law.

The living room of the dorm apartment came into view, worn couch, a small TV blasting a hip-hop music video.

"Wha—I ain't done nothing!" Shawn stammered. "Why you all up in my room trying to embarrass me like this?"

Lisa had heard countless stories of police raids gone wrong with innocent people caught up in the chaos. This wasn't that.

"Get down!" she said, gun pointing to the floor. Shawn wisely got down on his knees, hands raised in surrender. He knew better than to make any sudden moves.

Lisa stared into Shawn's eyes, badge in her left hand and gun in her right. "Mr. Wayles," she said. "You are being arrested on charges of rape and murder of Sheila Musinga. You have the right to remain silent. Anything you say today can be used against you in a court of law."

Shawn gaped, his eyes darting around the room as if searching for an escape from this nightmare. The officers swiftly moved in, handcuffing him without resistance. As they led him out of his dorm apartment, barefoot and dressed in sweatpants and a T-shirt, Shawn's fellow students had started to gather in the hallway, drawn by the commotion. They exchanged curious glances as whispers of speculation floated through the air. "You'll be bringing me back soon, and I better get a big apology for this embarrassment," Shawn barked to no one in particular. Lisa nodded, acknowledging but not exactly acquiescing to his demand. "We'll make sure to handle this *as quickly as possible*. And if you're innocent? We'll be sure to say we're sorry."

CHAPTER 2

Shawn

SHAWN sat in the police Cruiser, the world outside the window blurring into passing streets and buildings. His hands were still cuffed, the cold, unyielding metal biting into his wrists. In movies, they always seemed to remove the cuffs once the prisoner was safely in the police car, but here, they had left them on. Did they really think he was that dangerous?

"Can you take these off? I'm not going to run away in a car."

The driver, a stern-looking cop with a mean glare, shot him a withering look. "Do yourself a favor kid and shut the hell up."

As the cruiser rolled on, Shawn couldn't help but take in the world he was leaving behind. He recognized some of the roads they were on, from Boylston Street in Boston to the I-93 Highway and then Alewife Road and State

Route 2.

"Where are you taking me?" he asked. "I needed answers."

The cop sighed in irritation. "You remember the lady who read you your rights when you were arrested? She's the only one with answers to your stupid questions. Now, *please*, shut up and let me do my job."

"I didn't kill her—I didn't kill anyone," Shawn said, sounding desperate.

"My role is to transport you. Stop telling me what you did or didn't do. Understood?"

Shawn fell silent, not daring to utter another word. He couldn't shake the feeling that this cop might resort to violence, even with cameras in the police cruiser. In this crazy moment, anything seemed possible—they were racing down a dark road toward some uncertain destination, and fear was gnawing harder at the edges of his thoughts.

Suddenly, the car stopped, and Shawn was abruptly yanked out by the two stern-faced guards. As soon as his feet hit the ground, the cruiser sped away, leaving behind a whirlwind of dust.

The two officers ushered him into the imposing jail building, flashing their identification cards at every entrance and leading him past layers of security with zero questions asked. They passed through three imposing gates until they finally arrived in a crowded waiting room.

The atmosphere was chaotic, a confusing mixture of fear, frustration, and desperation. He could hear some of the new inmates still pleading innocence to anyone who would listen.

Shawn was about to crack, but just when he thought

he could not feel more vulnerable, another guard took charge, relieving the two officers who had escorted him. This guard led him into a small, sterile room and instructed him to strip down completely. Shawn felt violated as gloved hands roamed over his body, checking for any concealed items or contraband. With that unpleasant ordeal over, the guard tossed Shawn an orange uniform.

"Put it on. Now."

After Shawn got into the scratchy prison attire, the guard turned his attention to Shawn's personal belongings. The guard meticulously examined Shawn's clothes and then proceeded to empty his wallet onto a table. With dispassionate efficiency, the guard counted the cash—a whopping seventy-five dollars. He recorded the amount in a ledger before asking if there were any phone numbers Shawn needed to jot down from his mobile phone before he confiscated it.

Reluctantly, Shawn nodded. The guard watched closely as he quickly saved a single phone number under the name "Babe." He wasn't about to reveal his girlfriend's name to this invasive jerk. Then he scrolled and copied a second number, "Mama," even though he had her number memorized.

With his personal items cataloged and his dignity completely eroded, Shawn was ordered to stand with his back to the cold, sterile wall. The guard quickly snapped an unflattering mugshot.

"Go back to the waiting room," the guard said.

"And do what?"

"Wait for further instructions."

Shawn pressed, "What happens next?"

"The medical team will be here to collect samples and attend to any other orders they have from the forensics. Just go wait and stay put."

Hours passed in the dimly lit waiting area of the jail, each minute an eternity. Shawn watched as fellow inmates, each with their own stories etched into their faces, sat in silent resignation. Some muttered prayers under their breaths, while others exchanged knowing glances that conveyed fear and solidarity. His own thoughts drifted back to the raid that had led him here, to this place of uncertainty and despair. Sheila, murdered. And him, accused. A bewildering web—and now he was ensnared in this nightmare.

Finally, a pair of footsteps echoed down the hallway, breaking the oppressive silence. Two individuals dressed in medical attire entered the room. The man with a clipboard and the woman with a small metal case also carried with them an air of detached professionalism that contrasted starkly with the surroundings.

"Shawn Wayles?" The clipboard-man called out, scanning the room. Shawn raised his hand. The two made their way toward him, their steps deliberate and measured, and led him to a special room to do the tests

The woman stared him down with sharp eyes and introduced herself as Dr. Munro. "We are about to conduct a battery of tests and samples."

"To what end?"

"To establish your physical condition at the time of your arrest. Standard protocol."

Shawn nodded. Then he followed her instructions as she measured his height and weight, checked his vital signs, and examined him for any visible injuries or signs of distress. Her meticulous note taking felt like a strange invasion, as if every inch of his body was being scrutinized for evidence of guilt.

Next came a series of blood samples, urine tests, and swabs from various parts of his body. With every measure, Shawn twisted inside with the irony of the situation. Here he was, intent on proving his innocence, yet every procedure seemed designed to reduce him to evidence of guilt.

The medical team finally completed their job. They left with a curt nod and took their samples and their clinical detachment with them. Shawn was left to return to the waiting area, that much more dehumanized than he previously felt.

About a half-hour later, a stern-faced guard approached Shawn. He signaled for Shawn to follow him. As Shawn rose to his feet, his heart pounded in his chest, and anxiety clenched his stomach. This was it—the beginning of his life behind bars.

The guard led him through a labyrinthine maze of narrow hallways, the institutionalized odor of cleaning products and despair permeating the air. They passed by rows of identical steel doors, each one concealing a slice of someone's life, a story untold.

Finally, they reached a door marked *D-BLOCK*, and the guard unlocked it with a jangling set of keys. Beyond the threshold lay his new home—a cramped, dimly lit cell with two sets of bunk beds, one on either side—barely large enough to accommodate its occupants, let alone offer a shrivel of privacy. The cellmates lounging on their bunks looked up—a burly Latino man with a shaved head and a massive tattoo on his forearm regarded Shawn with a guarded expression. He looked like he had spent more time in jail than out of it.

The second inmate was a Black wiry, older man, his weathered face etched with lines that spoke of a lifetime of hardship.

Nobody introduced themselves. Shawn nodded to each of them, on best behavior. They assessed him with a mixture of curiosity and wariness, and he could sense the unspoken questions in their eyes. *What was he in for? Was he a threat or an ally?*

The Hispanic man broke the silence, "Name's Diego. Welcome."

Shawn nodded. "Shawn."

Diego said, "What brings you to this lovely establishment, Shawn?"

"I'm facing some charges… but I swear I didn't do what they're accusing me of."

The old Black man, who had been sitting silently, nodded in understanding. "I'm Ethan," he said, his voice soft and resigned, as if he'd long ago accepted his fate, "and we've all got our stories, kid. Doesn't matter much in here."

The guard locked the cell door behind him and left without a word. The door's metallic clang echoed in Shawn's ears.

CHAPTER 3

Bus

BUS got the call in the early morning—Chief Stephen Flores, summoning him to Acton to assist the state police with what he described as "a high-profile murder case." It was a surprise, considering he'd been on suspension for eight months after the allegations—falsifying overtime. But Chief Flores somehow had received a glowing recommendation from top CIA bosses, highlighting Bus's exceptional skills and valuable connections to Uganda, home country of the victim, Sheila Musinga.

"Bus, a police patrol will come get you in Quincy—precisely ten AM. Be in uniform."

"Chief, there's just one small problem."

"What's that?"

"I'm not in Quincy."

"Well then where the hell are you?"

"Downtown Boston."

"What for?"

"Well..." Bus hesitated. "I'm hauling around Uber clients." Since his suspension from the force, Bus had to do whatever he could to make ends meet. "But don't sweat it, I'll head home and be ready in about thirty minutes or so."

On his drive back, Bus took I-93, a road notorious for traffic, especially during rush hour. To his surprise, the mid-morning commute was unusually light, and he made it in just twenty minutes. He changed the radio station from Kiss FM 107.8 to 89.7 GBH, the news. The murder was already the main topic of discussion—the victim was the niece of the president of Uganda, Joel Katila Muaji himself. Everything clicked into place. His CIA contacts had clearly passed on his details to the Chief.

Bus's mother was a Black woman from Uganda. She met his father in Boston while working for his family as a Home Health Aide. They named him Basudde after the late Basudde Herman Semakula, the father of Ugandan music. It was a name that tied Bus to his roots, a name that carried the weight of two worlds.

When he finally arrived at the crime scene in Acton, dressed in a uniform he hadn't worn for eight months, the reporters and TV crews had already gathered, their cameras flashing and microphones thrusting at anyone who looked like they had a badge. Even as Bus rushed to gather his first impressions of the crime scene, the commander began advising on what and what not to say.

"Bus, we got a spotlight here," he said. "Let's conduct a full briefing in a couple of hours—*after* the squad sets up staging."

Bus was the name his co-workers used. He didn't

mind. What mattered now was cracking this case, bringing justice to a victim who had a direct connection to his ancestral homeland. He stepped closer to the scene, his mind racing, analyzing every detail, preparing to piece together the puzzle.

The victim's body had already been removed, leaving behind an empty, chilling space. But her car remained, and Bus took a moment to look at the vehicle. It was after midday but there were imprints of many feet around it, the impressions of a rushed and tense morning.

He turned to the team of forensic experts who were still meticulously collecting evidence. He watched as they gathered samples, took photographs, and measured every detail of the scene. They were professionals. He stepped forward to address them and flashed his ID.

"What can you tell me so far? We need something to tell the media—as you can see, they're hungry for a statement," Bus said.

A female technician stepped forward. "We've got samples of the interior, and we're documenting the possible points of entry. It looks like there was some struggle inside the vehicle, which might help with the investigation."

"So, this was not just the gruesome outcome of a random encounter?" Bus asked.

"No way. This was the work of someone looking for vengeance… and sadistic humiliation."

"Bus," Chief Flores said, pulling him aside. "You're going to be working with another detective, a woman named Lisa Garcia from the Concord State Police."

"Where is she now?"

"Arresting the victim's boyfriend."

Brett Wright, the forensics team lead, told Bus that they estimated that the murder had been committed sometime around midnight. It had taken motorists nearly five hours to notify the police.

"So how many morning motorists saw this and ignored it?"

"That's what I was wondering."

Bus's mind flooded with questions. Did the neighbors hear her scream for help? Did they ignore it? Could the perpetrator have escaped from the Concordstate prison nearby? Or—maybe he was a resident of Acton. Most importantly, *was he still in the area*? Whoever he was, if he wasn't the boyfriend, he was on the run. And dangerous.

Bus ordered his junior police staff to go out and retrieve a list of all of the guests registered for stays at the neighborhood motels for the night along with copies of their IDs. Then he briefed Lt. Bradley Anderson, the commander of the Acton Police, on his first impression of the crime scene. The amount of information that could be shared with the police was limited for the time being. What they had wasn't much.

To the press, Lt. Anderson ran down the basic details: A young college-age woman was brutally murdered after an apparent sexual assault. Police had yet to confirm the identity of the woman. Any other questions would have to wait.

Right after the press conference, Bradley pulled Bus aside. "Bus," he said, "I need you to move very fast while the evidence is still fresh. Coordinate with forensics and report back to me every hour—any findings, anything. I want to hear it."

"Understood."

"Otherwise, this media circus will overwhelm us—forty-eight hours will destroy our momentum. Acton isn't accustomed to all of this attention. The press will be haranguing around the clock. The quicker we get concrete answers, the quicker we satiate these parasites."

"You got it. I'm gonna round up any and every person of interest and start questioning, see who is and isn't already on our radar."

Dozens had descended on the cornfield acreage now that the news had been broadcast, shared, and reshared. The police cordoned off the road and blocked access completely. Traffic on School Street was rerouted to Hosmer Road, and the honking of frustrated commuters could be heard blocks away. It would be many hours before the busy intersection would return to normal.

Surveying the scene, Bradley placed a hand on Bus's shoulders. "Good to have you back."

CHAPTER 4

Lisa

LISA settled into the new office, gazing out the window at Chief Flores's convoy turning into the State Department offices. This was going to be her base of operations for the next few days, or maybe even months. The case had already garnered attention from the highest echelons of power, and there was plenty to do. But more than that, she had a nagging feeling in the pit of her stomach—a sense that things were about to get a lot more complicated.

For one, she knew she'd be sharing this space with her new partner on the case, a detective handpicked by the CIA named Bas or Bus or something like that, someone with both Ugandan and American roots. She couldn't help but frown at the thought of the CIA bending the rules to suit their needs. And just because the president of Uganda was considered an asset or an ally in diplomatic circles, that did not grant him the power to influence a murder investigation in the United States. After all, weren't we still an independent country? It was like a form of reverse imperialism, where foreign interests attempted to shape our internal affairs. Drag in the Feds, and it was like justice was something to be served from a selective menu for those with the right connections.

Still, as a detective, Lisa understood that her loyalty was ultimately to her boss, Chief Flores. If he thought she needed a half-Ugandan partner, well, who was she to say no?

Interrupting these thoughts, Chief Flores entered with a man he introduced as Detective Basudde. "But you can call him *Bus*—everybody does."

She stopped in her tracks. He was handsome, tall, middle-aged, well-built, with a presence that demanded attention. His police uniform clung to his well-defined physique, showing off his strong abs and chiseled features. If Lisa were to Google "sexiest detective alive," this guy might pop up. Maybe she shouldn't be surprised. The CIA had always been notorious for hiring exceptionally beautiful women, often raising eyebrows and fostering stereotypes about the agency's preferences. But Detective Bus was a revelation—apparently the CIA could play it both ways.

"Bus, this will be your partner, Lisa," Chief Flores said to the man. "I think you two may have met before. Detective Basudde comes out of our East Boston office."

Lisa leaned forward to shake his hand—he delivered a firm and manly grip.

"Nice to meet you, Lisa," Bus said, his deep voice resonating. She was instantly turned on and instantly knew it was a feeling she should suppress. She gave him a smile that was shy but not filled with attraction—even such thoughts could be dangerous these days, a breach of professional conduct. Detectives were not supposed to fall in love; it was a professional treason. It'd been a long time since she felt real attraction or allowed herself to. Her husband, the father of her two children, had been gone two years now. Ran off with their Salvadoran nanny. They were co-parenting—not exactly the life she had imagined, but it was the reality she had to accept.

"Pleasure to meet you."

"Your name is Bus as in B.U.S?" she asked.

"Si, senorita," he replied.

"Okay, pause there a bit. I'm not your Spanish instructor, and I don't want to practice your Spanish. If I speak to you in English, please do the same. Are we good?"

Her rudeness surprised even herself, but she had to set the boundaries. People often assumed she spoke Spanish because of her Colombian features, her tan skin and dark brown hair from her mother's side—and this assumption had become a full-blown pet peeve. She smiled again, this time more to break the awkwardness than anything else, as she settled into her seat.

CHAPTER 5

Bus

LISA'S little outburst had taken Bus by surprise. In the world of Uber, this would be a clear sign to cancel a ride and lose a troublesome passenger who might later leave bad ratings or complaints. But here, he didn't have a choice—especially with his ongoing overtime fraud case.

Solving the Musinga murder was his one shot at salvation, and he knew it. It would demonstrate his dedication and professionalism, potentially swaying the judges to be lenient with the fraud thing. Failing, on the other hand, could lead to a prison term, a fate that had befallen more than a few of his colleagues. If he had to endure this lady's rudeness, then he'd just have to suck it up; his career depended on it.

"So, what do we have on the case so far?" he asked, before taking a slug of water from his metal bottle. "I understand you already made an arrest."

"Oh yes," Lisa replied with a smile, revealing a pair of white teeth. "I arrested the presumed boyfriend. His name is Shawn Wayles. We'll go together to interrogate him tomorrow since it's already late." She glanced at her watch. "Also, I released the guy who had found the body in the car. He's a licensed nurse practitioner working in a senior home around here. His fellow nurses confirmed he worked until late last night, and in the morning, he was on his way to work a morning shift. The guy's a workaholic, doing twelve-hour shifts. His wife and daughter were his alibi—he'd been home all night, out in the morning."

"What do we know about the victim?" Bus asked, taking notes.

"Name's Sheila Musinga—a media studies student at Essex University in downtown Boston. She hails from Uganda, and her father, Bernard Musinga, is the brother of the president of Uganda. The brother serves as the foreign minister."

He listened attentively, marveling at how fast she was in collecting the details.

"I know the president," he said with a smile.

"Anyway," Lisa went on, "Sheila's mother met Musinga in Sweden during one of his official diplomatic visits. After a brief affair, she accompanied him back to Uganda. As you likely know, it's a common status symbol among accomplished Black African men to date and marry white women. Unfortunately, Sheila's mother died during childbirth, and she was raised by her stepmother, Joanita, a Ugandan-Rwandese woman and Bernard's first and official wife. Joanita also has five other biological children with Musinga—all older."

Bus listened respectfully, trying to hide his reaction to some of the generalizations Lisa was making about Black men and their preferences. As a bi-racial man, he knew things weren't always what they seemed. His own parents had been the subject of this kind of gossip—all generalizations. His Black mother had not *sought out* his white father; if anything, it had been the other way around. Even after his parents separated, he knew his father would do anything to win his mother back.

Lisa went on. "Sheila had been brought to the United States, along with her half-brother Amos, Joanita's eldest son. They were both here to pursue their studies, with Amos attending Harvard Medical School and living in Brighton. Later, Sheila joined her half-brother there and studied at Essex where she was majoring in media studies."

"Okay," Bus said. "Where's the uncle in all this?"

"Bernard, it seems, hadn't given up hope of marrying another white woman after losing Sheila's mother," Lisa said. "He has another white wife in New York with more children."

"Right."

"These people might prove useful down the line—but we need to exercise caution when approaching the grieving family members."

Suddenly the landline rang. Bus didn't reach for it. It was undoubtedly the CIA, the same caller who had contacted him earlier to check his availability and offer him the gig. A few minutes later, Chief Flores called. Again, Bus hesitated—he knew he couldn't step outside to answer the call without raising suspicion. Then the phone rang a third time, and Lisa stared him down. Bus finally pulled the phone to his ear.

"I know you're already at work," the caller began.

"Identify yourself," Bus said.

"Nevermind that. I just wanted to let you know the victim's family is our ally in Africa, and the agency would be honored if you helped find the person who killed their daughter."

Bus nodded, grunted something in Luganda, and continued to listen. ,.

He was familiar with these anonymous CIA calls, and he responded with a noncommittal "Uhhm," avoiding giving away any sensitive details in Lisa's presence. The caller then inquired about who had been arrested, but he couldn't disclose that information over the phone, especially with Lisa watching him intently. Instead, he promised to call back if any new information arose. The caller understood and hung up.

Bus had worked for the CIA on temporary assignments in Africa before, especially in Uganda, Congo, and Rwanda. On these gigs, he had helped train local intelligence staff in information gatherings, to infiltrate enemy circles. He'd also trained some battalions in key combatant techniques.

After the call, Bus grabbed a pad of paper and wrote down the number. Above it, he wrote *Virginia Man*, determined to keep this connection discreet.

CHAPTER 6

Lisa

DETECTIVE Lisa arrived at the State Police Forensics and Technology Center in Maynard with this new guy Bus in tow. The town was quiet, nestled in the neighborhoods of Acton and Concord, but this was the place where the digital and scientific puzzle pieces of their homicide investigation might begin to fit together.

At the Center, their first stop was the crime laboratory, cloaked in sterile white, where the air was heavy with the scent of chemicals and the promise of revelations. The forensic team was waiting for them, faces solemn.

"Detective Lisa, Detective Bus," greeted Dr. Brett Wright, the head of the forensic team. "We've prepared the report for you."

Lisa knew what came next: The gruesome tableau of a young woman's life, extinguished too soon. They wheeled out her lifeless body on a cold, steel gurney. Even in death,

Sheila was beautiful, haunting, her delicate features frozen in eternal slumber. Her lips were still pressed together, lipstick red. Her eyes were closed, as if she were merely taking a deep, peaceful nap. But the marks of strangulation marred the graceful curve of her neck with harsh, red welts on the left side of her throat, a silent accusation in the stillness of the room.

Then, together, they led the two detectives to the digital display where the photos were As they flipped through the photographs, Lisa's heart sank. There was Sheila, her lifeless body slumped in the passenger seat of a car. Her face was less peaceful somehow than now. Her blue jeans and underwear had been pulled down past her knees, an indignity that left a sour taste in Lisa's mouth.

"As these photos indicate, the corpse was initially found in this position," Dr. Wright said.

Lisa whispered, "Her name was Sheila," as a pang of sorrow gripped her heart. This stranger—Lisa felt an obligation to uncover the truth behind her brutal murder.

Bus and Lisa sat down in front of the screen, combed through the reports, noting every detail—the placement of Sheila's arms, the angles of the wounds, all the traces that had been so meticulously collected by the forensic team.

After about a half-hour reviewing, it felt like the initial shock had subsided, replaced by a resolute focus. The victim's hymen had been violated—it sent shivers down Lisa's spine. As Bus read transcripts, Lisa's gaze kept returning to the stark photographs on the screen. Deep grooves on the victim's delicate shoulder hinted at a ruthless grip.

"Strangulation." Bus said pointing up at the scar.

"That's what it looks like to me."

The word reverberated through Lisa's mind, its weight almost suffocating. The victim's final moments, as life slipped away under the merciless grasp of her assailant, flashed before her. She tore her gaze away from the photos and turned to Dr. Wright.

"Thank you for your work," she said. "We'll need copies of these for our records."

"Of course, Detective. We'll have copies ready for you."

With that, the two detectives left the laboratory. Their next destination was the Technology Center down the hall.

"Let's get those reports on the victim's phone," Bus said. "We need to trace her whereabouts and activities leading up to the murder."

Here, sleek computers and monitors lined the walls, manned by digital forensics investigators who sifted through terabytes of data in search of clues. This was a world where every click, every message, and every movement left a trace, a digital footprint that could lead them closer to the heart of darkness.

Bus and Lisa approached the lead digital forensics investigator, Agent William Reynolds, who was already engrossed in the reports. He greeted them with a nod.

"Detective Lisa, Detective Bus—we've been working on the victim's phone records and geospatial data. It's a mess, but we've made some progress."

He handed them a file—more than you'd imagine for just a few hours work. In this world of endless data, there were no secrets that could remain hidden forever. Every cellphone left a trail of breadcrumbs all day every day. A trained investigator could easily verify the trajectory of the phone signal and which cell towers in the service networks had been pinged along the way. Even if the phone was not being used, you could find out where the person was moving. "The person who had killed and raped the victim was known to her," Lisa said.

"Right," Bus said. "*Maybe* someone she could trust enough to sit in her car and drive off to an isolated cornfield in the dead of winter.

"Okay—maybe."

"But," he went on, "maybe she drove there under duress."

"How do you mean?"

"As in, *threatened at gunpoint*."

"But there was no gun used in the murder."

"So what? Crazy pervert threatens with a gun, but he's a cutter. Just because we didn't see it doesn't mean a gun wasn't there."

"So, she was strangled and asphyxiated… just for the hell of it?"

"Exactly."

"I still make Shawn for this," she said, "no matter the technique."

"Classic passion killing," Bus said. "I buy it."

"All I know is, that bastard better have a credible alibi to confirm his whereabouts the night of the murder."

Just then, John Adams, a bearded grey-haired engineer from the department, came in with a laptop. "Detectives, we've recovered some voice conversations from the deceased and her boyfriend taken shortly before the murder."

"Wow," Lisa said, "that should help."

"Are we talking about the last few hours of Sheila's life?" Bus said.

The engineer nodded and pressed play. A crackly voice played over the speakers.

SHAWN: Hello?
SHEILA: Shawn, I... I need to talk to you about something.
SHAWN: What's up?
SHEILA: Nothing. I... I heard something, Shawn. Something that really scares me.
SHAWN: Talk to me. What did you hear? You can tell me anything.
SHEILA: Are you really that angry at me?
SHAWN: About what?
SHEILA: You know. About me refusing... you know, about us not... you know.
SHAWN: Huh?!
SHEILA: You wouldn't *hurt* me for that?
SHAWN: Of course not! Where did you get such a crazy idea like that?
SHEILA: I heard it from a very reliable source, Shawn.
SHAWN: Reliable source? Sheila, you're being delusional. You need to see a psychiatrist or something. I can't believe you'd think I'd do something like that.
SHEILA: Shawn, please, just listen to me. I heard something. I wish I didn't.
SHAWN: Sheila, you sound crazy right now. Don't... don't go around making such ridiculous allegations about people without proof.
SHEILA: But Shawn...
SHAWN: I can't do this, Sheila. This is insane. I'm hanging up.
SHEILA: No, wait, Shawn! Please, just hear me out!

The line went dead.

Bus and Lisa exchanged a grim glance.

Back in the car, on the way back to police headquarters in Concord, they talked through the evidence.

"Still, one thing doesn't up," Bus said. "Why Acton—thirty miles from Boston, an hour in traffic? Even from her home in Brighton, the trip would have taken at least a half hour and likely forty-five."

"Did you expect him to rape and strangle his girlfriend in his bedroom at a college dorm?"

"No, but I also didn't expect him to cooperate."

"The guilty ones always cooperate, Bus. You know that."

CHAPTER 7

Bus

BUS sat alongside Detective Lisa in a dimly lit interrogation chamber, waiting for the suspect—Shawn. He didn't think this character did it. College boys didn't haul off and strangle their girlfriends, then go back to the dorm for a pizza. On the table before them lay the forensics report, a haunting testament to the brutality that had claimed a life… but Bus bet that when the college kid saw these pictures, he'd come up with a viable alibi real quick. The tension in the air was palpable. Within these walls, they would have to find some answers.

Two policemen brought him in, sat him down, and cuffed him to the chair. Dressed in orange, Shawn looked beaten, underweight, worried, and why not—he was facing the gravest accusations imaginable. Lisa cracked open the folder. She pulled three photos of the victim and slid them across the table.

Bus sat back and watched how Shawn reacted to each photo. The first two pictures showed Sheila's body in the passenger seat, face frozen. The third was Sheila and Shawn posing in Times Square, straight off her Facebook page. In that photo, Sheila appeared to have more layers of makeup than clothing. She wore a white blouse that just covered her breasts and left her midriff exposed and what appeared to be black booty shorts. Shawn's expression in the photo was like someone who received a gift they anticipated but never thought they'd actually get. He did nothing to hide how hard he was crushing on Sheila, and if a romantic crush could ever be classified as a poison, this interrogation would never have happened because Shawn would have already been six feet under.

Bus observed Shawn carefully, his eyes and hands twitched. The guy was obviously nervous, restless.

"I didn't do this," he cried. "I don't even know what the hell I'm doing here."

"Mr. Wyles," Lisa said, "this is a very serious charge you're facing. I need you to understand that you cannot just show up and tell us you're innocent and then expect to leave as if that's all we need."

"Let's be calm now, try to make yourself comfortable," Bus said, playing good cop. "We're going to keep you for a bit longer. So just… cooperate and be truthful."

Lisa looked without mercy into Shawn's eyes as he whimpered. "Shawn," she said. "One thing I don't understand… is how you can look at images of your girlfriend and not be even the slightest bit emotionally distraught. No tears, nothing."

Shawn scowled back at her, incredulous.

Lisa shook her head. "What can you tell me to make me believe that you are *not* someone who could have committed a crime like this without feeling any guilt or remorse?!"

"First of all," he said, voice measured, "she ain't my girlfriend. She was just a classmate of mine and… the daughter of my boss."

"Even if that were true," Lisa went on, "that doesn't eliminate *you* as a primary suspect—someone who could have easily raped Sheila Musinga before strangling her to death."

"I , , , did not… kill her," Shawn said, emphasizing each word.

"What happened, Shawn?" Bus said. "Let's get to it. I don't want to be here all day and my guess is you don't either."

"Like I said, I was not her boyfriend. We were just classmates. I always liked her. *As a friend.* And I would never hurt her, ever."

Bus leaned back.

Lisa said, "Not good enough."

Shawn, almost crying now, engulfed in shock, said "I still don't know why you arrested me. Do you have anything? What makes you think I did it? What evidence could you have when I didn't do it?"

Lisa pulled in closer, staring him down.

"Shawn, believe me, we have evidence. And it's piling up against you. And yet, here you are—you have yet to tell us one thing that would give us pause and reconsider the possibility that maybe you aren't the suspect."

"You've got to show me that evidence!"

She shook her head. "We'll submit it first to the grand jury—first-degree murder with aggravated specifications. You could end up with… prison for life, without parole. You think about that."

CHAPTER 8

Shawn

THE two detectives left Shawn alone to simmer. He shifted uneasily in his chair, his gaze flitting away into memory. He knew that his feelings for Sheila had run deep, deeper than he'd liked to admit to those two interrogators.

Shawn met her in the classroom, but their friendship had quickly grown far beyond the confines of academics. Shawn remembered that day vividly. It was a beautiful New England early fall day, and he was eager to begin this new chapter in his life. The first day he met Sheila was his first day at Essex University in Downtown Boston. The school was prestigious, *the* destiny for creative individuals. The lecture room was buzzing with anticipation as the packed classroom of students all settled into their seats. He could feel the excitement in the air as the clock inched closer to the start of the lecture and the room fell into a hushed silence.

He was exuding confidence that day—a young Black man, with the presence to command attention. Heads turned, and eyes lingered on him. Whispers rippled through the air, some curious, others judgmental.

Shawn was there to pursue a bachelor's degree in creative writing, and he couldn't have been more excited. There were about twenty students in the class—he was the only Black man. At six-one, he was also the tallest, the most athletic, and the most well-built. Besides, he had always been told that he was handsome, but he wasn't the only one who stood out that day. Sheila Musinga was the only other person in the room who wasn't white, but actually, with her light-toned skin, he initially thought she was. He guessed she could be from Mexico, Puerto Rico, or some country in Latin America or the Caribbean, but he never would have picked an African country. Then he heard her accent—deep African. A little eavesdropping let him know that her father, Bernard, was the brother of the president of Uganda, serving as the foreign minister. This was one young lady he had to get to know better.

As they went around the classroom, introducing themselves to the professor, Shiela spoke and Shawn marveled at her beautiful voice, and he felt connected to her. In that moment, Sheila and Shawn seemed like the two genuine outsiders among the other eighteen students in the course, connected even though they were from opposite points on the globe.

And Shiela was all class—she displayed the vestiges of her family's wealth and social status in haute couture clothes and expensive-looking jewelry that was definitely not fake. Unlike most of the students, she wasn't at the mercy of financial aid, scholarships, or grants; her family could probably afford to pay the staggering $80,000 a year in tuition.

But what struck Shawn even more was how Sheila defied the stereotypes that many Americans might associate with the continent of Africa. The American schools taught little about the history, culture, and politics of Africa. News from Africa rarely made its way into the American media, except for stories about extreme poverty, starvation, and deprivation. Most Americans probably thought the place was one big desert of hunger. Sheila defied it all. She was beautiful, elegant, well-spoken. She was like royalty. And she seemed destined for a life where she would never have to work. Shawn guessed that she probably had a serious trust fund. After all, her dad was in the government.

Shawn had to admit that he looked like a different sort of outsider that day, probably looking out of place in a college setting. He couldn't help but notice how every set of eyes in the classroom was trained on him, scanning and judging. Many, if not every one of these so-called peers, probably just assumed that his presence in the classroom was a result of affirmative action. But that wasn't the case, and he wanted them to know that he was there because he was funding his own education just like the rest of them, augmenting expenses with student loans. One thing about everyone in this room but Sheila: They all shared one major thing in common—they would all be negotiating installment payments after graduation to pay down a big mountain of student debt. It was a burden that would likely take many years to relieve.

That first day, Shawn was seated in the roundtable arrangement the instructor had set up, and Sheila was just three seats away from him. Their eyes locked onto each other, and he couldn't help but smile slightly as he noticed her. Her hair looked so different from the American girls he knew, braided with a maroon hue. He couldn't help but notice how the pink on her fingernails matched her lipstick perfectly. He was momentarily lost in his thoughts, and his attention was pulled back to reality when the lecturer called upon him to comment on the class discussion.

"I'm still trying to piece my thoughts together, you know what I'm saying?" he mumbled awkwardly, trying to save face. Truth be told, he was completely driven to distraction by Sheila.

Throughout the class, he couldn't help but steal glances at her. Sheila would look away, but when she looked back again, their eyes would meet once more. It felt like a flirtatious dance of visual gestures.

And what did she think of him? He couldn't tell. Maybe she just thought he was full of lust, or maybe she thought he was focusing on her because she was the only other student of color in the classroom.

As soon as the class ended, Shawn walked over to her, extending his hand and introducing himself.

"Thank you," she muttered shyly. "Though I already know your name from the class introductions." And then, with a smile, she said, "You haven't done much work today besides looking at me."

Shawn tried his best to seem genuinely apologetic. "I… I'm real sorry," he stammered, trying to suppress his embarrassment. "It won't happen like that anymore, I promise. I ain't no creepy stalker, for real."

Despite this, he followed her out of the classroom and toward the stairs. She said, "So, do you look at all girls like that?"

"No," he replied, sounding like a boy who had been caught doing something he shouldn't.

But her slim, athletic physique with toned thighs and hips seemed to mesmerize Shawn. And her voice—her African continental accent, he found this trait to be her sexiest one.

Now, sitting in a jail cell, chained to a chair, his memory leapt forward. A week or two later—after class one day, a small group of white students stood by the elevator as Sheila and Shawn entered. Sheila called out to them to enter, but one of the students said they would wait for the elevator to return. It was as if they sensed that a love match was in the making.

Then the elevator closed, and Shawn caught a whiff of Sheila's perfume. His eyes were pinned on Sheila's chest when she said, "Are you looking at my boobs?"

Shawn immediately looked up, saying with a sheepish smile, "Nah, I'm looking into your heart, trying to see if you've got any love secrets."

"Haha, and what body organ is doing your thinking?" Sheila said, taking quick command of the moment.

And just like that, the elevator door opened, and they walked out casually, as if nothing had happened. They were just two fellow students who coincidentally shared an elevator ride.

They began to hang out in Boston Commons Park across from class. Most days, the chats only lasted a few minutes or sometimes as much as a half-hour. Sheila wanted to make sure to not miss the Green Line subway train to Brighton—he lived close to the park in the dorm on Tremont.

In those park bench chats, Shawn was always cordial, compassionate, a good listener—but truth was, he was steadily pursuing a strategy to capture Sheila's heart. One time, he told Sheila he wanted to work for the CIA when he graduated.

"What will you do for them? Be a lethal assassin?" she asked.

"Oh, nah. Not that. You know CIA be hiring writers too, right? You ain't heard 'bout Ernest Hemingway, the novelist? He used to work for the CIA."

"Yeah? Good for him. But that's not me."

"What's you?"

"*You* want big money to chill with the big boys," Sheila said, standing up and pressing her hands on her dress which was about to blow south with the fall wind.

Shawn never did understand why most people considered the CIA a cash cow, and some even joked that CIA stood for Cash in Advance. But he explained to Sheila that his motivation was altruism, not greed.

"Sheila, the CIA got a lot of influence in this world. If you're trying make a positive impact and stand up for folks' rights and freedom everywhere, the CIA be the spot to be. If the CIA got good-hearted folks looking out for lives, they gonna make policies that uplift the people."

He knew his responses could be charming, but he was also learning what could perk up Sheila's interest in him. He was like many young idealistic college students who believed in American exceptionalism and the CIA's role in maintaining the US and its superiority. Sheila listened to him as if she fully believed in his wide-eyed ideals, often nodding affirmingly.

"You are a very smart boy, you know," she said. "My family has good connections with the CIA. Complicated to explain, but you know, I maybe could help you."

Next time they hung in the park, she promised him that she would talk to the director of a lobbyist firm that worked with the government in her country. Maybe the firm would have a spot for him to gain some experience if he ever wanted to really pursue a career track with the CIA. The lobbying firm occasionally had several job postings for writers and researchers to work on topics of security and intelligence.

Shawn had expected that Sheila's background from Africa was richer than what other students in the US had, but he was also surprised that she apparently was even better plugged into a network that was serious about such matters. Up to this point in his education, he had encountered readings explaining how CIA agents had infiltrated the governments of many African countries, especially during the Cold War.

But Sheila painted a different picture, which rattled what he thought was a concrete view of African politics. Sheila was telling him that it was less the CIA influencing the governments than the ability of African leaders who knew precisely how to manipulate the CIA's support for the sake of keeping themselves in power for potentially the rest of their lives.

On the outside, he did little to show just how surprised he was by what Sheila told him. Never challenging her, he merely said a few words of thanks for her insights and always played it cool.

But the truth was, Sheila Musinga intimidated him in ways that no other woman could.

Then, he stood up, raising himself to his full height, as if he was about to say something significant to Sheila, but then he closed his mouth, like a shy boy who saw his one surge of confidence vanish in an instant. He could never catch Sheila off guard, as she smiled broadly at him, making it clear that she knew what his game was.

He paused for a moment, mustering once again the grains of confidence to say something—something romantic. But, not missing a beat, Sheila motioned for him to stay silent. She said, "Please keep it to yourself; I don't want to hear it."

His eyes could not hide his disappointment. She admonished him by reminding him that their friendship was academic and professional.

With that, they ended the chat. Sheila promised that she would call him the following day once she contacted the lobbying firm in Washington, DC. He escorted her to the deep stairwell leading to the Green Line subway train.

This was as far as they ever walked together. He rarely used the subway, so he didn't even have a regular rider's pass.

Before they could separate, Sheila opened her arms in an invite for a hug and said, "You know, I don't often hug tall boys because I don't want to hug their stomach instead of their chest." But at five and a half feet, Sheila was just tall enough in heels to meet Shawn's broad chest.

He felt the sparks as they hugged. If he felt fireworks like this just from a hug, just imagine what it would be if their bodies were entangled in bed. "The right passage to my heart is asking," she whispered into his ear while they were still embracing each other. "Forcing those big eyes through my clothes and chest to find my heart is cheating," she said with the stern manner of an elder.

Sheila pulled herself away from his embrace and muttered that it was enough for now.

Looking back, getting lost in these memories, it seemed like almost every guy in the class was vying for Sheila's attention. One particular guy was Greg, a white classmate who always seemed to be trying to flirt with Sheila.

There was that one day when fate put Shawn behind Greg and Sheila as they walked down a hallway. He couldn't help but overhear their conversation.

Greg wondered where Sheila was staying, and when she mentioned Brighton, Greg's eyes lit up.

"Oh, I also stay in Brighton," he said.

"Where exactly?" Sheila asked with an extra curiosity in her tone that Shawn did not like. He was chafing, wanting to interrupt their hallway chat, as jealousy mounted inside his body. Remembering what happened in the classroom earlier, Shawn thought about how he should warn Sheila that all this white boy wanted to do was jump on her to fulfill some exotic fantasy. Shawn knew exactly where Greg stayed in the dorms in Boston. And he knew Greg's roommate. But with a deep breath, Shawn settled himself down, realizing that disrupting their chat would be a big mistake.

Before Sheila and Greg parted, they exchanged phone

numbers and promised to call each other. Shawn waited for Greg to disappear then he strode immediately up to Sheila and asked if she didn't mind him escorting her to the subway station.

Sheila agreed, but on the walk, his rage of envy returned.

"That dude is a complete jerk," Shawn remarked. "Every word he speaks is a blatant lie, and what's even crazier is that he resides in my dormitory."

"Are you jealous?" Sheila said in a stern voice.

"I swear, he is not staying in Brighton."

"You see, you are just being nosy. And you got it wrong. He said he was from Brighton as it was his parents' home, you know," Sheila said.

"Oh, for real? But why would someone that close be staying in a dormitory? It still does not add up."

"Who needs it to add up? Just get over it and leave him alone." She shot him a withering look. "Come on, Shawn. You and I know that every junior at Essex is required to stay at the dormitory. My family just secured a special exception for me to stay off campus. You know that, Shawn."

"Yeah but—"

"But nothing. You're just mad because all the boys in the class are hitting on me."

"Who's all the boys?"

"There is this other boy named Ben. You know him?"

Shawn nodded. "Benjamin Clarence."

"He is sending me texts asking to take me out. Last night he texted me that he has two tickets for Jonas Brothers at Fenway."

"How do they all get your phone number?"

"It's on the class sheet, stupid."

Shawn grunted. "So, you going out with him?"

"No. I can't. My brother Amos will literally kill me or report me to Dad if I do go dating, you know, but why are *you* so concerned?"

"So, are you not into Black boys?" he asked.

Sheila stopped walking and turned to look at him, a hint of amusement on her lips.

"I have no experience with boys, Shawn."

"Ok, we're friends. Let's talk about that."

"But Shawn, you're asking me very personal questions," she protested, though her tone remained gentle.

"Okay, just tell me, do you like Black guys as much as you like white boys?" Shawn pressed.

Sheila laughed softly, shaking her head.

"We are not talking about sex, are we?"

"No, not at all. Just social life," Shawn clarified.

"Anyway, I don't care because I don't have a sex life yet to talk about," Sheila said.

Shawn's mind raced. There was no way this beautiful girl was celibate. But he didn't want to argue or annoy her.

"So, is it Black or white boys?" he asked, pushing his luck.

Sheila sighed.

"You want me to be honest?"

"Yes."

"I prefer white boys."

"Why?"

"They are more romantic, like in movies," Sheila explained, her eyes drifting off as if imagining a scene from her favorite film.

Shawn's mind was racing with the urge to promise Sheila that he was also romantic and nice, but instead, he asked.

"Do you agree with the movies' depiction of Black guys being less?" His voice unintentionally rose a notch.

"Eh, eh, don't raise your voice," Sheila cautioned, glancing around. "People are going to think we're fighting. I don't understand why you are taking this so personally. It's not about you and me because we are not anything, right?"

"I'm sorry."

"It's not just movies," Sheila continued, her tone softening. "Also, my girlfriends who have done it with Black guys told me they are rough and more aggressive."

"So, it's about your Ugandan girlfriends' experiences?"

"Not exactly, but yes, somehow," Sheila said, shaking her head and shrugging her shoulders. "All my friends in Uganda had Black boys, and I have always wanted to be different."

"Like I want my first experience to be special and smooth. My friends told me their first experiences were tough with Black boys. Like they just tore into them. I want my experience to be a process and enjoyable, gentle, like what you see in movies."

"You want your relationship to be like that in a movie," Shawn repeated, his voice tinged with frustration.

"Enough of these questions, oh god. You are too much," Sheila said, her laughter breaking the tension.

Shawn kept silent and stewed. The fact was, he hated every white guy in the class for making it seem easy to get Sheila's attention, especially once they figured out she had a thing for white boys. *Damn, that white privilege*, he thought. Shawn did not like the lecturer in class either—another damn white man Sheila paid close attention to.

As Shawn seethed, working through every male student in the class, he realized that there was just one white boy who did not seem interested in pursuing Sheila. *Ryan*—she never mentioned him.

Shawn said, "Do you happen to have Ryan's phone?"

"No," Sheila responded. "I don't think that one has ever even said hi to me. Do you talk to him?"

"Yeah, *he* is a solid friend, no doubt," Shawn responded, sounding bitter. And anyway, it was a blatant lie. Shawn had never spoken a single word to Ryan. Now, all of a sudden, he felt some sort of camaraderie with the guy just because he happened to be the only male classmate who did not lust after Sheila.

For Shawn, that was good enough to call him a friend.

CHAPTER 9

Lisa

LISA, waiting in the lobby during a break from the interrogation, spotted a woman entering who seemed instantly familiar—she'd seen her photo. It was Shawn's mother, Jasmine Wayles, arriving alone at the police station. Lisa peeked at her through the waiting room door. She could see plain as day that the weight of a mother's love and anguish rested heavily upon the poor woman's shoulders.

Mrs. Wayles approached the reception desk, her voice quivering as she addressed the receptionist.

"Excuse me I… I need to speak to someone about my son. They… they say he's been arrested."

"I'm so sorry to hear that, ma'am," the receptionist said. "Let me find someone who can assist you. Please have a seat." The receptionist signaled over to Lisa, blowing her cover.

Mrs. Wayles's eyes welled up with tears as she took a seat in the waiting area.

Lisa emerged from her office, conscious that she was dressed in the uniform of the Massachusetts State Police, a badge of authority that could only underscore the seriousness of the situation. Mrs. Wayles stood up as she approached her.

"Mrs. Wayles, I'm Detective Lisa," she introduced herself, extending a hand. "I understand you're here about your son?"

"Yes, Officer. They… they say my boy got caught up in some crime. I'm sure it's a mistake. My boy Shawn, he ain't capable of doing something like that."

"I understand your concern, Mrs. Wayles," she said. "We're still in the early stages of the investigation, but I can assure you that we'll do everything in our power to uncover the truth."

"Please, Detective Lisa," Mrs. Wayles said, sounding desperate. "I know my boy. He's a good boy, got a heart of gold. Ain't no way he'd be doing messed-up stuff like that. Y'all gotta find the truth, for his sake and for mine. We need justice up in here."

Lisa guided the lady to a private room. She knew this would be the best opportunity to learn more about Shawn and his life, his education, his background, whatever Lisa could get before going back to the kid and turning up the heat.

Lisa held a newspaper article that had been published just that day, featuring a sensationalized story about Shawn and his father. The article was judgmental and titled "Dorchester's Notorious Drug Lord's Son Arrested for

Girlfriend's Murder."

"So, Jasmine, let's start with Shawn's family background. Can you tell me about his father and what he did for a living?" Lisa said.

"Sure, Shawn was born in 2000 in Dorchester, Massachusetts. His dad's name was Marquis Wayles, and I actually knew Marquis back in high school. We both graduated, but despite our academic success, neither of us could secure full scholarships. So, we ended up taking entry-level jobs at grocery stores and starting a family."

"Ma'am, I don't mean to sound accusatory. But they're saying your husband was a drug lord. In Dorchester."

Mrs. Wayles glanced at the article briefly and then shook her head. "I don't bother with newspapers. They're all full of lies. Let *me* set the record straight, Marquis was no drug lord. Sure, he messed around with drugs at some point, but it wasn't entirely his fault."

"How so?"

"Back about twenty years ago, Marquis injured his leg in a car accident and a physician prescribed OxyContin. That nasty shit. It didn't take but weeks for Marquis to develop a serious addiction—first more opioids, then straight heroin when he couldn't get a script. Inside maybe a year, his habit had already spun *way* out of control. I'm talking fifteen baggies a day. Which cost him an entire week's take-home pay."

"That doesn't mean he wasn't a drug lord."

The grey-haired woman shook her head. "He was a good, polite man. And he wanted to bounce back quick from the accident, to support us. But I could tell something wasn't right."

"Tell me more."

"Well, Marquis initially seemed like he was functioning despite his addiction. He only injected heroin at night because he wanted to be sober during the daytime for his job as a delivery driver. But over time, I could tell his usage was increasing. And no matter how many times I warned him, he never listened about driving while high.

"Now, I can't help but feel regret for enabling his addiction. I even volunteered my urine for his drug tests and kept a small bottle of it in the medicine cabinet to make sure he was always prepared for screenings at work. Living like that was constant fear.

"I knew deep down that time was running out.

"The overdose episodes started happening more often," Jasmine shared. "He used to pass out maybe once a week at first, but then it started happening three or four times a week."

"There were times when Marquis would overdose. Whenever it happened, I'd give him large amounts of water and stay by his side until he regained consciousness. But one evening, I came home from work and found him unconscious on the floor next to the sofa with a syringe and needle still in his hands."

"That must have been terrifying," Lisa said.

"It was," Jasmine responded. "And it wasn't the first time I feared the worst. But I couldn't take him to the hospital because we couldn't afford the medical expenses. I kept Marquis's addiction a secret, you know? I was afraid of how embarrassing and shameful it would be if anyone found out. I just wanted to protect Shawn's dad as much as possible."

"I understand. It must have been a long night for you," Lisa said.

"Oh, it was. I spent the entire night pacing the house, checking on Shawn every now and then. I couldn't bear the thought of him seeing his father like that.

"For the first time, I realized how destructive enabling my husband's drug addiction had been," Jasmine confessed. "I decided that I couldn't sacrifice Shawn's quality of life for Marquis."

"What did you do?" Lisa asked.

"I went to the bathroom and emptied the reserves of urine specimens kept in the medicine cabinet," Jasmine said.

"I made up my mind while my husband was knocked out in the living room that I couldn't keep covering up his drug habit," Jasmine told Lisa. "It was tearing everything apart, and I couldn't take the risk of Shawn getting hurt.

"I remember drifting off to sleep for a brief moment in that old reclining armchair across the room from where Marquis lay. And then, in my dream, I saw his coffin being lowered into a grave… It felt so real, like a punch in the gut. I jolted back to reality, heart racing, filled with fear and tension.

"Maybe he was already gone, and I didn't even know what a dead person looked like," she said. "I thought he was on his deathbed. I wasn't prepared to be a single mom or a widow. I don't know why I waited so long, but I finally dialed 911. I was desperate, lost, angry, and damn frustrated. At that moment, I didn't care if the ambulance came with the police trailing right after. I was saving him from death. Even if they arrested him when he woke up, at least in jail he couldn't overdose. He would be alive, and Shawn would still have his father."

Lisa pressed further. "If you're saying that your husband was just using drugs for himself, why was he arrested? What did the police say?"

Mrs. Wayles sighed and leaned back. "All right, let me fill you in on that part of the tale.

"After Marquis was taken to the hospital, the police returned a couple of hours later. I was trying to figure out arrangements for when I could make it to the hospital, but first, I needed to take care of Shawn and determine my boss's stance on me taking time off work. When I first saw the cops, I was sure they were going to inform me that Marquis had died, but instead, they presented a search warrant. One officer informed me that Marquis had been under surveillance for a long time as a drug trafficker, and they had witness reports that he had orchestrated many heroin deals. In shock, I allowed the police in to search our home.

"The search yielded numerous small bags of heroin and black tar heroin, all cut with substances that made overdosing dangerously easy. The warrant also included Marquis's mobile phone. It revealed countless messages from drug suppliers, runners, and evidence of many drug transactions. I didn't know about all this until the police were presenting it to me. I felt like someone had planted heroin in our home and altered Marquis's phone just to convict him.

"I was crushed. How could I be so dumb? I always thought Marquis was just a user going through some hard times—I couldn't believe that the quiet, respectful dude from high school would be a straight-up dealer, not giving a damn about me or Shawn's safety. I screamed and screamed, Officer. The tears wouldn't stop streaming down my face."

"Don't you think the way you were wrong about Marquis's drug use and trafficking is the same way you are wrong about Shawn and this crime?"

Jasmine shook her head "No, no. Shawn is my son. I know him inside and out. I carried him in my womb and breastfed him. There's nothing he never tells me."

"Okay, let's leave Shawn for now. Please tell me what happened to Marquis after he was arrested?" Lisa said.

"Marquis was recovering in the hospital, but it became clear that the police would detain him and put him in jail once he was well enough. The charges went beyond just possessing dangerous narcotics. They said he had been dealing and trafficking for a long time, and many witnesses, who were part of the long list of contacts who had texted him about drug deals, decided to cooperate with the authorities to avoid facing charges themselves.

"I knew that everything I had done up to that point had failed," Jasmine said. "He eventually pleaded out, hoping that his prison sentence might be reduced. He became a convicted felon, sentenced to ten years in the Massachusetts pen. I was thinking maybe he was going make it out on parole one day, you know?" she added.

Lisa was torn. On the one hand, she was happy Jasmine was opening up to her at her own pace. On the other hand, she had managed to avoid the real subject at hand—her son.

"What happened to Shawn after his dad was arrested? How did all this affect him as a kid?"

"I had to hold it down for my son, Officer, make sure he stayed focused on school. I found a second job working nights, which meant that Shawn was alone in the house. If social workers found out, they might have taken my son away. But Shawn, even at seven, seemed to understand his momma's troubles, and he just went to bed when I left for work. No tantrums, nothing."

Jasmine's voice trembled as she painted a bleak picture of her daily life to Lisa. "It was not easy," she admitted. "Every morning, I barely had time to see Shawn off to the school bus before rushing off to my daytime job. But even with all the hours I put in, it was never enough to keep up with the bills. Rent, utilities… they ate up more than three-quarters of my wages."

She sighed heavily, "Sometimes, the utility company cut off our electricity and water. It would take me up to two weeks to scrape together enough money to get them turned back on.

"Rent's another struggle," she continued, "Our landlord, Lucas Thompson, didn't bother with repairs anymore. The apartment was falling apart—clogged plumbing, roach-infested sinks. It was a nightmare.

"The kitchen sink was dripping, and we had a bucket sitting under it to catch the water," she said. "The bathroom wasn't draining, and you had to wait for minutes before you could flush the toilet. We had to throw wet toilet paper in the trash 'cause it wouldn't go down."

"Why didn't you ever bring these issues up with your landlord?" Lisa asked.

Jasmine let out a weary sigh. "I tried," she replied. "But every time I brought up repairs, he'd just brush me off. Said I needed to be patient and reminded me of all the times he'd let me slide with late rent payments." She shook her head, a bitter edge to her voice. "It felt like he was just using my financial struggles against me."

"I also knew calling a building inspector would just bring more trouble," Jasmine added.

"Did he threaten to evict you?" Lisa asked.

Jasmine nodded, "Yeah, he did," she confirmed. "He said if I couldn't pay the rent, he'd start eviction procedures right away. And he made it clear that having an eviction on my record would ruin my chances of ever finding another place to live."

"Did you see this happen to other people in the building?"

"Oh, definitely," she replied. "I know several single mothers who went through the same thing. It's like a never-ending cycle of eviction threats and court battles. And most of the time, the landlords come out on top, leaving the tenants with nowhere to go and their belongings left out in the cold."

"So, what did you do when he threatened to evict you?" Lisa asked.

"Honestly, I didn't want to deal with the stress of fighting it," she admitted. "So, I decided to accept his offer to move out within a month, before he could start the eviction process.

"It's alarming how easily landlords can wield that power," she mused. "Especially considering the disproportionate impact it has on Black women. An epidemic of incarcerated Black men has led to an epidemic of evicted Black women, a problem often overshadowed by the focus on incarcerated men."

"So, what did you do next?" Lisa asked.

"I was hoping to find a single-bedroom apartment where Shawn and I could stay together," she explained. "But every time I called about a listing, as soon as they heard I had a child, they turned me down."

"That must have been incredibly disheartening," Lisa remarked sympathetically.

"One landlord told me, 'Ma'am, let me understand you clearly: you have a seven-year-old son, and the father is in jail?' When I confirmed it, the landlord apologized and indicated that the apartment was no longer available. I couldn't understand whether having an imprisoned husband or a seven-year-old child became the reason for my struggle to find a new apartment."

"What did you do when the month was up and you still didn't have a new place?" Lisa asked.

"I didn't know what else to do," she admitted, her voice tinged with sadness. "I started considering going to a homeless shelter with Shawn. I kept telling myself it would be temporary, just until I could find us a cheap apartment. I had hoped to stay in a subsidized home, but when I went to the city housing authority, they told me the list was closed to new applicants. I realized I'd have to wait several years just to get on the list."

"How long did you end up staying at the homeless shelter?"

"Just one month," Jasmine replied. "It felt like an eternity, though."

"And how was Shawn during that time? Did he make any friends at the shelter?"

"He was still a boy" she explained. "So, he didn't really interact with the other kids there. Besides, we were only there for a month, so he didn't have much time to form any real friendships."

"So, how did you manage to get out of the homeless shelter?"

"Well, I was lucky to meet a man named Willie at my daytime job," she said. "He was looking for a roommate for his two-bedroom apartment on Blue Hill Avenue in Dorchester."

Lisa nodded, encouraging her to continue.

"He offered me a single room in his apartment for a thousand dollars a month," Jasmine said. "And we'd split the utility bills, which came to about three-hundred dollars a month."

"That sounded like a decent arrangement," Lisa commented.

"It was," Jasmine said. "But what really appealed to me was that Willie was open to me bringing Shawn into the apartment. He understood the challenges of being a parent. He even offered to keep an eye on Shawn if I ever had to work a night shift.""What was Willie like as a father figure to Shawn? Lisa asked.

"Willie became a surrogate father for Shawn. He didn't just see him off to the bus in the morning when I was at work, but he would also wait for him when he returned home. Sometimes, he would even go to his school and attend his soccer games. Willie seemed to thrive on having a new child on board."

"Did this new closeness between Shawn and Willie also lead to something more between you and Willie?"

"Oh, why would you ask that, Detective? Well, the answer is yes. Willie and I started sharing not only the utility bills but also the grocery bills, with me taking on the role of the cook. At the dinner table, Willie, me, and Shawn would sit down as if we were a normal family. Shawn stayed in my room, but Willie offered to move Shawn to his bedroom, as they were both men, which would give me some quiet time and privacy.

"And you were okay with your son staying with a stranger in his room for your privacy?" Lisa asked.

"No, no, that's not what happened. Actually, Willie quietly moved into my room, and Shawn had his room to himself. It wasn't long before Shawn started realizing that he was essentially staying alone in Willie's bedroom, and that Willie had just pulled him out of his mother's bedroom to make space for himself to join me in bed. I know Shawn was young, but I believe he understood. He must have muttered to himself, 'Stupid adult games,' unfazed. He had long been accustomed to being alone.

"When Shawn was about fifteen years old, Willie stopped working and stayed at home most of the time due to various medical conditions stemming from diabetes. He had retired and was now living on his Social Security check. The monthly check helped cover a portion of the rent for the entire apartment, and I could now afford to cover the difference. Willie's daughter sometimes brought us groceries. But, for the second time, I was the main breadwinner in the family."

"Let's get back to Shawn's real father. Did Marquis ever return into his son's life?" Lisa asked.

"Marquis served his entire sentence of ten years, while

Willie and I had been staying together for almost nine years, sharing a bed as if we were common-law spouses. But I remained officially married to Marquis, regularly visiting him in prison and uploading money to his commissary account.

"So, after Marquis finished his prison sentence, I made space for him to join us in the apartment. Willie moved out of my bedroom and back into his own room to make room for Marquis."

"How did that go?" Lisa asked.

"It was tense, to say the least. I mean, you can imagine the tension when you have two men who see themselves as the head of the household under one roof. The moment Marquis walked in, there was this immediate clash."

"What happened?" Lisa asked.

"Well, Marquis walked in and saw Willie sitting at the dining table eating breakfast. He flipped out, asking Willie what he was doing in his wife's apartment. But Willie, being Willie, fired back, telling Marquis it was his apartment too, and he'd been taking care of me and Shawn all this time. It was not the smooth reunion I'd hoped for, that's for sure."

"Shawn told me later that he observed Marquis telling Willie, 'Look here, I don't give a damn who rented this place first, but if I ever catch you getting too close to my wife, I'll whoop your old black ass and toss your stuff out on the street,'" Jasmine recounted.

"Did they really have that kind of altercation with Shawn in the house?" Lisa asked.

"Yes, of course. That's why I was so bitter and told them both to stop.

"'I ain't taking this bullshit no more. If the police come 'round here, we all gonna be damn homeless,'" Jasmine recalled.

"Then I demanded that Marquis apologize to Willie," Jasmine continued, shaking her head. "I said there was no room for violence in the house.

"But even after the apology," she paused, "Willie always avoided Marquis. He kept himself locked in their bedroom and asked Shawn to have a spare key. Sometimes Willie would watch from his bedroom with the door slightly open to make sure Marquis wasn't in the living room before coming out into the hallway without encountering him.

"I believed in old-school discipline," she explained, a hint of pride in her voice. "I managed to monitor Shawn from elementary school all the way through college. I was generally strict about him not roaming the streets and having fewer friends."

"In the community," she continued, "I was a role model. People saw my son, who had gone to college, as proof that despite the odds, Black kids with similar broken family experiences didn't have to end up in the school-to-prison pipeline.

"'Listen up, son. Don't mess with them drugs, and stay away from them white girls. That's how you keep your ass out of a prison.' That's what I would tell Shawn."

Jasmine looked Lisa dead in the eye, like she was trying to read her thoughts. Then she said, "To make long story short, Marquis went back to his old ways and ended up dead within a year of getting out of prison. And Willie passed away about a year later because of diabetes. It was a hard time for me and a harder time for Shawn, but soon as we became roomies, he started working part-time to help with rent "My son ain't capable of killing nobody. He ain't never harmed nobody in his whole life. He can't even squash a cockroach."

"Jasmine, I'm glad you've shared so much with me. But there's one thing from this newspaper article I need to ask you about. It says your husband left behind a will, asking his friends to have his body cremated and his ashes mixed with cocaine for mourners to… well, you know."

"Oh, those tabloids, always making things up. My husband had a proper burial, no cremation, and definitely no cocaine snorting at his funeral."

Her story had moved Lisa—but only to a point. She had already heard countless versions of the innocent's plea. This is what anyone expected for any mother of a murderer to say. Lisa was also expecting Shawn to paint himself as the good guy. The most nefarious despots even had their moments of compassion. Even Adolf Hitler supposedly cried when his cat died. He became a vegetarian. Big deal.

"Jasmine," Lisa called, "I appreciate what you've shared. And I know this is a difficult time for you. But we need to ask you some questions about Shawn and his relationship with Sheila."

Jasmine nodded, tears welling up in her eyes.

Lisa leaned forward, her tone gentle but probing. "Can you tell me about Shawn's *relationship* with Sheila? What was it like?"

Jasmine hesitated, her gaze dropping to her lap. "Well, they were friends, you know. They met at the university, and Sheila was always so kind to Shawn. She helped him a lot."

She raised an eyebrow. "Are you sure it was just friendship?"

Jasmine's face flushed and her voice quivered. "Yes, of course. Just friends. They never had anything more than that."

She decided to press further. "Shawn… admitted to having feelings for Sheila during his initial interrogation. Why would he confess to something like that if it wasn't true?"

Jasmine fidgeted in her chair, her fingers twisting the tissue. "Well, maybe he misspoke or was confused. It's been stressful, and he's been through so much."

Lisa took it in, careful not to overheat. "Shawn told us about a job in Washington that Sheila helped him secure. Can you tell me more about that job?"

Jasmine hesitated once again, and her voice dropped to a near-whisper. "Yes, she did help him get that job. It was a… a good opportunity, and she knew he needed it."

"Are you saying that the job was the only connection between them?" Lisa asked.

Jasmine was visibly flustered, her eyes darting around the room. "Well, yes, that's the main reason they were close. Sheila was generous, always looking out for others."

Lisa leaned back in her chair, studying Jasmine carefully. "I appreciate your time today. but one piece of advice, just between me and you," she said. "Please do lawyer up. I'm not supposed to be telling you this, but… I'm also a mother. Your son is facing charges for a capital crime, and as touching as your story is, it doesn't do much to help prove that Shawn is innocent."

CHAPTER 10

Shawn

BACK in the interrogation room, Detective Bus turned his attention to Shawn, with his sharp gaze.

"Alright," he began, "Let's talk a little bit more about your interactions with Sheila *in your college classes*—I know you and Lisa spoke some but… there's more to it, isn't there?"

Shawn nodded, nervous, with Lisa also present in the room, looking on.

"Look," Bus said, "We understand that there were… *racial tensions* on campus. And I'd like to understand how Sheila's being bi-racial played into all that. In a white majority university."

Shawn shifted in his chair, meeting Bus's probing eyes.

"Well," he said, "we definitely had some heated discussions in class. Lotta times, I was the only Black person surrounded by a sea of white faces."

"How'd that make you feel?"

"Feel? I made it my mission... to challenge stereotypes and prove that being Black didn't set me apart."

Bus's eyebrows furrowed on instinct. "Tell me more about these debates," he said.

"I could feel the tension every time I stepped into that classroom," Shawn said. "All eyes were trained on me, ready to pass judgment whenever I dared to raise my hand or even just join in on a class discussion. It was like... like my white peers expected me to be twice as good as they were, just to convince them I deserved my little place at Essex University. They thought I just slid in on affirmative action."

Detective Bus said, "Okay. And how did Sheila fit into all of this?'

"Well," Shawn said, "Sheila... had a unique perspective. She kind of... added another layer to our discussions

"Can you be more specific?" Lisa asked.

"Well... like, I remember this one particular assignment where we all had to write essays on hybrid languages, right? We'd been assigned two essays to prepare. The first was *Nobody Mean More to Me Than You and the Future Life of Willie Jordan* by June Jordan, a—she's a... a poet, and an activist. Anyway, her whole thing delved into the legitimacy of Black English, formally referred to as, uh, African American Vernacular English—that's A-A-V-E. Second essay was *How to Tame a Wild Tongue* by Gloria Anzaldúa, focusing on the legitimacy of Chicano Spanish, you know, spoken along the US-Mexico border."

"Okay," Bus said. "So *where does Shiela fit in*."

"Well, our instructor was this middle-aged white man

named Donald, and he had asked us to write our perspectives on the usefulness and value of hybrid languages. We were to share our work with our peers, and everybody was talking with each other about their different contributions. Katie… that's Katie Saoirse, one of our classmates, had read my essay and launched into this *scathing* critique. She was totally out to bust my ass. Everybody's ass!

"First, she dismissed my essay as a collection of disorganized rants more suited for a rap song than a literary essay. Then she went on this tirade about how hybrid languages existed only because people failed to speak proper English. I remember, she said, *"We will be rewarding failure if we acknowledge these languages. English must be spoken correctly and properly.'* And she was confident.

"Anyway, Greg Smith, this white student, stepped up to Katie. He called her a racist. He stood up for me and Sheila, *insisting* that we deserved equal treatment in the class as Black individuals. I was happy to hear it. But you know what? Things were different for Shiela. For one, she didn't even consider herself Black! I mean, her mom was from Sweden, that freaked us out. Maybe the whitest place in the world. But here in America, she was *consistently* classified as Black—and it frustrated her. Like, it clashed with who she thought she was."

"So, this Katie launched an attack. Greg defended. How'd Sheila take it?"

"Greg, like, wanted to snooker Sheila into a classroom war about racial identity by grouping her with me, the only Black male in the course, but Sheila protested. She was all like, *'I'm not Black!'* She was pissed."

"Then what happened?"

"The classroom went silent. Everyone started exchanging these perplexed glances… like, trying to process the revelation. It was an awkward moment that stuck with me."

Bus took it in. The kid before him wasn't all bad. He was beginning to like him or at least appreciate that he was being candid. Bus said, "Was Sheila always this confused about her race?"

Shawn said, "I think so—in fact, she once told me a story that, while filling out forms at the admissions office, an administrator questioned her choice of marking 'white' as her race, assuming it was a mistake. And here's Sheila, she just couldn't fathom why she had always been referred to as white in Uganda but was labeled as Black in America."

Bus probed further. "Did you ever talk to her about it?"

"Hell yeah. I told her about the injustice of the one-drop rule, which had been used socially and legally throughout the twentieth century in the US. It weighed heavily on her."

"Remind me," Bus said.

"A single *drop* of nonwhite blood meant you ain't white. Sheila could hardly believe it."

"Okay, Shawn," Bus said. "I get it, you're the only Black person in the classroom… but c'mon. The school definitely had some more Black people. Did Sheila ever interact or become friends with any *other* Black people at the school, that you know of?"

"No. Sheila was… irked by the way American Black men often called her *sister* in public. '*Why do they have to claim me? I'm not one of them!*"

"All right, all right," Bus said, getting impatient. "Let's get back to the class debate on race, what happened next?"

"To regain control of the class discussion about the assignment, Donald, the lecturer, steered the conversation back to my essay," Shawn said. "Expertly." I countered Katie's arguments by highlighting that even English was an improper linguistic descendant of German and Latin. I said, '*If the Germans had blocked all the folks who couldn't speak their language right, we wouldn't be having English today.*'"

Bus interrupted again, his tone more serious and focused. "Shawn, all that's fine. But… look. You're an educated man, and I know you're familiar with the term *Black on Black crime*. We're trying to establish if there's any dimension of racially related hatred connected to Sheila's murder. As you can see, I'm biracial like Sheila—my mother is also from Uganda, just like Sheila's father. And I'm the right person to ask you these questions."

Shawn felt anger rise within himself as he responded, "You seem like you're already taking sides, Detective. I still don't get it. Why is my race and her race even relevant here?"

Tears welled up in Shawn's eyes, and for the first time since his arrest, he broke down. He was embarrassed to cry in front of Lisa, but the weight of the case had become overwhelming. Lisa and Bus both looked on, their expressions seemingly unmoved by his emotional outburst.

Bus cleared his throat, changed his expression and said, "Please, Shawn, collect yourself and talk to us like a man. Crying won't help you here."

With his face still hidden in his palms, Shawn said, "You don't have a single piece of evidence—nothing!—but you're already bragging about your biracial and white complexion stuff. Is this for real?"

Bus's voice hardened. "We do the questioning here, and you answer, not the other way around, Shawn. Stop pushing."

"Get me out of here. I'm innocent. Why can't you people understand that?"

Lisa entered the conversation, playing good cop. "Shawn, are you okay? Do you need to rest?"

"No, no. Okay, fine. What do you want me to tell you?"

"Tell us about Katie. Did she continue being racist toward you? Was she racist toward Sheila as well?" Bus said.

"No," Shawn replied, a faint smile crossing his face. "We actually became friends with Katie from that point on."

This fell like a thud. Without further ado, the detectives collected their files and told Shawn that they were done for the day.

As they exited the room, Shawn settled back, waiting for the guards to escort him to his cell. His thoughts drifted back to that class debate and how it had ultimately led to his friendship with Katie. Katie had followed Shawn into the hallway. Her steps were hesitant, but her apology was sincere. She admitted that her comments had been out of line, and she reassured him that she was learning how her responses and reactions, even if they seemed not to be racist on the surface, could end up being just as hurtful and offensive. She told him not to hesitate to call her out in the future if she said something hurtful, even if it was accidental or unintentional.

Shawn listened to her, and despite his initial frustration, he felt open-minded about the subject and accepted Katie's apology as genuine. After all, he remembered the saying, "Judge not, that ye be not judged."

Katie told Shawn that she came from a less privileged background herself, with economic struggles that many other white individuals didn't experience. Besides her studies, she worked at a coffee shop and had hoped for a better job. She once interviewed for a clerk position that would have paid more, only to learn that a Black woman was chosen for the job. The manager who interviewed Katie confided in her that, despite her better qualifications, the company needed to diversify its workforce due to new diversity initiatives.

At that moment, Katie had felt vulnerable and had blurted out to the manager, "I am from a poor white family, and my family never owned any slaves. Why is a Black candidate being hired for a job ahead of me just because I'm white?"

Shawn understood the plight of poor whites struggling to make a living, and he had already prepared his standard response to those who pointed out that there were other successful Black individuals who didn't need a racial card push, without acknowledging the broader issue.

He explained to Katie that while there were indeed poor white folks, they couldn't claim their poverty was due to their skin color. They had racial privilege that wouldn't hold them back. On the other hand, Black people often found doors closed to them solely because of their race, making it harder to bounce back or get second chances.

Katie nodded, absorbing his perspective. It seemed that he was the first Black person she had encountered whom she could trust, especially when she felt vulnerable. He also talked to her about how income inequality was a growing problem for both poor white and Black individuals and he stressed the importance of setting aside their differences and uniting to fight against economic inequality.

He turned to Katie, who seemed more sympathetic. "We're all in this economic mess together, you feel me? There are poor white folks just like a lot of us Black folks who've been struggling forever. This fight for fairness and living with dignity—it's not just about Black folks, and it shouldn't be. We gotta come together, work side by side instead of fighting against one another if we're gonna make it through."

Katie realized how much she still had to learn, and she was grateful that he took the time to explain it, especially after what had happened in class. He tried to remain as positive as possible, talking about how Blacks and whites had come together in movements like Occupy Wall Street and Occupy Boston to address issues of disenfranchisement not just at home but also in school and the workplace.

As they continued their conversation, they didn't realize how much time had passed. Katie had one more question, though: "Are there no Black people who are racists?"

CHAPTER 11

Bus

A WEEK later, Detective Bus sat in his office at the police station with maps and crime scene photos. He adjusted the earpiece of the listening device, the wire trailing down to a recorder on his desk. He had just received information that Shawn, the prime suspect in the Sheila murder case, was making a phone call from the jail. This was an opportunity he couldn't afford to miss.

Katie's phone buzzed and a recorded message played instantly. *This is a call from the county correctional facilities in Acton, Massachusetts, To accept the call please press "one."*

"I'm locked up in Jail, Katie."

"Yes, I know. You are all over the news." A long pause. Then, "What do you want, Shawn?"

"I need a good lawyer, obviously. Someone who specializes in criminal defense. Can you help my mom find one for me?" Shawn said. "These detectives just wouldn't lay off. They kept saying they couldn't wait forever for me to appoint a lawyer before they started their interrogation."

Bus furrowed his brow, his focus unwavering as he scribbled down notes. Shawn sounded terrified.

Katie said, "Shawn, I don't know how to do that. I've never been in a situation like this before."

"Katie, please, I need you to figure this out with my mom. You're the only two I can trust. I don't have anyone else. Nobody. And… I… I can't stay in here."

Bus began to wonder who this Katie was—and who she was to Shawn. The desperation in Shawn's voice suggested a deep connection, one that went beyond the confines of friendship.

Katie hesitated, and then her voice softened. "Okay, Shawn, I'll do my best. I missed a call from your mother. I will call her back tonight and see,"

"Thank you."

There was a silence, then the line clicked—they both seemed to know that any casual chatting was out of the question.

Bus knew that he now had to find this girl. On the phone she sounded white, and this mystified Bus even more. She also sounded like she was still in shock.

Bus could not fathom her relationship with Shawn. He quickly dialed the tech guys and asked them to search the line.

The tech guys came back to Detective Bus with a report showing that Katie had been making numerous calls regarding Shawn's case since his arrest. They had a log of all the calls she made. However, one call she placed to

Jasmine right after speaking with Shawn stood out as particularly significant.

"Hey, Jasmine," Katie said.

"Hey Katie," Jasmine replied, relief evident in her voice.

"I went to the jail today and had a chat with Lisa," Jasmine continued. "I thought she'd let me meet Shawn, but she mentioned needing some time to sort out paperwork for the visitation. Then, Shawn called me later today and said they had allowed two days for visitation. You down to roll with me and visit him someday?" Jasmine asked.

"I'm not sure what I'm supposed to do right now, Jasmine. He called me and wants us to find him a criminal defense attorney. I think let's focus on that now," Katie replied.

"My friend hooked me up with this attorney named Martin. He's got his office in Quincy. I was thinking of going to see him tomorrow at 10 a.m. You down to roll with me?"

"Yes, send me the address. We will meet there at nine-thirty before the appointment."

Two days later, Shawn was going to receive his first visitors. Bus had already been notified about this visit and was again determined to see and listen to it from afar in his office.

Detective Bus turned his attention to the live surveillance screen before him. The screen displayed the crowded waiting area of the county jail, a place filled with a mix of emotions, from tearful goodbyes to anxious faces waiting to see their loved ones.

His attention was focused on a particular individual,

Katie, who had arrived at the jail. She was nervously shifting from foot to foot, glancing at the heavy security doors and the stern-faced guards. Her eyes betrayed her anxiety.

Bus adjusted the earpiece in his ear, ensuring he didn't miss any of the conversation. He knew that Katie's visit to Shawn, the prime suspect in Sheila's murder case, could potentially reveal more about the events leading up to the crime.

Katie was ushered into the visitation area. She clutched a small bag tightly to her chest, her fingers trembling slightly.

Through the small microphone on the table in the jail's visiting room, Shawn and Katie began their conversation. Bus listened intently as their voices came through the speakers.

"Shawn, I've been so worried about you," Katie's voice quivered as she spoke.

Shawn, on the other side of the glass partition, managed a weak smile. "I've missed you, Katie. I didn't expect to see you here."

Bus jotted down notes.

Katie's voice dropped to a whisper as she continued, "I had to come, Shawn. We're all so worried. Your mom, your friends… we want to help you get out of here."

"I know, Katie, but it's not that easy. I've been talking to the others here, and I've realized how serious this is. We need a good lawyer, and we need bail money."

"So, I went with Jasmine to see this lawyer yesterday…" Katie said as Shawn listened intently.

Bus was eavesdropping from the other side

"Friends in the Black community had told Jasmine he

was one of the best criminal lawyers, especially for representing Black individuals arrested for felonies and crimes including murder and rape."

"I didn't do it, Katie, I—" Shawn protested.

"I know. Anyway, Martin Sterling was already familiar with the case, as it had been all over the news. He also had been gathering details about the investigation. Jasmine and I were pretty impressed that he already seemed so familiar with the case and agreed that he could successfully defend you, so we agreed to let him defend you, provided that that… there was nothing that had been suppressed."

"I don't understand."

"He just wanted to make sure that we didn't hold anything back that might raise further suspicions. Martin Sterling is a high-profile defense attorney with a solid track record. He's dealt with major national news stories before, and he knows how to communicate with public affairs programs. He also knows how to overwhelm critics who resisted criminal justice reform. But… we knew that his price tag would be high."

"How high?"

"In cases like this, you need to set aside a budget of up to $100,000 for legal representation. He said he'd take $20,000 as an initial deposit to start working on the case and the remainder would have to be paid at the conclusion."

"My mom doesn't have that kind of money."

"Well, she considered selling your new car, which would raise less than $20,000 as a second-hand sale. And if she sold her car as well, she could raise another $10,000 but she also could not guarantee she would be able to raise the remainder of the funds."

"Even if she could," Shawn said. "there's no telling that it'll work. We are not sure what the large sum of legal representation costs guarantee for us. Was the lawyer promising if my mom could raise $100,000 that I would be free? Was the lawyer going to help negotiate down the bail amount needed to get me out of county jail until the trial?"

Katie ignored his burst of frustration and continued. "Martin explained how he had arrived at calculating your fees. Your case was unique and complicated. It's a murder with aggravated charges of rape. In Massachusetts, if convicted, you could face life in prison without parole. The local and state media have already descended into a frenzy, and they're casting you as a likely suspect who was a guilty and jealous boyfriend—"

"Katie, I did not *do* this!"

"I know that, Shawn. But the headlines are *sensationalized*. They don't even know if you can even get a neutral jury—that's what the lawyer told us."

Detective Bus set aside his notes. He couldn't help but feel the weight of the situation. If Shawn's family and friends couldn't afford a defense attorney or the hefty bail fees, it added a layer of complexity to the case.

"Martin brought up something important that has to be resolved. He mentioned that someone in the prosecutor's office had already leaked transcripts of those controversial phone calls. You know, the ones that paint you in a really negative light," Katie said. "They might have leaked just the bits to make you look bad. Martin thinks the prosecutors will want any defense attorney to agree to keep things secret if the case goes to trial. He's also planning to ask the state attorney general's office to look into the leak. Martin wants to make sure that the prosecutors didn't twist those leaked bits just to make you look guilty. He wants to clear things up before anything else happens."

Shawn continued to listen in silence, his mind likely filled with thoughts about how all this chaos had suddenly descended upon him and how what was supposed to be a quick exit turned into something much more complicated.

"Mr. Sterling told us that a female victim's pleading voice in these transcripts can become strong evidence in the minds of potential jurors," Katie said.

He asked us to consider your situation in light of the Biblical story of Joseph and Potiphar's wife, where the temptress's word alone was enough to put Joseph in jail.

As a criminal lawyer, he explained that it would be a complicated task to neutralize the weight of such evidence in your case. He also mentioned the need to probe deeper into why this information was leaked and why someone would take such a risk that could potentially damage the prosecution's case.

As Bus listened in, he could hear Katie's voice, tender and filled with a mix of uncertainty and reluctance.

"Shawn, I'll do everything I can to help. We'll find a way to get you out of here. Just hang in there."

Then changing the subject, she said.

"Hey, Shawn, I've got another story for you," Katie said.

"What's up?"

"Well, I'm pregnant."

"Real?" Shawn asked.

"Positive, I had intended to terminate the pregnancy?"

"Yeah, go on."

"So, I walked down Park Street to catch the green line train from Boston Commons to Commonwealth Avenue. As I was walking, I passed by that spot where you and Sheila used to sit and chat after class in Boston Commons. It's funny how things change, huh? Anyway, then I remembered how Sheila would take the same train home."

"I… I decided to go to the local Planned Parenthood clinic," Katie said.

"Oh, okay. Are you okay?"

"Yeah, I just… I wondered if you had anything to do with Sheila's… you know… her death. I suspected I might be pregnant, and I was so scared I'd end up like her."

"Katie, I would never…"

"I know, I know. Sorry. I'm just so anxious lately. Anyway, at the clinic, there were these anti-abortion protesters outside. One elderly woman came up to me with a sign saying, 'Abortion is a sin' and said, 'Please don't kill your baby, give her to me, and I will raise it.' I didn't say anything, just went inside."

"That sounds intense," Shawn said.

A nurse appeared and led me to the waiting area and asked me "Do you have an appointment today?"

"No, I didn't realize I needed one. Do you take walk-ins?" I replied.

"Actually, we don't, but I'll let you speak to a counselor. Just fill out this form with your details," she said, handing me a clipboard.

"After that, the nurse took me to this separate area and checked all my vitals and stuff. Then she told me it would cost $1,100 for the procedure, and I only had $500 saved up."

"That's rough," Shawn said.

"Yeah, but the nurse said there were some options to help with the costs. She gave me some contacts and then escorted me out of the clinic. I didn't want to stick around too long. Those protesters outside were something else."

When she took the train to return to campus, she replayed in her mind the whole string of scenes that had brought her to this moment. She thought about how Shawn always bragged about his prowess in sex, knowing when to pull out when he was about to ejaculate. In fact, Shawn often climaxed on her thighs. He even joked about how popular he was in Texas, a state notorious for having among the nation's most stringent bans on abortions. "If I put a profile on a dating app and mentioned that I was a master of withdrawal, my app would be jammed with notifications," he'd said.

Katie had laughed off the joke, as she took a tissue and wiped her thighs. She always had believed that sex with Shawn was worth it and that she would never get pregnant. Now, he was in jail, awaiting trial on a first-degree murder case. And she was desperate to end this pregnancy as soon as possible. *If he was here now, I would punch him so hard.*

Katie believed that Shawn had betrayed her by not telling her that he had once failed to withdraw before climaxing. Moreover, Shawn occasionally talked about how withdrawing before climax never satisfied him. He talked about how states like Texas were anti-orgasm. But he conveniently forgot that in states which still accepted abortion as legal, access to the procedure still cost too much for people who often sought it out the most. The rich could always get an abortion. But there were many single women like Katie, including those who were in even much direr circumstances than her.

"When I got back to my dorm room, I called the number the nurse gave me."

"And?"

"It turns out it was a place in Worcester, which is pretty far from here, and when I talked to the woman there, she explained that their services were all about finding homes for babies of troubled pregnancies. They'd support me until I gave birth, and then the baby would be taken for adoption."

"That's… a lot to take in."

Katie said, "It is. But I just can't do it, Shawn. I couldn't bring a child into the world just to have them taken away like that. I'd always feel guilty knowing my child was out there somewhere, maybe even too far away for us to ever reunite if they ever wanted to find their biological parents."

"I understand, Katie. It's our baby. As soon as I leave this prison, we'll take good care of them."

"Yeah. So, I thanked the woman and decided to hold off on anything until I could raise the rest of the money I need for the abortion."

Bus watched the screen intently. Just as Katie's visitation came to an end and she got up to kiss him goodbye, the heavy steel door creaked open once more, revealing

Shawn's mother, Jasmine. Bus's eyebrows went up in surprise. This, he wasn't expecting.

Her face bore the lines of worry and sleepless nights, but her eyes held a fierce determination.

"Mama," Shawn called.

She rushed forward, enveloping him in a tight hug through the cold, metal bars that separated them. "Oh, Shawn, we'll get through this. I promise."

Shawn had tears welling up in his eyes as he held onto his mother.

Katie and Jasmine exchanged a few words, their voices hushed and filled with concern.

Then visitation time drew to a close, Katie kissed Shawn softly, her lips lingering on the glass for a moment before she reluctantly pulled away.

"Take care, Shawn," she whispered, her eyes brimming with tears.

"I will, Katie," he replied. "Thank you for everything."

She nodded, and with one last lingering gaze, she turned to leave. Jasmine followed, casting him a reassuring smile filled with love and resilience.

The heavy steel door closed behind them, and Shawn was once again alone. Bus also closed his notebook and stood up to reflect and think through his plan of visiting Katie.

CHAPTER 12

Shawn

SHAWN lay on his jail bunk, staring at the ceiling, remembering things. He understood that his arrest was tough on Katie, just as much as it was tough on him, and nothing had prepared her to be in a relationship with a murder suspect. It had almost been a month since she'd taken him to meet her parents in Springfield for dinner at a restaurant.

As Shawn and Katie stepped into her parents' home in Springfield, her parents greeted them warmly. They exchanged kisses with their daughter and then extended their hands to Shawn, welcoming him to join them at the dining table. "We are already late for our reservation. We shouldn't be sitting. Why don't we just get ready to go," Katie announced.

"But how is school, Katie? Are you planning to major in journalism or creative writing?" said Katie's father Edward, leaning on his chair. He walked sometimes with an unsteady limp, but he was too proud to use a walker.

When Katie didn't answer, Shawn chimed in. "She's gonna do creative writing, you know? She's grinding hard, trying to write her heart out and make a difference in this world."

"I'm not talking to you," her father said, his tone instantly sharp, terse. "I'm just trying to have a private conversation with my daughter. Please stay out of it,"

"Dad. Please be nice."

"Don't take it personally, Shawn," Katie's mom, Carol, said. "Edward is always hostile to his daughter's boyfriends. He thinks they are going to take his daughter away from him. Katie, do you remember how he treated Ryan at first? Oh my god, Edward was furious when Ryan came to pick you up to go out. And the other boy you dated in high school, what was his name?"

Katie waved her hand dismissively, hoping to stop her mother from spilling more tea at the table.

"Okay, Mom, that's enough. Let's go. Don't start counting off my boyfriends to Shawn. Let's get out of here."

Edward, the father, limped off to a nearby corner. Katie went to him and begged him to rejoin the family, but he said he wanted to go to another restaurant. He didn't want this Asian restaurant because he could not stand the spicy food.

Shawn offered to drive the family to another restaurant but when they arrived at the second location, Edward was still not in the mood for eating. He demanded to be taken back home. Carol insisted she wanted to eat, and Shawn was confused by this family drama playing out in front of him.

"Dad, thank you so much for behaving so well today," Katie said, the sarcasm so blunt that it seemed to anger her father even more.

Carol was always quick to explain her husband's erratic behavior as non-racist but then added he was just mad at some Black folks who had wronged his family.

Shawn had heard stories from Katie in the past about her parents' fallout with their Haitian Black caretaker. She told him of when Edward almost beat this poor woman who had left her mother to go back to school.

Her name was Marie, and she had taken care of Edward's mother, Linda, for five years and Linda had become fond of her. She asked the caregiver's agency to replace all their aides with women just like Marie. It was Marie who regularly took Linda to doctor's appointments, social gatherings, family parties, mall shopping, and regular walks for exercise.

Every family member and friend of Linda came to know Marie, and whenever they would see Linda, Marie was always besides her. One day, Marie decided she would enroll in nursing school, and initially, she cut her working hours. When the school workload intensified, she decided to resign and concentrate on her studies.

Linda was heartbroken. For several days, she didn't get out of bed because no one could lift her into her wheelchair. The family decided to take her to a nursing home, but the staff there were rude and often left her unattended for hours. Every day, she cried about losing Marie as her aide and told all her visitors that she was dying because she missed her caregiver, who happened to be Black. Linda always made it a point to announce that her beloved caregiver was Black.

After two months in a nursing home, she was found dead. Edward was distraught. He asked the nursing staff what time his mother died, and they said sometime between two and five in the afternoon. They were not even certain of the exact time she had left the world, as a testimony that they consistently had left her alone, often all day, without bothering to check on her.

Marie attended the funeral, and Edward was so angry that he stopped short of punching her, as he furiously accused her of murdering his mother.

"She would not be in that casket waiting to be lowered in a grave if this dirty nigger had not gone to that stupid nursing school and abandoned her," he shouted, in a fury that caught everyone's attention and they stared at Marie who had just walked into the viewing room.

Carol tried to apologize for her husband's outburst first to Marie and then explained to others in the room. Yet, she still managed to blame Marie, even if it was not intentional, for deciding to go to school and leave the family. But, still she offered nothing to explain how her husband's irrational anger justified suddenly becoming so antagonizing and racist against Black people.

Edward did not make the embarrassing situation in the restaurant any better. He scolded his wife, telling her that he did not need anyone to speak on his behalf.

"My daughter was only seven when they urged her to apologize to Black kids in her school for slavery. What did *she* have to do with slavery?" He was practically shouting. "No one in my family ever owned a slave. My father and grandfather were all poor people who worked their asses off in factories for a living but because we are *whites*, we are targets and our children are forced to apologize. The Black people are taking over this country, and it is not funny. It is now a crime to be white. At the college, my daughter again was not selected for an assistantship because some Black students had applied, and they are *privileged* because of affirmative action. Maybe they hired your sister, and now you come here, buying me dinner, and you want me to be grateful. The Black people are asking for reparations, and they will cut our social security checks to give them the money. Forget it! Why can't Black people move on like anyone else?"

The tirade had left Katie's father angered but also nearly in tears. Katie offered him a tissue and rubbed his shoulders. "Dad, Shawn does not have a sister and you should not be so rude to him. He is a good guy and if you just got to know him… I bet you'd come to respect him. And maybe even love him."

Needless to say, her dad did not answer this.

The trip to their home was uneasily quiet. No one spoke a word. When the family returned home, it was Carol's turn to speak up. She halted Shawn on his way to the bathroom.

"Oh honey, don't use this bathroom," she said, as she stood up and raised her hands to block him from entering the bathroom. "Edward uses this bathroom and is so vulnerable to infections. You would be fine using the toilet outside—the contractors put it up there. Does that sound okay, honey?"

After this, Shawn and Katie left immediately. As soon as he started the car, he told her that he'd never visit her parents' home again. After another grueling silence, he said, "Why didn't you speak up—why didn't you defend me?"

"Because it wouldn't have done any good. They're just… major cranks. That's how they are. But they eventually will be fine with you, you'll see."

Her excuse seemed weak to Shawn, and she picked up on his skepticism.

Katie went on. "Look, my parents are just… parents. They're not perfect. But all parents have their biases. You told me your mother warned you against dating white girls. *'White devils that will only put a Black man down.'* C'mon Shawn, it's the same thing."

And now, laying on his hard bunk under the cracked jail-cell ceiling, with the sounds of the guards walking up and down the hallway, he pictured Katie helping his mom find the legal representation. And it was true—mom didn't like her much… it was barely better than the way her parents had treated him.

Another memory, days later, Katie said her father called a day after the visit and apologized for his behavior but still made it clear that his daughter was making a terrible mistake dating a Black guy. She imitated her dad for Shawn.

"*Katie, you went to school at Essex University—not Howard University. Of all the people you could have picked out to date, you went to a single Black boy in class to be your boyfriend. I'm not being judgmental or being racist but are you sure about what you're doing?*"

Now Katie was probably wondering if he was right.

CHAPTER 13

Bus

BUS stepped out of his state police patrol car, the brisk evening air hitting his face as he glanced up at the aging apartment building. It loomed like a silent sentinel over the city streets, its cracked facade revealing the wear and tear of decades. Tonight, this building held secrets that Bus was determined to uncover.

Sheila had lived here, in this modest apartment, until her life had been cruelly snuffed out. Now, Bus had come to gather evidence, and he had a hunch that Amos, Sheila's half-brother, knew more than he was letting on.

Bus entered the dimly lit building, the flickering fluorescent lights overhead casting eerie shadows on the walls, and a chill ran down his spine. He climbed the creaking stairs to the second floor, stopping in front of apartment 205. He pulled on a pair of latex gloves before knocking on the door.

The door creaked open, revealing Amos, a disheveled and grief-stricken young man. His eyes were red-rimmed from crying, and he clutched a tissue in one trembling hand.

"Mr. Amos Musinga, I'm Detective Bus. I'm here to investigate your sister's murder, and I'd like to ask you a few questions."

"I don't know if I should talk to you without permission from the family," he said.

"I understand your concerns, Mr. Amos," Bus said. "But we're doing everything we can to find out what happened to your sister. I promise to be discreet and respectful."

Amos nodded and stepped aside, allowing Bus to enter the apartment.

The room was a reflection of the way people described Sheila—warm and inviting. A soft, lavender-scented candle flickered on the nightstand, casting a gentle glow across the neatly made bed. Bus noted every detail, from the family photos on the walls. He asked to see Sheila's bedroom and followed Amos down a narrow hallway, where the atmosphere grew even more somber.

The bedroom was a stark contrast to the rest of the apartment. It was tidy and covered with soft pastel colors. Framed photos of Sheila and her family and friends adorned the walls, capturing happier times.

Bus knelt by Sheila's desk, where her laptop sat in silence. He carefully placed it in an evidence bag and sealed it, all the while noting the meticulous organization of her belongings. It was as if she had been preparing for something, but what?

"Amos," Bus said, turning to face the young man standing in the doorway, "I need to take this laptop for examination."

Amos nodded again, his expression a mix of despair with his loss.

"Amos, can you tell me about Sheila's recent activities? Did she mention anyone who might have had a reason to harm her?"

Amos hesitated, his eyes welling up with tears. "I want to help, Detective, but I think you should talk to my father first."

Amos seemed torn, his internal struggle evident in his furrowed brow. Finally, he reached for his phone and dialed a number. Bus watched intently as Amos spoke in hushed tones, mixing English and his local African language, explaining the situation to the person on the other end. After what felt like an eternity, Amos handed the phone to Bus. "It's my dad," he said quietly, avoiding eye contact.

Bus took the phone and put it to his ear. "Mr. Musinga?"

"Hello, Detective," he replied.

"You may remember me, Mr. Musinga," he said. "I worked with you in the Congo."

"Really?"

"That's right—you used to call me by my full Ugandan name, Basudde."

"Of course, Basudde *Herman*!" Mr. Musinga said—it was a nickname he'd given Bus after the popular Ugandan singer. "It's good to hear your voice again, though I wish it were under different circumstances."

"I'm so sorry for your loss, Mr. Musinga," Bus said. "I'm a detective with the force here. We're hoping to find out who murdered your daughter."

"Thank you, Detective Basudde," Musinga replied in his usual polite way, just as he had always been during their time together in Africa. "Is there a way I can help you?"

"Well, it would help if you could let your son know that it's best for him to share everything he can with us," he said, his gaze shifting to the young man who stood silently beside him.

"Detective Basudde," Musinga said, sounding a little hesitant. "There's something you should know."

"Please—tell me."

"Your main suspect, Shawn, was working on 'The General's Project.' It's a very sensitive project here in Uganda," Mr. Musinga explained cautiously. "We are trying to have my nephew, the president's son, General Mlevi Kainewaragi, replace my brother as the next president. We have invested enormous resources into promoting this project to the people in Washington, and Shawn was helping with the publicity."

Mr. Musinga hesitated for a moment before continuing "We don't want this to go in any news that the suspect was working on this project or to have this project be affected negatively in any way. That's why we are being careful with whatever we say and don't say. And that is why we want my son, Amos, if he is ever going to give you any information, to be in the presence of a lawyer. I think you understand, having worked in Africa yourself, how these things work."

"I do," Bus said. "Do you mind giving me the cell phone of the lawyer so that I can schedule an appointment? Time is of the essence."

"Give a business card to my son, Mr. Basudde," Mr. Musinga said. "I'm going to ask the lawyer to call you ASAP."

As he left the apartment and settled into his car, driving through the bustling streets, Bus could not stop imagining how the voice of Mr. Musinga was still familiar. He had been one of the contacts in Uganda when he worked with the CIA's clandestine operations in the region. Five years securing the Shinkolobwe uranium mines—it was all coming back.

Bus's cover position had been the UN-Congo security analyst based in Entebbe, Uganda, but in reality, he spent most of the week in Katanga, traveling on a UN aircraft. When he returned to Uganda on the weekends, it was Mr. Musinga who was responsible for providing him and others with the necessary supplies. He called him by his full name, Basudde, and even once offered Bus a music cassette of the popular singer Basudde Herman Semakula. It was a peculiar gesture, but he understood that it was Mr. Musinga's way of acknowledging his importance in securing the Shinkolobwe mines.

The Shinkolobwe mines were of utmost significance to American interests in the region, thanks to their uranium deposits. The United States couldn't afford to let it slip into Russian hands. Mr. Musinga handled Bus as if he were special because of his role in securing this vital mine. He used to remind Bus when Bus visited Uganda, "You can have everything you want because that mine is the most important thing for all of us."

Mr. Musinga's voice on the phone brought back memories of those covert operations. The dusty landscapes of Katanga, the long nights strategizing with the operatives, and the constant tension of keeping the uranium mine out of enemy hands. It was a time of secrecy and danger, and it had changed Bus profoundly.

But now, years later, he found himself on a different path, working as a police detective in Massachusetts. Yet, his past had a way of catching up with him. Mr. Musinga's call meant that Bus's past life and his current one were about to intersect in a way he hadn't anticipated.

From Sheila's home, Detective Bus went straight to Katie's college dormitory. It was like a field day for him to check out all the evidence outside the crime scene. From the moment he'd heard her talking to Shawn on the wiretap, he knew he'd have to question her. It was a crisp afternoon, and the campus was bustling with students, most of them oblivious to the grave matters he was about to inquire into.

He followed the directions he'd been given to reach Katie's room. The atmosphere was tense, and Bus could feel the weight of the conversation even before it began

He knocked on the door gently, and after a moment, Katie opened it. She looked surprised but not entirely shocked to see a detective at her doorstep.

"Katie, I'm Detective Bus," he began, his tone measured and sympathetic. "I'd like to ask you a few questions about your relationship with Shawn and some details about what's been happening."

Katie nodded and stepped aside, allowing him to enter. As he took a seat on her unmade bed, Katie perched on the chair by her desk.

"Katie, we know you've been in contact with Shawn," he said gently. "We need to understand your relationship. Can you tell me how the two of you got close?"

Katie sighed and looked down at her tightly clasped hands, "We… we met in class," she began. "We had some common friends. And, uh, I guess… I guess we just started hanging out."

Bus leaned forward. "And your romantic involvement?"

"We, um, we started dating a few months ago. But it was never that serious. More like a fling, you know?"

"And what can you tell me about the pregnancy, Katie?"

"How the F do you know that?"

"Shawn mentioned it during your conversation in the jail."

"Did you wiretap my visit to him? I mean, do you do this to all inmates?"

Bus nodded positively

"Ok. I was… I *am* pregnant. But Shawn didn't know about it until recently. I hadn't told him."

Bus raised an eyebrow. "Why didn't you tell him, Katie?"

"I was scared, Detective. I didn't know how he'd react. We were never that serious, and I didn't want to burden him."

"I see. I understand why you kept it to yourself. Now, we're also looking into something very serious, Katie. The murder of Sheila. We need to know if you had any information or if Shawn mentioned anything to you about her."

"Detective Bus," she said. "I can't believe all of this is happening."

Bus nodded, trying to convey some sympathy.

"I just can't wrap my head around it, Detective. Shawn… I mean, he's not perfect, but I can't believe he's capable of murdering anyone, let alone Sheila."

"Katie, we have evidence that points to Shawn's involvement. We need your help to understand what happened that night. Can you tell me everything you know?"

"I didn't see him that night," she said, tears streaming down her face, "I never thought I'd be in this situation. My parents warned me about Shawn, about the risks of being in a relationship like this."

"Your parents were concerned about your relationship with Shawn because he's Black, weren't they?"

Katie nodded, wiping away tears. "Yes, they were. My father cautioned me about it, and now… it's all coming back, and it feels like they were right."

"It's important not to jump to conclusions, Katie. We're investigating, and we'll find out the truth. But I need your cooperation."

"I know, Detective. I want to help, but it's just so overwhelming. My friends are calling me, asking about Shawn. I'm having nightmares about what might have happened that night."

"Katie, it might be a good idea to seek therapy to help you deal with all of this. It can be a lot to handle on your own."

"I think you're right, Detective. I need help to make

sense of all of this."

Bus looked at Katie, concern etched on his face. "Katie, I know this is incredibly difficult for you, but it's essential for us to understand everything we can about what happened that night. Can you tell me about the nightmares and dreams you've been having regarding Shawn and Sheila's murder? Every detail, no matter how small, could be crucial in our investigation."

"I had a dream that startled me in the middle of the night," Katie said. "I was in the living room with a baby in my hands. Shawn, in his jail uniform, opened the door and entered the house, with a bloodied knife in his hands and his shirt stained with fresh blood. I screamed and dropped the baby. That's when I woke up, shaking and crying."

Bus listened intently, taking in the dream's symbolism.

Katie continued, "I couldn't stop thinking about that dream and what my subconscious was trying to tell me. I remembered that I had purchased a pregnancy test kit a week before Shawn was arrested and had put it in my purse. I thought about taking the test periodically, but I kept postponing it, maybe fearing what the result might be. I had forgotten about it until Shawn was arrested.

"I saw that dream as a reminder that I had the test kit in my purse. So, I pulled it out and went to the bathroom in my dormitory. In a matter of moments, the result was what I already knew: I was pregnant."

Katie's vulnerability was evident, and Bus couldn't help but sympathize with her. Her life had taken a sudden, unexpected turn, and the weight of it all was taking a toll on her.

"I struggled to go back to sleep," she continued. "But I knew that first thing in the morning, I would meet with Shawn's mother to go to a lawyer. I left the light on, fearing that the darkness would bring back another nightmare I've been having since Shawn was arrested."

Katie took a deep breath, her eyes finally meeting Bus as she concluded, "In another dream, I saw Sheila coming to me, in the Essex University's Main Building on Washington Street. Sheila's neckline was covered in blood, but otherwise, her clothes were white and pristine. I tried to run away from her, but Sheila pleaded for me to stay, and she said she wasn't coming to me for a fight or an argument. That's when I woke up."

CHAPTER 14

Shawn

SLEEP in the jail became a struggle for Shawn. As his two roommates snored in a syncopated rhythm, Shawn lay awake on his narrow bed, the hard mattress offering little comfort. Deep into the night, he found himself immersed in a whirlpool of thoughts, unable to escape the harsh reality of his situation.

The weight of the murder charge pressed heavily upon him, suffocating him with its gravity. He couldn't shake the disbelief that he, Shawn, could be accused of such a heinous crime, especially against Sheila, someone he had cared for deeply. The betrayal stung him like a thousand needles, leaving him feeling more isolated and alone than ever before.

Pulling the thick cover of a scratchy blanket over his body, Shawn sought solace from the biting chill of the cell. But even the fabric failed to provide the warmth he so desperately craved. It felt as though the icy tendrils of despair had permeated every inch of his being, leaving him shivering despite his efforts to bundle up.

His mind drifted back to his last conversation with Sheila, the memory a haunting specter that refused to be banished. The accusations she had hurled at him still echoed in his ears, each word a dagger to his already wounded heart. How could she believe he was capable of such betrayal? And yet, her words had become the damning evidence that sealed his fate.

He longed for another chance to speak with her, to unravel the tangled web of accusations and discover the truth hidden beneath. Who were these supposed sources she had mentioned? Surely, they held the key to unraveling the mystery of her murder.

But Sheila was gone, her voice silenced forever, leaving Shawn alone in the darkness with only his memories for company. He remembered their last intimate moment together, before Shawn started dating Katie.

That day, Sheila asked him to take her out for a night in Downtown Boston. Near campus, where he stayed, Sheila had noticed the nightclubs in the neighborhood. But with school, she didn't have the time to stay out late and enjoy the club scene. And her brother Amos was so strict that she regularly returned home at the same hour on those nights. Whenever her brother was visiting the family in New York City, she could get away and stay out late without worrying about him snitching on her.

When Shawn and Sheila returned to her place after covering the nightclub circuit near campus, he stumbled through the front door of Sheila's apartment, his heart still racing from the night of dancing and laughter they had just shared. The pulsating beats of the music still echoed in his ears, and the energy of the night coursed through his veins. As he stepped into the apartment, he couldn't help but take in the atmosphere that greeted him.

The apartment, nestled in a high-class building, boasted an air of sophistication. Yet, as he glanced around, he noticed the signs of neglect. The once pristine space seemed burdened by disarray. Dirty plates and cups were scattered across the dining table, creating a chaotic mosaic. Clothes, both clean and dirty, littered the floor and draped over the furniture like forgotten treasures. It was as if the apartment carried the weight of its occupants' busy lives.

His eyes roamed over the scene, but his attention quickly shifted to Sheila, who was ahead of him and seemed to understand what was on his mind. She emerged from the depths of the apartment, her presence captivating. She smiled at him, her eyes filled with affection, and his heart skipped a beat.

"Sheila, where can I sit?" he asked.

Sheila's fingers gracefully plucked clothes from the sofa, revealing glimpses of vibrant fabric beneath the disarray. With a playful gesture, she directed me toward the vacant space. It wasn't the pristine seating area he had expected, but in that moment, it didn't matter. He could only see her, and everything else faded into insignificance.

As Sheila disappeared into her bedroom, he sank into the sofa, feeling the soft cushions envelop him. He glanced around once more, the disorganized chaos somehow reflecting the essence of Sheila's spirit. Her world may have been a whirlwind, but he found solace in being a part of it. The messiness of the apartment seemed to whisper stories of her vibrant personality, a reminder that life wasn't always neat and orderly, but it could still be beautiful.

Lost in his thoughts, he awaited Sheila's return, anticipation growing with each passing second. He knew that within the bedroom's sanctuary, she transformed into a different version of herself, shedding the day's burdens and embracing vulnerability. It was a privilege to witness these intimate moments, to be invited into the depths of her world.

The sounds of rustling fabric and the faint hum of a melodious tune drifted from the bedroom. His heart fluttered as Sheila reappeared, now wearing a different outfit, a pink see-through nightie that accentuated her every curve. It left nothing to the imagination; He was instantaneously aroused. Her eyes sparkled with a mischievous twinkle, inviting him into her realm of shared secrets and unspoken desires.

Sheila approached him, her steps filled with a graceful confidence that never failed to mesmerize him. With a tender touch, she traced a finger along his jawline, leaning in to place a gentle kiss on his lips. In that moment, all the clutter and chaos around them seemed to fade away, leaving only their connection, their love, and the undeniable magic that drew them together.

As they sat side by side on the well-loved sofa, he took in the imperfect perfection of the apartment. He asked if she had anything on hand that he could change into, and Sheila laughed as she explained that there was nothing in her closet for a man to wear.

"I don't mind rocking Adam's suit," he said as he took

off his T-shirt.

"No! Put your shirt back on. We need to talk first."

He did as Sheila instructed, figuring there might be a reward for being obedient, and then signaled that he was giving her his complete attention.

Sheila told him she was a virgin; it was a cultural thing in Africa for young women to preserve their virginity until the first night of their marriage. Though Sheila was not a cultural traditionalist, she had other reasons for remaining celibate until the proper time. She wanted to lose her virginity only to her husband, someone whom she would be convinced would not see any other woman in his life besides her.

"I want to be the last woman for my first man," she said.

That night, Shawn was on the edge, ready to swear that he would not see any other woman in the future if Sheila agreed to let him. He said that he would abide by Sheila's request, adding that the combination of her beauty and brilliant mind was irresistible to him. He had come prepared because he thought that endorsing whatever she had to say would help speed things up and lead to the moment he had fantasized about ever since he met her.

"I don't care if you've had sex before, but if I let you inside my body, I have to be your last," she said emphatically.

Shawn nodded with an automatic reflex, not yet sure of what he had agreed to in Sheila's expectations.

"Shawn, I know you are not ready for such commitment, and we have to go slow. You are just agreeing because your dick is standing right now, and this would be different if you were not erect."

He looked as if he were an innocent boy, confused but with a pleading sense that if she gave him this, he would be on his best behavior. There was so much to process in this short exchange, and his brain seemed not to be catching up to the adult realities of Sheila's words. He simply looked on, without saying anything else.

Sheila decided there was a compromise. They could make out and engage in some foreplay but leave it at that. No intercourse and no penetration whatsoever. The arrangement also would require him to keep his clothes on, and she would only bare the part of her body that was open for play.

Shawn was intrigued by her suggestion, but he also wanted to show her that he could be patient, so he decided not to ask questions that would antagonize her. He let her do all the talking and responded only with words such as "I'm fine with that."

Sheila agreed and slowly stripped off her pink nightie. He could barely contain himself, but he followed her instructions. He was seated but he was breathing hard, his eyes and mouth wide open. The carnal instincts were strong. He realized that Sheila was giving herself to him. No matter what the priests and moors said was heaven, they were all wrong. His heaven was between Sheila's legs, and he was ready to go to church every Sunday of his life, if Sheila admitted him to her corporeal paradise that moment.

Sheila turned to him and helped him pull down his jeans and underwear to his knees. She reminded him the agreement didn't require removing clothes completely, so he left his shirt on, not wanting to breach her instructions. She eased him to lie on his back and face upwards. She grabbed his dick and massaged it first with her hands and then she moved on top of it, grinding on it but without allowing even its tip into her body. She told him this kind of sex was called "Kachabali" in her country, which means sexual activity that is permissible for virgins. To Shawn this was the equivalent to frottage in America.

This virgin got skills with the hand game, Shawn thought.

He fancied being the first man inside her, and his dick became fully erect. Even though he had not penetrated, the action had obviously worked on Sheila. She was so dripping wet that his shirt was more than just damp. "Don't worry. I will buy you a new shirt," she said. She returned to Kachabali, her moans more frequent and louder.

Every time he tried to change positions, she warned him to stay still and not to try to enter.

"It's slippery when wet, if you try to move your dick, it will slip inside," she said. "I don't want any accidents there."

She kept massaging his dick on her clitoris which was like a tap of water every time she tapped it.

With every action, his dick twitched and enlarged in anticipation that she was soon throwing away her guard and letting it inside.

"This thing is huge, oh god! You know! My fingers are too small to hold it round." she moaned as she continued rubbing her front.

"Look how big it is Shawn; do you ever put all this inside a girl?"

"It becomes small as it disappears inside a girl," he answered breaking his silence.

"Liar," Sheila said. "This thing would suffocate and choke a girl's cookie."

Her breathing grew louder as soft moans pushed through her lips. He thought this girl was about to orgasm on frontal sex, not good for all his waiting.

"Please push just a tip inside," he begged as he closed his eyes fighting his erection giving away to a release. If he released outside of her, it was like a defeat.

"Just a lil' tip like this," he said with emphasis on showing a tip of his second finger.

"You can do whatever you want so long as you didn't enter," Sheila reminded him.

As ecstatic as the moment felt, he was also unhappy and felt cheated. He blamed himself for not being convincing enough for Sheila to give in and not follow her cultural custom. There was nothing material he could offer to entice her. She was so rich that it would not make any sense for him to offer her some gift.

Finally, he had a chance to blurt out his frustration. "I think you just using me for your pleasure. I thought we both gonna enjoy this."

Those words halted everything. Sheila pulled away from him, and without saying a word, she went to the bathroom.

When she returned, she was dressed in long sweatpants and a sweater to indicate that business was over. She also had a wet warm cloth in her hand. She gave it to him to clean himself and then told him he had to leave. He cleaned and then dressed and kissed her like friends who are calling it after a night out in the town.

CHAPTER 15

Lisa

LISA'S phone rang, and she reached into her handbag on her office desk and pulled it out. She glanced at the caller ID, recognizing the name of Martin, a criminal defense attorney she had dealt with on previous cases. She picked up, her curiosity piqued.

"Hello, Martin," She greeted.

"Detective Lisa," Martin responded. "I'm calling to inform you that I'll be representing Shawn in his murder case."

"Shawn's case? You're taking it?"

"Yes," Martin confirmed. "I just became aware of the situation, and I've decided to represent him pro bono."

Lisa took it in. She had crossed paths with Martin on several cases before, and she knew he was a skilled defense attorney. Still, this was unexpected news.

"Is there a particular *reason* you're taking this case?" she inquired.

"It's complicated. I have my reasons, but I believe Shawn deserves a fair defense." Before she could probe further, Martin continued, "There's something else, Lisa. I thought you should know that Shawn's mother passed away a few days ago.",

Lisa's eyes widened in shock. "Please, Martin, tell me everything, what happened?" she said, her voice trembling with concern.

"Katie, Shawn's girlfriend, informed me that Jasmine's last days were challenging," Martin said. "She described how Jasmine's heart sank as she paced back and forth in those cold, sterile offices. The arrest of her son shattered her world, leaving her consumed by frustration and desperation. Despite her tireless efforts to secure his release, each office door seemed to close in her face, leaving her feeling increasingly exhausted and defeated."

Lisa asked, "But how was her health? She seemed fine when she talked to me like two weeks ago. In fact, my colleague Bus recorded her meeting with her son, Shawn, a few days later, and she didn't seem sick, only anxious."

"Her health was taking a toll too. Diabetes and high blood pressure had plagued her for years, and the stress of her son's situation only exacerbated her conditions. To make matters worse, she had lost her health insurance, which her son used to sponsor, leaving her without the crucial medical care she needed. Martin explained

Lisa listened intently as Martin continued.

"You know, one night, when the world was asleep, Jasmine's breathing became labored. She tried to put on a brave face for her niece, Agnes, who had been staying with her during these trying times. 'I'll be fine, don't you worry,' she would say, forcing a smile on her weary face. But the pain in her chest and the shortness of breath were relentless reminders of her deteriorating health."There was a moment of silence before Lisa responded, "Is there more?"

"Jasmine's condition worsened. Agnes could see her aunt's struggle, the beads of sweat on her forehead, and the fear in her eyes. She wanted to call for help, but Jasmine refused, not wanting to burden anyone further.

"As the hours passed, Agnes felt torn between obeying her aunt's wishes and seeking help. She stayed by Jasmine's side, unsure if she should wake her up or let her rest. The uncertainty gnawed at her, and she couldn't shake the feeling that something was terribly wrong.

"Finally, as dawn approached, Agnes mustered the courage to wake her aunt. She called out her name softly, then louder, but there was no response. Panic set in, and Agnes ran out of the house, seeking help from their neighbors."

"Oh my god," Lisa exclaimed. "She didn't get any help all night? But was she still alive?"

"A grey-haired woman from next door hurried into Jasmine's bedroom. She checked for a pulse, her face solemn, and gently broke the news to Agnes. 'Call 911,' she said, her voice trembling. 'Your auntie is gone.'"

Bus walked in as Lisa was on the phone with Martin. He tried not to disrupt the conversation but stayed close to Lisa to listen in.

As Martin concluded the story, Lisa exchanged a shocked glance with Detective Bus. They had interrogated Shawn's mother not long ago during their investigation. This sudden turn of events was both surprising and unsettling.

"Thank you for letting us know, Martin," she replied. "We did speak to her recently."

"I'm on my way to see Shawn now. If you and Detective Bus would like to meet and discuss the case further, I'm open to it."

"That might be a good idea. We'll coordinate with you."

With that, Lisa hung up the phone. She turned to Bus, her mind racing with questions about the sudden change in Shawn's legal representation and the passing of his mother.

Two hours later, Lisa was standing in the sterile hallway of the Concord Jail, glancing at her watch, noting that Martin, Shawn's new criminal defense attorney, would be arriving soon. She was eager to hear more about Martin's motivations and his approach to the case.

Moments later, she spotted Martin approaching. It was clear by his gait that he knew his way around the jail. They exchanged nods in greeting as he drew near.

"Thank you for meeting me here, Detective Lisa," Martin said.

"Of course, Martin," she replied, leading him to the jail's reception desk. "I appreciate you reaching out to us and your willingness to represent Shawn."

As they approached the desk, she explained, "I'll help you fast-track the procedure to meet with Shawn. It's best if you meet him as soon as possible."

The jail receptionist, a stern-looking woman with years of experience in her position, greeted her with a nod of recognition. "Detective Lisa, what can I assist you with today?"

"We're here to arrange a meeting between Mr. Martin Sterling and the inmate, Shawn," she explained. "Mr. Martin is Shawn's new attorney."

The receptionist quickly checked her records and made a phone call. After a brief conversation, she nodded and said, "You can go in. I've informed the officers in charge of Shawn's block."

Martin and Lisa followed the receptionist through a series of secured doors, finally arriving at a small meeting room. She gestured for Martin to have a seat and assured him that she would arrange for Shawn to join. Lisa wanted to express her condolences for Shawn's recent loss. To her surprise, Martin asked her to stay for their first meeting.

Soon, Shawn—dressed in the standard orange uniform—was escorted into the room by a corrections officer. Shawn's face a mix of curiosity and tension as he took a seat across from Martin.

Detective Lisa cleared her throat.

"Shawn, we have some difficult news. Your mother passed away recently."

Shawn's eyes widened in shock, his breath catching in his throat.

"What? What happened?" he asked, his voice trembling.

The room fell silent, the weight of the news pressing down on everyone present as Shawn struggled to process the devastating information.

"Shawn, I'm sorry for the loss of your mother. Please accept my deepest condolences. This is your new attorney, Mr. Sterling," Lisa continued. "He's asked me to be present for this meeting."

Martin nodded in agreement, pulled out a pencil, and

tapped his notepad.

"Shawn, let me be straight with you 'cause our time is tight. This case is… riddled with inconsistencies, contradictions, and what I might describe as… betrayals of the facts. The bad news is, in the eyes of the public you are already guilty."

"But I'm not."

"I know that. But there's only one way to prove your complete innocence: Find the true killer."

Shawn shook his head, exasperated. "So how am I gonna do that? In here?"

"That's what we need to figure out. Because the only person who completely believed you were innocent is gone."

Shawn looked crestfallen.

"I need you to tell me that you have not held back any information or detail in your questioning by the two detectives. I don't want any surprises once this case goes to court. Surprises… will finish us. Are we on the same page?"

Shawn nodded.

"Did you kill her?"

Shawn shook his head.

Lisa watched closely as Shawn repeated all the information in the same detail that he had shared with the detectives. He seemed exasperated that no one wanted to believe him despite his honesty.

"The prosecutor claims Sheila called you twice, scared that you were going to murder her," Martin continued. "You told her you were not a murderer, but she was murdered anyway. Why do you think Sheila would say something so dramatic like that?

"I can't understand why she accused me of planning her murder," he said. "I repeatedly assured her that I had no intention of harming her, but she simply wouldn't believe me."

"Shawn," Martin said, "is there anything else you want to share with me? Is everything fine in your cell?"

Shawn's gaze met Martin's, and a flood of memories from his first day in jail washed over him. His voice trembled as he spoke, the weight of his experiences evident in every word. "Martin," he began, his voice barely above a whisper, "that first day… it was hell." His eyes, once vibrant, now mirrored the darkness of his ordeal. Tears welled up as he recounted the horrors he had endured behind bars.

"It was straight-up hell, Mr. Sterling," Shawn said. "Soon as them iron bars clanged shut behind me, I knew my life ain't never gonna be the same no more."

"Take your time, Shawn. I need to hear what happened, so we can build a strong defense."

Nodding, Shawn took a deep breath, trying to compose himself before delving into the nightmare that was his first day in jail. The room seemed to shrink around them, the walls closing in as Shawn's memories flooded the space.

"I got put in a cell with two big dudes, both standing well over six feet, built like brick walls. They eyeballed me like I was fresh meat in a den full of hungry lions," Shawn said. "Man, their eyes drilled into me, and before I even had a chance to react, they had me trapped up against that cold cell wall. I tried to talk some sense into them, begging for mercy, but all they did was laugh, straight-up mocking my fear like it was some kind of a joke.

"They threw the first punch, and from there, it was on. I didn't have a chance against their raw power," Shawn said." They beat me without mercy, pounding on me 'til I couldn't even feel my own body 'cause of the pain."

"Did anyone come to your rescue?"

"Nah, nobody. The guards acted like they didn't see a thing, like it was just another regular day in this cursed place. I was nothing to them, just another inmate caught up in the messed-up power games of this jail's cruel hierarchy." He looked down at his hands, his fingers tracing the faint scars on his knuckles. "They left me there, messed up and beat down, with a limp that still haunts me to this day. That was only the start of my nightmare.

"They came back on some other day, looking like they from a whole other world. Once again, they trapped me in a dark corner of the cell block. I could feel their pure hatred oozing through their eyes, man."

Martin knew that Shawn hadn't told him everything, not yet.

"Don't hold back," Martin said. "The time to get this out there is now."

"They demanded to know why I was locked up in here," Shawn said, his words catching in his throat. "I told them the truth, Martin. I told them they falsely accused me of raping and murdering some college girl. But they didn't wanna believe me. They said I was lyin', and that I deserved to suffer just like they claimed I harmed that girl."

A shiver ran down Shawn's spine as he remembered

the chilling promise they made to him. Their intentions were clear—they sought vengeance, to inflict upon him the pain they believed he had caused another.

"They said they gonna make me suffer, doing to me exactly what they thought I did to her," Shawn whispered. "And then it all started, Martin. The torture began."

The room seemed to grow darker, the weight of the memories bearing down upon them all. Shawn's body trembled as he struggled to regain his composure, his vulnerability laid bare in the dim light.

"They... they straight up whooped me, Martin. They was getting a kick out of it. And... there was times when I couldn't defend myself, when they was doing stuff to me that I can't even say out loud, you feel me?

"They took turns, Mr. Sterling," Shawn's voice quivered. "Every day was like a living nightmare. The pain was too much to bear, but I couldn't show no weakness. I had to tough it out, had to keep on surviving.

"I'm feeling violated, Mr. Sterling," he choked out, his voice tinged with shame and anger. "I feel filthy, like I can't ever wash off the mess of what they did to me. I thought I could deal, but... it's tearing me up inside, man."

Martin's eyes bore into Shawn's, the fire of determination flickering within them. "We won't let them get away with this, Shawn. I promise you, we will fight for justice."

Shawn nodded, gratitude swelling in his heart for Martin's unwavering support. "Thank you, Mr. Sterling. I can't handle this all by myself. I need someone to have faith in me, to have my back and stand up for me."

"You're not alone, Shawn," Martin reassured him. "I'll fight tooth and nail to expose the injustice you've faced in this place. We'll get to the truth, and those responsible will be held accountable."

Martin and Lisa patiently waited for the jail guards to take Shawn away before they stood up and moved outside. The dimly lit corridor of the jail seemed like a world away from the questions that had been swirling around this case. As they walked, Martin turned to her.

"Lisa, there's just one thing I need to ask."

"Shoot."

"Why are you working with a CIA mole on this case?"

"Do you mean my colleague, Bus?"

"Exactly, Lisa," Martin said as they continued to make their way out of the jail. "I don't want to be nosy, but something is off in this case—and I say it's *because* of that guy. And anyway, you folks can't let the CIA influence and listen in on this investigation, it's not legal. Their jurisdiction is supposed to be *outside* the USA. They shouldn't meddle in our internal affairs the same way they do with these third-world countries."

Lisa listened carefully—as someone who had been opposed to Bus's hiring, she felt a pang of guilt for not resisting his recruitment more vehemently. However, she also realized that she hadn't had the final say.

"Think about it, Lisa," Martin said. "The murderer you're looking for has nothing to do with this Shawn kid."

"What do you mean?"

Martin stopped in the doorway to face her. "This girl was a loose target. She's related to our propped-up dictator in Uganda. You can't possibly think that's a coincidence."

Lisa twisted in frustration. She knew he had to be at least partially right. "Fine, I've wondered that myself, but what do you want me to do *now*?"

"Investigate the CIA's interests in this case. It's the only way to—"

"Martin! I can't question the CIA! *All* their agents are secret operatives."

"You're free to follow any lead, Lisa, and no one has a right to block your access. You *already know* your colleague is a CIA operative who has been on CIA missions in Africa, Cuba, and the Middle East. Start with him."

. "But Bus has nothing to do with this. He could have been chosen to do some cover-up, but, for God's sake, he was just driving Uber five minutes before they pulled him. With all due respect, Martin, you're talking as if we're in a Hollywood movie where the detective happens to be the killer."

Martin breathed in the cool air, but he didn't budge. "I understand why you think it looks that way, but it doesn't change my position. Investigate why the CIA is interested, why they're meddling. You might be surprised at what you find."

With brisk determination, she walked back to her office, her thoughts a whirlwind of questions. She crossed the SR 2 road on foot and entered her office building. Her destination was Chief Flores's office.

Without knocking, she rushed straight into the room.

Flores looked taken aback. "Everything okay, Inspector?"

"Chief, who is this man I'm working with? Is he a detective or just a CIA mole?"

Flores shook his head but stayed calm. "Please… sit down."

As she took her seat, she said, "People are going to talk, Chief. I've just met the defense attorney, Martin, and all he said to me was whether I'm working with a CIA mole. He suggested I either get rid of him or investigate him and even the CIA itself for this murder."

"Lisa," Flores said "Martin doesn't give you leads for this case. You two may be friends, but you are adversaries here. Bus is a trained and qualified detective like you, and he has been operating in the state. You'll have to get used to working with him."

"Maybe," she said, "but I need to start following my new leads without him."

"Why?"

"Because I'm going to Washington to talk to the suspect's bosses and inquire about all the work he did for the Ugandan government. There is a political dimension to this—and I can't afford to keep looking the wrong way."

Flores stayed cool, swiveled his chair toward her. "There's no problem. Let me arrange your flight. But… you'll still have to go with Bus; that's how it works."

CHAPTER 16

Bus

DETECTIVE Bus sat in the VIP waiting lounge at the Concord Airport, mere miles from their workplace. Chief Flores had arranged for him and Lisa to fly on a private jet to Washington, where they would interview the directors and staff of the lobbyist firm that employed Shawn for a side gig he'd picked up while still in school, all thanks to Sheila's introduction. The particular lobbyist firm they were headed to represented several African and Middle Eastern governments, with Shawn primarily working remotely.

Bus found himself connecting the dots, understanding why his colleague Lisa had been acting so suspicious lately. Sheila's family had some solid connections in Washington. It made sense that the CIA might be keen on influencing and overseeing the investigation into Sheila's murder.

He also understood that the private jet they were

about to board was owned by Sheila's well-connected family. And Lisa didn't like that.

"How much independence could we maintain when this family appears to be funding the investigation?" Lisa said.

"Lisa, let's get to Washington and see," Bus replied.

"Are these people genuinely motivated to expedite the search for their daughter's murderer, or is there something more at play? How honest was this family in the investigation of their daughter's murder when, up to now, they had even refused their son, Amos, who stayed with Sheila, to speak to us?"

"Lisa, the family promised their lawyer will call us."

"When? And why are you and Chief Flores accepting the family's generosity?"

"It's nothing. It's a free flight."

"No. It's a morally gray area that doesn't sit right with me."

"All the answers will be in Washington from this lobbyist firm, Lisa. Let's go."

Lisa went mute. Bus thought she was annoyed because she had initially planned to travel on this trip alone, but Chief Flores had insisted they travel together. So Bus gave her some space.

He returned clutching two cups of Dunkin Donuts coffee in his hands. He'd remembered Lisa's preference—green tea with two bags, no sugar, and no cream.

"This is yours, Lisa, exactly as you like it."

"I don't understand, Bus. Why do you always go out of your way to show me that you're such a caring gentleman?"

"Because I am, Lisa. Despite our differences at work, I genuinely care about you."

"Really? Is this part of the CIA training, trying to soften up your women suspects? Because, unless you're treating me as a suspect, I'm just your colleague."

"Lisa, let's forget about the CIA for a moment. Just enjoy your tea."

Suppressing a smile, Lisa accepted the cup of tea from Bus. As their eyes locked, a victorious smile crept across Bus's face. Lisa's suppressed smile couldn't hold any longer, and she burst into laughter.

"And you sit alone in that private jet of your friends," she said. "I don't want you too close to me."

Bus ignored her. "That man over there is our pilot. Let's go."

Michael shook Lisa's hand and escorted them through expedited security as if they were true VIPs. They crossed the tarmac and stepped into the aircraft—the Falcon 50, a French super-midsize long-range business jet with a capacity for up to ten passengers.

Bus stopped for a moment to absorb the sight of the inside of a private plane for the first time. Michael guided them both to a seat in the middle before taking the pilot's seat in front of them.

"The cheapest seats are in the front," Michael said, with a sly smile.

"Come on, man! I would pay with my life to be a pilot," Bus said.

"It's not as glamorous as you think, especially in a private jet," Michael said. "Let me ask you: Do you know who wipes down the seats, mops the floor, and cleans up the toilet in this jet? It's the pilot."

They both laughed as Michael started the engine for takeoff. Bus somehow liked this pilot, a decent, gentle guy. Moreover, Michael shared something he could relate to—work everybody thought was glamorous but wasn't. Michael was a white man with a talent that many others envied him for, but he also was like any other hard-working guy struggling to make ends meet and get through the day without being so disgruntled that it made the day less tolerable.

Once the plane reached its cruising altitude, Bus said, "Michael, I was surprised when I saw the customs and immigration offices up in this private airport. Like, even the rich go through all that immigration stuff and pay customs fees?"

Michael almost choked, laughing so hard. "Yes, of course they do. My bosses are from Uganda, and whenever I bring them in the States, they need to get their passports stamped. I carry their passports to immigration because... well, because they *are* VIPs, you know. I'm supposed to do everything for them except wipe their asses after taking a dump in the jet toilet. Which, by the way, I still have to clean."

It was just an hour-long flight. They would have yet another chance to be awed after landing—the firm's chauffeur was assigned to pick them up from the airport and take them to the offices.

CHAPTER 17

Lisa

DETECTIVE Lisa, flanked by Bus, entered the spacious office of Conrad Taylor, the owner of Mercurial Global Relations, the lobbyist firm that had employed Shawn. Despite being in his early sixties, Taylor maintained an impressive physique, a testament to his resilience despite a lifestyle probably filled with extravagant lunches and dinners among Washington's power players. His reputation preceded him as a master of strategic public relations, particularly in the art of transforming the public image of African leaders, no matter how tarnished. All around him, the place was opulent, reflective of its owner's close connections with powerful figures in both Washington and Africa, including, of course, Sheila's father and his brother, the president of Uganda, General Joel Katila Muaji.

"Thank you, Taylor," Lisa replied, shaking his hand.

"It's good to see you again." She took a seat as Taylor launched into an explanation of Shawn's role within the firm. This guy didn't beat around the bush.

"Shawn," Taylor began, "was assigned to what we in the firm call The General's Project."

"What was it about?" Lisa asked.

Taylor leaned forward, slightly hesitating, "Well—The General's Project is centered on crafting creative pieces."

"What kind of pieces?"

"Creative pieces aimed at bolstering the image of General Kainewaragi Mlevi, the president's first son."

"Why does he need… bolstering?"

"General Mlevi is expected to succeed his father in leading the Ugandan government."

Lisa nodded, absorbing the information. "It sounds like important work," she remarked.

Taylor smiled. "Indeed, it's crucial, especially considering that President Katila Muaji has been in power for over four decades now. The General's Project plays a significant role in ensuring the Muaji family's enduring role in Uganda's politics remains intact."

Lisa said, "One thing… I notice you refer to these men by their middle and last names," she said. "Why is that? And… what about the first lady, Nanjovu?"

Taylor chuckled. "Ah, Nan-*jo*-vu," he said with a slight struggle in pronunciation. "Personally, I call her Jessica Muaji. But to answer your question, it's a naming style that's caught on among the firm's staff. Don't ask me why."

"So, Taylor," she continued, "what exactly is the core of your firm's work when it comes to these African leaders?"

"What we do here is ensure a quote-happy-ending-un-quote to all of the political crises these leaders face in Africa, Asia, and other regions. In fact, I don't like to brag, but we have a stellar record in managing crises and safeguarding the reputations of our clients. Lisa felt her sense of unease growing. "But what about ethics? Do they play a role in all this… crisis management?"

"Our focus is on what political circles in Washington and London think, rather than what the people in the countries led by our clients *believe*," he said confidently, but Lisa wasn't sure he'd answered her question. He quickly shifted topics. "We even pitch major Hollywood movies, including The Last Man, did you see it?"

"No," she said, "no, I haven't."

"The film portrays some former Ugandan dictators as cannibals and savages who rejected international cooperation."

"And," she said, "I suppose it also glorifies the current president, Katila Muaji."

Taylor was undeterred. "President Muaji may not be a saint, but he did welcome international corporations into his country and the neighboring regions where his armies operated. Frankly, President Katila Muaji has become one of our most successful transformational projects. Senators, White House advisors, even senior US military leaders sing his praises, describing him as one of the United States' most valued allies on the African continent. Now look—I'm not a man of illusions. I know that the term *ally* is a temporary state of affairs, often exaggerated for political correctness. But I do consider the man an essential asset in American foreign policy. Proud to be a part of it."

Lisa was becoming restless with the lesson in geo-political wheeling and dealing. She came out with it. "Mr. Taylor, I know you're a busy man, and we have a case to solve. Can you please explain Shawn's *specific* responsibilities within this... *General's Project*?"

"Certainly. Shawn, along with two other ghostwriters and an editor, worked on the project full-time. Shawn's primary role was to craft op-ed pieces with General Mlevi Kainewaragi's name on the byline. These pieces were strategically placed in some of the most widely read newspapers and magazines in the US, including The New York Times, Washington Post, Los Angeles Times, Boston Globe, and San Francisco Chronicle. We also had a strong presence in digital publications with large social media followings and tens of thousands of email subscribers."

"So, how often did Shawn need to publish these pieces?"

"Shawn was expected to publish at least two pieces every month," Taylor explained. "However, he often worked on multiple pieces at the same time. In any case, the minimum requirement was two published and audited pieces per month. It was crucial to maintain a consistent media presence."

Lisa nodded. "And for one of these pieces... you mentioned he met and interviewed General Mlevi. How were these meetings arranged?"

Taylor leaned back in his chair, remembering. "Our office handled all the preparations," he replied. "When General Mlevi came to New York for a family visit, we made sure Shawn got some face time."

"And what about Shawn's compensation?" she asked. "What was he earning?"

"Shawn received a monthly salary of $6,000, every two weeks. Additionally, he enjoyed full health insurance coverage for himself and any immediate family members. Plus, he was eligible for a year-end bonus if his work met our standards. And because Shawn didn't have a wife and children, we also allowed him to enroll his mother in the health insurance plan. This was particularly important to him, given his mother's deteriorating health."

"All around, not a bad deal for a young college kid," Bus said.

"I'd say so," Taylor said.

"In your well-informed opinion," Lisa said, "given your extensive work with this family over the years, do you believe they would pay Shawn to carry out such a heinous act against their own daughter? Or do you think Shawn might have acted independently?"

At this, Mr. Taylor became tight around the eyes, dead serious. "Look, I've given this some thought. The only conceivable reason for Sheila's demise for political reasons would be if she posed a *direct threat* or actively worked against The General's Project. The way things are in Uganda now, The General's Project is a red line."

"What's that mean exactly?"

"It means that anyone seen as an obstacle to it faces grave consequences. General Mlevi, the president's son, commands an army of ruthless goons who are ready and willing to eliminate any opposition in preparation for his impending rule. Harrowing tales of citizens being abducted by his militia in vans, often referred to as drones, have become alarmingly frequent."

"And these… militia… do they kill their hostages?"

Taylor nodded solemnly. "Yes. But not before enduring brutal torture. Some end up being prey for crocodiles and lions."

Bus and Lisa stared back at him in shock.

"Look," Taylor went on, "American to American, I want to be perfectly frank with you. As gatekeepers of the nation's image, we've been compelled to suppress numerous accounts of abductions, murders, and torture by The General. It's widely acknowledged among Ugandans that he is even more uncompromising than his father."

Lisa went point blank. "Do you think that's why Sheila was killed?"

"No. No, I don't. Whatever dissenting views she may have expressed—and I haven't heard of any—hardly seem reason enough to warrant her death, especially when you consider her familial ties. I know of many other family members, including the first lady of Uganda, who hold much louder opposition to this project, yet they continue to go on unharmed."

Lisa scoffed. "Mr. Taylor, we understand that this family is your *client*, but we implore you to be completely candid with us. Tell us anything that might lead us to the killer. This is about a homicide on American soil."

"I genuinely want to assist you as much as I can, detectives," Taylor said. "But you must understand that if the government of Uganda is indeed involved in this murder, it transforms the case from a homicide into an assassination. And if that's the case, it won't fall under the purview of state police detectives. Assassinations of political figures orchestrated by foreign governments are *not* within your jurisdiction."

Lisa and Bus exchanged a grim look—things were going sideways faster than anyone expected.

Lisa said, "I understand all that. But if our prime suspect and your employee acted on orders from Uganda, then it *does* become a matter for the CIA. This family has strong ties to the CIA, as you know damn well. We might as well be in Langley, Virginia, speaking with the CIA's top brass."

"Detective Garcia, you can't expect their director to sit down and explain their actions to you. The CIA reports directly to the president of the United States. Even the State Department can't question their covert operations."

"Why would the CIA hire one of your employees for such a task?" Lisa asked.

"The CIA recruits from everywhere and everyone. In Africa, just like any other business working with foreign governments, we maintain a close working relationship with the CIA. Several CIA agents operate from our offices as cover for their covert operations. Your colleague here, Detective Basudde, also worked in our Ugandan office as a cover when he was with the CIA."

Bus raised his eyebrow and smiled. Lisa's suspicions were confirmed, and she smirked back. What perplexed her, though, was that Bus's CIA affiliations were public knowledge, when CIA agents typically operated undercover. She'd have to take this up later.

"Mr. Taylor," she continued, "it's my understanding that President Katila Muaji is… not just a client. He's a close friend of yours. Do you believe he would ever issue an order to eliminate his niece in the name of The General's Project?"

"I've known President Katila Muaji for over four decades, ever since he sought representation after meeting President Reagan in the eighties. While I can't definitively say that he was involved in his niece Sheila's murder, I *can* tell you that there's nothing he wouldn't do to protect his power and his son if provoked. That's as honest as I can be, ma'am. Whether the president is capable of such an act or not is not for me to speculate on."

"Mr. Taylor, have you had any recent meetings with the president, particularly since you began this work?"

"I saw him about six months ago. The president and his wife Jessica had come to Washington specifically to express their gratitude. The purpose of the meeting was to thank me for orchestrating a highly effective media campaign in Washington. What we did played a crucial role in preventing their government from collapsing, mostly because we quieted certain politicians in Washington who had been advocating for a change in leadership. It was an unexpected visit to tell you the truth. The whole thing was a private, rather than official, meeting. We met at the Sheraton where they were staying."

"Anything unusual during the visit?"

"Unusual? Well—Jessica did start a conversation that caught me off guard. She just came out and said, 'My husband wants you to alter the project.' I said 'How?' And she said, "We'd like you to promote our son-in-law, Ronnie, as the next president—that's Ronald Mwizi Kuharibika.' I never saw that coming! But as soon as she said it, her husband quickly interjected, saying they hadn't reached a conclusion on the matter and so forth. Not a word of it was mentioned again. And I didn't want to be party to a marital dispute, where I might be unexpectedly cast as the judge or referee, right? That's just not in my contract. But she went on. She said, 'Bubu'—that's what she called her husband—'Bubu, you yourself admitted your daughter Desire is really your favorite child.' Anyway, the president got a little raspy, he's an older guy, almost eighty now. 'Yes, yes, I'm well aware,' he said. She said, 'Don't you want her to become the First Lady, like me?'"

Lisa then asked "Did this mean that the first lady and Sheila were both against The General becoming the next president? Was this anti-general sentiment common in the family?"

Taylor replied, "That's a good question. Actually, the First Lady's opposition to The General's ascension to the presidency is partly because she is a stepmother of The General. Since she has no sons of her own, she wishes that at least her son-in-law becomes the next president. That way, her daughter would be the next First Lady."

Taylor continued the story saying, "Again, I tried to change the subject. I didn't want to see them fight. Suddenly, out of the blue, the president starts asking about Shawn Wayles. I explained that he was writing for The General's Project. And that's when the wife got really mad. She said, 'Don't bring up The General's Project stories here. We're here to discuss the future of our children, Desire and Ronnie, as the future president and first lady of Uganda!' And then President Muaji responded with, 'I told this Ronnie boy to surrender to me all the children he has had from all his housemaids and secretaries, but he has not done so.'"

"Why do you want his children, Muaji?"

"Those children are bastards, and my daughter alone has given him legitimate children who would take over from him when he gets old."

"Do you want to say you don't have bastard children from secretaries? And what about this general boy, is he a legitimate child?"

Taylor observed as the conversation spiraled deeper into a tumultuous discussion about succession. Jessica continued, her words pouring out like a marathon runner who had waited her entire life for this opportunity.

"Mr. Taylor, all these men are pigs! Sorry, sir, I mean *these* African men. They sleep with their employees, whether housemaids or secretaries. They don't distinguish between their offices and bedrooms, or even their office desks and marital beds, just imagine that."

When Taylor paused, Lisa initially thought he was finished, but then he continued explaining how he and the president found themselves bewildered, unsure of how to halt Jessica's spewing rant of family secrets. They simply stared at her as she lamented, feeling as though she had been waiting for the perfect moment to unleash its total impact.

"And that's not all, Mr. Taylor. At our wedding ceremony, one of his exes, the wife of his personal medical doctor, showed up in a bridal gown. Can you imagine?" Jessica paused, allowing the weight of the moment to sink in before continuing. "As if she wanted all the guests to admire her beauty and judge it against mine. I asked the security to escort her out, but this man you call your friend insisted she stay, as if our wedding had room for a threesome."

"Enough, Jessica. Stop embarrassing me in front of my friend," President Muaji implored.

"Ah, Mr. Taylor, you see? He's trying to silence me. He can talk about all his other women, but not that woman. He still loves her and writes glowing recommendations for her to work in the African Union and the United Nations. Bubu Muaji, do you think I don't know how she landed those positions? No wonder your former personal doctor despised you, which is why he resigned."

The president stared at his wife in disbelief, unable to silence her and prevent her from revealing his marital secrets. His facial expression conveyed his thoughts: "You're lucky we're in front of this white man in a foreign country. If we were in Uganda, I would show you how to remain silent." Instead of voicing his thoughts, he resigned himself to looking down at his plate, meticulously chopping a piece of meat into small bites.

"Mr. Taylor, please talk some sense into your friend. He only listens to you," Jessica pleaded.

At that moment, Bus cleared his throat as if he had something to say, but then he stopped abruptly. Lisa had a feeling he wanted to blurt out something like, "Let's get out of here," and if he had, she would have been quick to agree and follow his lead. However, he remained silent, opting to continue listening instead.

Taylor, who had remained mainly silent throughout the dinner conversation, finally spoke, addressing the president.

"Mr. President, would you inform me of your decision after you two have spoken to Ronnie?"

"There's nothing more to discuss with that boy Ronnie. Jessica should handle it," the president responded in a sharp tone. "Listen here, Mr. Taylor," President Muaji continued, with frustration making his voice sound even more hoarse. "I know my son, The General, struggles with alcoholism, and we're trying various therapists to help him overcome it.

"I don't trust my son-in-law to inherit the presidency because he has children with other women. Once he assumes power, he might choose one of his other bastard children as the next president, instead of one of my grandchildren."

Taylor asked, in a calm tone, "So, what do you suggest we do? You make the decision, and I'll implement it."

"If my son, The General, doesn't recover from alcoholism before the next election, I will run again and remain as the president. I'd rather hold on until one of my grandchildren is old enough to assume the presidency themselves." With that, Taylor understood that Uganda's fate had been sealed. He decided to focus on his plate for the remainder of the meal.

"Was succession the only reason they came all the way from Uganda, or was there something else they discussed that could aid our investigations?" Lisa inquired. Taylor paused for a moment, deep in thought, before responding, "Actually, now that you mention it, there was something else."

"What was it?" Lisa asked, intrigued.

"I wanted to discuss this media frenzy in New York regarding the allegations that I used the IMF loan to purchase an armored toilet truck," the president said to Taylor.

"The one where they claim your driver ran over a protester?" Taylor asked.

"Yes, that's the one."

The press had published shocking images of the deceased under the headline: "This is what IMF money does to poor Africans." Another newspaper ran a damaging piece with the headline: "The US's key ally can no longer contain himself." Alongside the tanker images, they published photos of the president with a bulge on the left leg of his trousers, insinuating it was a catheter.

"Is there a way to mitigate this frenzy?" the president inquired.

"Yes, Mr. President," Taylor responded. "One of my staff members is currently working on the issue. He has proposed a solution that I've asked him to put in writing."

"What does the proposal entail?" the president asked, sounding impatient.

"He suggests compensating the family of the protester your toilet truck driver ran over during the political campaign. Once they are compensated, we can run articles and op-eds depicting the incident as an accident rather than intentional."

The president grew furious. "There's no way I'm going to give a single coin to that opposition family. Do you have any other plans to address this?"

Taylor asked, "Could the plan be to reduce media coverage of the toilet incident?"

"Yes," the president replied, adding, "Have your staff speak with the editors of these newspapers in New York investigating and publishing damaging pieces. Once the media stops covering it, the public will eventually forget about the unfortunate incident, and we can move on."

In Taylor's observant eyes, the realm of Ugandan social media seemed to have transformed into an unsettling gallery of graphic imagery—militant figures wielding weapons with abandon, the streets of Kampala awash in crimson streams of blood. A disconcerting contrast emerged as mainstream media outlets remained seemingly indifferent to these harrowing scenes of civilian suffering and military brutality.

Among the disturbing visuals that Taylor stumbled upon was a particularly gut-wrenching video. It depicted a group of military personnel subjecting a hapless man named Fanta to an unfathomable ordeal. The violent encounter culminated in a sickening display of brutality—the man's skull cracking open like a macabre work of art, torrents of blood mingling with the dust. Heart-wrenchingly, Fanta's journey ended there, his life extinguished amidst the grim spectacle.

"What an asshole!" Lisa blurted out, catching both Bus and Taylor off guard. They exchanged surprised glances as Lisa quickly apologized, saying, "Forgive my language, but I feel like kicking that president in the balls and making him eat his own shit."

Taylor chuckled and replied, "You wouldn't kick a seventy-eight-year-old man in the balls, even if he still had any left." They all shared a laugh before Taylor resumed his story.

In another grim incident etched into Taylor's memory, the presidential unit guard seized the headlines. The victim, Yaseen Kawooya, a mere driver for the opposition leader, faced a tragic and undeserved fate. A fatal barrage of bullets from the guard's weapons cast a pall over his dreams and aspirations, leaving the nation to mourn another senseless loss.

Engaging in a private conversation with Taylor, Uganda's president expressed his desire to manipulate the media's attention. "Let's conjure a distraction," he suggested, his voice carrying the weight of his intentions. The plan was simple, if chilling—orchestrate an incident that could be attributed to elusive terrorist factions, inciting a frenzied shift in the spotlight from the grim realities at home.

For Taylor, such machinations had always been a point of moral conflict. These premeditated maneuvers, often involving the sacrifice of innocent lives, gnawed at his conscience. Yet, he acknowledged the undeniable gains his clients like President Muaji derived from these orchestrated diversions. The twisted calculus of power and influence played out, urging Taylor to grapple with the shades of gray that clouded his convictions.

Lately, however, the frequency of President Muaji's men launching ruthless assaults on unarmed civilians, especially those picked up in "drones," had begun to chip away at Taylor's own resolve. The toll on innocent lives and the relentless waves of human suffering left him wrestling with the very foundation of his ethical principles. The lines between duty and morality blurred, as he confronted the consequences of decisions that seemed far removed from the moral compass he had once upheld.

Lisa noticed Bus been yawning throughout the meeting. She knew her colleague was already tired of the details Taylor was providing. Lisa herself was weary but had one more question about the recent Kenyan president's visit to the White House. She wondered if it was a sign that Washington was growing tired of Uganda's brutal aging dictator and was looking for a fresh alternative in the new Kenyan leader.

"Will the Ugandans be free from this monster if President Lutalo is recruited to do the international community's projects in Africa?" Lisa asked.

Taylor laughed before composing himself to answer. "I don't know why people think that once Washington hires a new puppet, it has to let go of its old ones," he said. "Seriously, there's been panic everywhere, even in Africa, regarding this Kenyan president's visit. In fact, when our client, President Katila, learned that President Lutalo was coming on a US state visit similar to the one the CIA had introduced him to Reagan in the eighties, he panicked. He called me himself and asked what was going on in Washington. He told me that the CIA boss had first visited Kenya, and now their president was going to Washington. There was no way to say it meant nothing."

Lisa looked surprised as Taylor continued, "I understood his fears stemmed from the fact that the CIA had not been so enthusiastic about his choice of succession—his son—but they are also not saying no. So, I advised him to go on a fact-finding state visit to Nairobi and have a word with President Lutalo before he comes to Washington."

"And what did he find?" Lisa asked.

"Let me tell you what I personally think," Taylor said. "Washington is trying to widen its network in Africa, especially since some West African countries have been turning to Russia and China, kicking out US military bases from their territories. For Kenya, the deal is not just about finding more willing puppets to fight our wars with boots on the ground, like what Katila Muaji is already doing. It's also about securing a military base that will accommodate some of our troops and equipment from bases like Niger, where the radical government has asked us to leave.

"When President Muaji introduced President Kagulire of Rwanda to the corridors of power in Washington, we saw him starting to behave like Muaji—stifling democracy and assassinating political dissidents."

"Are we going to see Kenya behaving like Uganda after taking this key US support?" Lisa asked.

Taylor replied, "And there was Mobuto of Congo before these two. In fact, President Katila Muaji got his political playbook from Mobuto. People unfamiliar with the region think Muaji is the master, but he's not. Mobuto assassinated his political opponents, organized sham elections, operated torture chambers, and ruled his country and neighboring ones with fear and impunity.

"But to get back to your question about President Lutalo behaving like President Muaji—yes, there are all the signs. We've already seen something like President Lutalo trying to change the constitution. All we need to do now is watch and see how much he takes from Uganda," Taylor replied.

"But what is your role as PR lobbyists in such African leaders' state visits to the White House?" Lisa probed.

Taylor smirked. "Did you see the focus of the media on the Kenyan First Lady begging America's celebrity Steve Harvey for a hug?" he responded with a question, then continued, "Yes, that's the role of public relations—

to refocus the public on those small, humorous things and leave behind the big issues agreed upon in the partnership. The public shouldn't know much about what this partnership is bringing to Kenya or the whole African region or even what it is going to take. Instead, the Kenyan public will be shocked a few weeks later when their leader introduces a repressive and exploitative finance bill and fast-tracks it through parliament."

Lisa leaned in, intrigued. "So, it's all about distraction?"

"Exactly," Taylor nodded. "We shape the narrative. While everyone's talking about a harmless hug, the real deals are being made behind closed doors. Deals that could reshape the political landscape of a continent."

"And you think President Lutalo will follow the same path as Muaji and Kagulire?" Lisa asked.

"It's possible," Taylor admitted. "The US has a pattern of supporting leaders who align with their interests, even if it means compromising the local democratic processes. Lutalo might be the next in line, and Kenya could start mimicking Uganda's political playbook."

Lisa sighed, the weight of the implications settling in. "So, we just sit and watch?"

"Pretty much," Taylor said, leaning back. "Until the next move is made, all we can do is observe and be ready for whatever comes next."

The revelation about the Ugandan family's malevolent deeds to maintain their grip on power weighed heavily on Lisa's mind. It was a chilling thought that this very family, seemingly entrenched in political self-interest and ruthless ambition, could be connected to their daughter's murder.

In her mind, she began to construct a tentative hypothesis: perhaps Sheila posed a threat to their power, especially The General's Project, in a way she hadn't yet uncovered.

Back in the hotel, Bus and Lisa separated.

Lisa took her room and flopped on her bed. Her mind raced with questions and doubts as she considered what Sheila might have known, and whether it had led to her tragic demise. Sheila had possessed knowledge of the family's sources of power, the CIA, and the lobbying firm. But what troubled Lisa was the possibility that Sheila had been attempting to reveal or compromise these sources. How could she have gone about it? Was she trying to persuade them to abandon their support for General Mlevi, the family's chosen successor?

The more Lisa thought about it, the more she believed Martin might be right about the CIA. This case had too many layers and too much intrigue to dismiss the possibility of covert intelligence involvement. Senior CIA officials might indeed hold some crucial answers, but the question was, how could she, a detective with the local police force, go about investigating another formidable security arm like the CIA?

The complexities of the case were becoming increasingly daunting. Still, Lisa was determined to get to the bottom of it. Her best course of action, she decided, was to keep probing the relationship between the lobbying firm, the Ugandan government, and Shawn. This seemed to be the heart of the matter, and with each layer she peeled back, the more she was drawn into a labyrinth of deceit, power, and conspiracy.

Lisa had asked Taylor if there was anyone else in the

firm they could reach out to. She was looking for someone who had a deep understanding of the Ugandan first family's strong connections with the international community. She hoped to find someone who could shed light on how they should approach this relationship in the course of their investigation. Taylor had mentioned an instructor, Larry Sanchez—Shawn's direct report. He was, however, only available to talk in the afternoon. Lisa and Bus returned to their hotel briefly to prepare for the meeting.

After a failed attempt to nap, she returned to the hotel lobby where she found Detective Bus engrossed in a phone call. Startled, he abruptly ended the call and laid the phone on the table, its screen still lighting up, revealing the name VIRGINIA MAN. This wasn't the first time she had caught her colleague having what seemed like a suspect conversation with this mysterious being.

Bus broke the silence, "Do you have any specific questions you want to ask when we talk to this Sanchez character?"

She considered for a moment. "Nothing too specific, besides delving into the topics of the ruling family, Shawn, and the CIA."

"Great," Bus said. "I'll take the lead."

CHAPTER 18

Bus

BUS entered after Lisa as Larry warmly welcomed the two detectives into his office and offered coffee or water. Bus shook his head; Lisa poured herself water. After settling into their seats, Bus reached for the right tone—it wasn't easy.

"Mr. Sanchez," he said, "I know this is a difficult time. But… we're told you have a close association with this family, and it's important for us to understand…"

"Tell me."

"Well… it's important for us to get an understanding of *why* this family has such deep ties to the international community."

Larry sat back and sighed.

"It all began with the British," he explained. "Back in 1978, maybe 1979, they were the colonial masters who discovered Katila Muaji and groomed him to become the president of Uganda. Later, they introduced him to the US foreign offices to work closely with the CIA as the key figure in the region."

Bus took it in. He looked to Lisa—she was taking notes.

Larry went on, "You remember Idi Amin? You may be too young. But during his tumultuous reign, Amin constantly clashed with the international community. It was a mess, so a team of intelligence officials was sent to aid Ugandan fighters stationed in neighboring Tanzania. These fighters were waiting for the right moment to overthrow Amin's regime."

"Did they do it?" Bus asked.

"During this mission, the team encountered a young soldier named Katila Muaji. He was known for his unwavering loyalty to the international community… and his brutal methods. In one training session, another soldier, Julius Kayiira, questioned the trustworthiness of these international operatives, which wasn't so strange given the history of colonialism and its lingering scars."

"And?"

"Mauji didn't hesitate. He drew a knife and plunged it into Kayiira's chest, then twisted the blade, right there on the spot, in front of everyone."

Larry allowed the gravity of this revelation to sink in before adding, "Can you fathom that level of brutality? Even the British intelligence team was taken aback. After his friend's death, he told the intelligence operatives that the time for questioning the international community's interests in Africa had ended with the likes of Patrice Lumumba and Kwame Nkrumah. African leaders now had to embrace the international community wholeheartedly, without reservations."

"Where'd he get the name?" Bus asked. "It's an unusual one."

"One member of the intelligence team asked him his name, to which he initially responded with something like Joyeri. However, another team member corrected his pronunciation, suggesting Joel. The young soldier, however, seemed unable to pronounce the English name correctly, so he persisted in calling himself Joyeri."

"He sounds like a rough piece of work," Lisa said.

Larry nodded. "The intelligence team wasn't seeking an intellectual or a brilliant mind to lead a strategically important African country for our interests. They needed someone loyal, somewhat mediocre, and naive enough to consult the international community for every decision. They recommended him to the CIA, which at that time was just beginning to expand its involvement in the region, and a plan was set in motion to ensure he rose to power through… what you might call persuasive force.

"If he was such a significant figure back in the eighties," Lisa said, "why is the international community still so tightly connected to him, even after nearly four decades? Why can't we let go and encourage his son to take over?"

Larry leaned back, tapped his pencil anxiously, and took a moment to gather his thoughts before answering, "The international community's biggest concern, and what's kept them closely aligned with these African dictators, is *stability*—It's that 'devil you know.' At bottom, we're afraid of what a change in leadership might do to our business interests and, unfortunately, these dictators are well aware of our fears, and they're *always* quick to play on them. The constant unspoken suggestion is… if they lose power, we can expect war and a serious disruption to our resources and business interests."

Bus was taking it all in, assembling the pieces. The true nature of the regime in Uganda was more corrupt than he realized and… this Shawn kid, in advocating for that regime, was right in the heart of it. The more Larry revealed, the more Bus realized that the work Shawn was doing was, in fact, aiding the cause of imperialism. Imperialism—the very force that perpetuated slavery and colonialism.

Bus said, "Mr. Sanchez, I just don't get it. Why did this idealistic young Black man continue working for what he knew was an imperialist government?"

"Well," Larry said, "he put his imperialism on ice. For two reasons. One was money and the other… was patriotism."

"His aspirations to work for the CIA?"

"Exactly. And I told him, if Central Intelligence is your career goal, you need to understand patriotism, at the deepest level. It requires supporting the position your country has taken in the global debate without questions, without conditions. You can still be 'anti-colonialism,' but you *must* support our role in the effort to stabilize these former colonial states."

"Sounds immoral to me," Bus said.

Larry snickered. "When dealing with Africa, the right approach to morality is flexibility—that's the golden rule for lobbying on the behalf of African rulers. But I see we've gotten far afield. Do you two have any more questions? Because I've got a busy afternoon."

"Yes," Lisa replied. "I was checking out the tweets of that young general—Mlevi—and from what I read, he seems to be more a pro-Russian communist than an American capitalist. Why would this country be so hot to support a Russian pundit?"

A broad smile stretched across Larry's face—like he'd been waiting for this. "Good question, Lisa—what you didn't catch is that The General's tweets were *aimed* at misleading and firing up the African masses. Crazy, but not unusual. In fact, his father, the president, used this very ploy in the eighties and fooled *everyone* that he was a heavy-duty Marxist. Meanwhile, behind the scenes, he was busy begging the international community for support to reinforce his political standing. When the British legitimized his political status and introduced him to President Reagan in the eighties, he emerged as the most fervent advocate for capitalism *on the continent*. In just one year, he had privatized all his countries' parastatals bought and paid for by the international community. Same time, the US extends over a billion dollars in security aid every year."

"To what end?" Lisa asked.

"The Pentagon isn't paying Africans to work for Russia or China. They work for us—all for the Yankee dollar. Katila Muaji's family are… not exactly our allies, but they are *assets* across the region."

"But the international community—"

"Yes, yes, I know—the international community *benefits* from these political stooges while publicly distancing themselves. The international community knows damn well that these are criminal regimes who murdered their way to power and overstayed through corruption and even more murders."

"So, we turn a blind eye," Lisa said.

"That's right, we turn a blind eye. And we play the key role. The African dictators love us, they need us. They're always trying to cozy up to us because *that's their way of staying in power*, indefinitely. It's like they're practically on their knees, begging us to give them military assignments, offering up their troops to go as far as Iraq and Haiti. They wouldn't even think of doing that for Russia because they're well aware that Russia itself is facing its own challenges, and they can't rely on an unstable superpower to secure their own grip for the long haul."

"This is… a lot," Bus said. "But I'm still not sure how it ties in."

Larry wanted the detectives to fully understand. "There's no way to be sure," he said. "But it's important that you explore the political rhetoric on the African continent if you aim to see through their manufactured images and not be deceived by what this family claims to be. All imperialist stooges will claim to be independent from the international community as well as the pan-Africanist community. And I mean all of them. Mobuto Seseko, the former president of Zaire. changed the country's European chosen name of Congo to Zaire and banned Christian names, including his own. He called himself Mobutu Seseko Kuku Wazabanga. He banned European fashion styles; now the people can only wear his own design—*abacost*—a lightweight short-sleeved suit, often worn without a tie, just like the uniform worn by Chairman Mao. There's some bad actors out there. You need to know what you're getting into."

Larry stood—the meeting was adjourned.

CHAPTER 19

Lisa

DETECTIVE Lisa sat in a car outside the lobbyist firm's office, awaiting her return to the airport and processing the information she had just gathered. Her mind was a whirlwind of thoughts, and it was proving difficult to piece together the puzzle that was Shawn's involvement with this politically dubious family. The surprising revelation was that Shawn's affiliation with this dictatorial government seemed utterly incongruous with his young, idealistic, and deeply anti-establishment personality.

She couldn't help but be intrigued by this glaring contradiction. Shawn had ardently professed his convictions about Black empowerment and the injustice of historical white imperialism, but he had spent a significant portion of his time working for an entity that seemed to be the antithesis of his beliefs. It was as if Shawn had been on a relentless quest to contribute to something he despised.

The question that loomed large in Lisa's mind was why did Shawn persist in this role despite despising it? Had he embraced the notion of taking matters into his own hands, seeking a form of revenge for his family's involvement with a government that he considered a betrayal of Black independence? Or was there a more complex narrative at play?

And if this family was responsible for the murder of their daughter, what could possibly have made Sheila a target within her own family? Did they know about her relationship with Shawn, the boyfriend who had vehemently anti-imperialist beliefs? Had Shawn's influence sparked a transformation in Sheila, leading her to question the family's actions and perhaps even uncover some of their dirty secrets? These were questions that swirled around Lisa's mind as she contemplated the family's potential motives for harm.

Furthermore, the interviews had unearthed a new enigma: "The General," General Mlevi Kainewaragi, who Shawn had been assigned to work with and promote. This mysterious figure held the potential key to unraveling Shawn's motivations and actions. However, Lisa felt a pang of regret that General Mlevi was not within her immediate reach for interrogation. He was back in Uganda, which presented a significant obstacle to her investigation.

Yet, Lisa couldn't wait to probe Shawn about his dealings with The General and the extent of his involvement in promoting this shadowy figure. She knew that as soon as she returned to Boston, the following day, she would need to have an intense interrogation session with Shawn. The questions were stacking up, and she was determined to get to the bottom of this complex web of motivations and actions that seemed to surround the enigmatic "General" and his role in this intriguing case.

Another layer of mystery had woven itself into the fabric of this complex murder case, and it was one that kept her awake at night: the possible involvement of the CIA. She was acutely aware that delving into the CIA's operations was far beyond her jurisdiction as a detective. Still, the intrigue pushed her to seek answers from those within her purview who might provide some insight.

It was a tangled web. The CIA operated under a shroud of secrecy, but if they were ever involved in this case, it would undoubtedly fall outside the bounds of their jurisdiction as well. Their mandate was to deal with foreign threats on foreign soil, not within the United States. Theoretically, they could argue that Sheila, as a foreign national, fell under their purview. But the question remained: how could this seemingly innocent college girl pose any significant threat to the United States?

She knew that the lines of jurisdiction and responsibility would be muddied in this murder case. If the media ever caught wind that both rogue foreign government operatives and the CIA were potential suspects, it would be a field day for them. Yet, she couldn't bring herself to be the one to leak this information. Not only would it jeopardize the investigation, but it would also risk exposing her as the source. And no doubt, her colleague, Bus, would immediately know she was the one behind it.

Despite their differences, she did have a soft spot for Bus. To him, apparently, the CIA was just another gig, not unlike the Uber gigs he had done before. As a person and a colleague, he was good, very good. And he was attractive in many ways; she had to admit that. But what of it?

Lisa's unease about Bus's previous involvement with the CIA persisted, especially since theirs was supposed to be a covert operation. Determined to uncover the truth, she conducted a swift Google search on her phone using Bus's name alongside "CIA." The results left her utterly shocked.

An article headlined "USAID threatens to withdraw aid to Congo if it doesn't release its staff" revealed that Bus had been arrested in Congo alongside two other USAID personnel, accused by Mobutu's faltering government of being CIA spies. This event likely occurred before Mobutu's downfall, as he had turned against his former Western allies, including Uganda, accusing them of plotting his overthrow. Another article titled "USAID staff arrives in Kampala and is received by the head of USAID in the country," prominently featured Bus's name. Furthermore, Boston newspapers mentioned Bus as a former CIA operative involved in overtime frauds within the Boston state police. Lisa couldn't help but wonder how she had been so naive not to investigate her colleague online. While the entire world seemed to know his past, she was finally in the know as well. She decided to keep it under her hat—for now.

When she returned to their offices the next day to work alongside Bus, their routine began as usual, with customary morning greetings. To her surprise, his response carried an unexpected indifference, an attitude that caught her attention. Lisa couldn't help but wonder what had put him in this mood. She also wondered why she was dissecting his moods and responses, as if each nuance held a hidden meaning. She was getting ahead of herself, putting on more makeup, treating herself like a woman and not just a detective. She had to keep her focus on the work.

"We're going to talk to Shawn about The General this morning," she said, hoping to engage him. "I've prepared some questions and shared a Google Doc. Take a look and see if there's anything you'd like to add."

Bus's response was far from enthusiastic. "Unfortunately, Lisa, I won't be joining you this morning. I'm working on a write-up of our Washington visit report. Just keep me updated if you find anything new during your interview."

Her concerns were confirmed: Bus was annoyed about their recent trip to Washington. She had sensed his resentment and detachment during the interviews in the capital, and throughout, she felt like she was navigating those treacherous waters alone. She couldn't help but recall Attorney Martin's accusations about Bus being a CIA mole and silently noted how his behavior during the interviews had only fueled those claims.

As she entered the prison to arrange for Shawn's interview, Lisa couldn't shake the strange void she felt without Bus by her side. His presence had always provided a sense of security and an undeniable allure, even in the midst of disagreements. The unspoken connection was just undeniable. Nevertheless, her duty was clear. She took her seat and faced the prisoner alone.

"Shawn," she began, her voice steady, "I'm here today to ask you about The General Project you were involved in with the lobbying firm in Washington. And I need you to tell me everything, including every detail of your interactions with the president's son—the man known as The General, during your assignments."

CHAPTER 20

Shawn

TODAY, Shawn found himself facing Detective Lisa, and she was eager to learn about his involvement and interactions with The General. The detectives' leads in this case were far from straightforward, but the story of The General was an intriguing one, and he was ready to share it.

He and Sheila had arrived at The General's home in Brooklyn Heights a few minutes past noon on the day in question. Sheila disappeared into one of the upstairs bedrooms upon arrival and remained unseen by him until it was time for them to leave.

His appointment was scheduled for 1 p.m., but when they entered The General's home, General Mlevi appeared as if he had just woken up. He greeted them with shorts and no shirt, without a word of welcome. His first order of business was to instruct the staff to prepare his breakfast immediately, stating, "I need my breakfast before heading to the pool. My princess is already in the water waiting."

The General was a tall, obese man with a substantial potbelly and drooping "moobs," a stark contrast to the images of him Shawn had seen online. In preparation for this interview, Shawn had taken the time to study The General, as he was known in his home country. He had learned that The General had attended two international military academies in the UK and the US. However, the image of him at home struck him as bizarre.

He couldn't help but think to himself, *If he really been to any of them military schools, he must've been doing it all on Zoom. Ain't nobody going to them schools without skipping that tough physical training and daily exercise. That potbelly of his just be showing otherwise, man.*

Douglas Mwesige, a slim man with graying hair who had received him and appeared to be a top aide to The General, intervened between The General and the chef and asked The General to meet Shawn.

"I think you will be happy to talk to Shawn while taking your breakfast and then have your swim an hour later. I have communicated to the princess in the pool, and she fully understands there are going to be some delays," Douglas said.

But The General resisted, and he seemed distracted. All he could think about was the pool and the young beautiful woman waiting for him. After a few exchanges of murmurs with The General, Douglas told Shawn that the meeting would proceed poolside so The General could go swimming as soon as the interview was finished.

Douglas was a radio journalist before becoming a

mentor and publicist for The General. He had pushed for change and transparency in Uganda as a reporter but eventually relented, knowing that the forces of status quo were far stronger than the chances for any independent journalist to inspire changes through their investigative reporting.

"As a journalist, I was once onsite where a surface-to-air missile struck down the jet of Rwanda's president, Pious Habari. The missile remnants were found in a valley near Masaka in Uganda, the spot from where they were supposedly fired. When I arrived on the scene, I could see Rwanda's air traffic landing at Kigali International Airport, making it so easy to target. I was the first to break the news of finding the missile debris, and my reports soon brought international investigators who confirmed the details of what I had reported," he said.

Douglas added, "My last assignment as a journalist also involved a plane crash, this time with South Sudan's former president, Paul Garunga, which occurred shortly after takeoff in Uganda. I reported the crash as an orchestrated assassination by Ugandan officials.

"Soon after, I was arrested, tortured, and threatened that my own 'accident' would be forthcoming—not in a plane, but in a car. I believed they were serious, so such threats could not be dismissed. If they could arrange two plane crashes involving presidents of other countries on the continent, then the assassination of a recalcitrant journalist in a car accident was almost certain to happen."

Instead of waiting to die, he renounced his previous work as a journalist and begged for mercy from President Katila Muaji, the father of The General for whom Douglas now was handling publicity and the young man's image campaign. Douglas was working for the family, which did not hesitate to use the most extreme measures to snuff out its critics or political rivals, regardless of whether they were in Uganda or elsewhere.

Douglas had resigned himself to becoming a sycophant. Instead of mentoring the young general to develop as an enlightened political leader, he became his mouthpiece, aware that the young man was impulsive and often sounded crude and tactless. Douglas, though, subtly worked to make sure The General would definitely rely on him.

He didn't believe the imperialist sponsors of power wanted an intelligent leader for Uganda. He remembered a familiar story he used to tell his radio audiences. Britain had sponsored Idi Amin to become president because they wanted a pliant stooge which they could easily manipulate. It was a situation of great risk. Indeed, after becoming president, Amin was so thoroughly stupid to comprehend the agenda of his masters and engulfed by his own megalomania that he resisted. He chafed at anyone telling him what to do, believing that the president was the ultimate arbiter of his country's well-being. Amin expelled all foreigners in the country, fearing they were scheming to replace him. The British often preferred to tell the story of only Indian expulsions, as they didn't want to be part of those expelled.

So, it was important for Douglas to keep The General an idiot, because being smart was not so much a quality the imperialists wanted in an African president.

Moreover, if The General remained an idiot, Douglas envisioned his role as being the brains in The General's government. He saw the possibility that he would not just be close to power but also that he would possess power.

The likelihood of that happening could never be sure because men like The General were too wrapped in the idea of creating a cult of personal ego as leaders rather than as prudent stewards for the citizens in their countries.

At the poolside, Shawn noticed that the beautiful young woman in an orange bikini was Princess Shaki, supposedly The General's date, who had consumed his attention. He also learned that she was a pop music idol in Uganda, who had taken on the stage name of Princess Shaki, after Shakira. But the princess, however, looked like a prisoner of her thoughts, completely distracted and unable to concentrate.

A few minutes into the interview and before The General could even say anything to Shawn, seated across from him and Douglas on the side, The General noticed the princess seemed lost in a sea of thoughts, as she stood in the pool.

"Are you fine my princess?" he asked, slightly raising his voice to be heard.

The princess replied something in accented English that sounded like she hoped that The General would join her in the water. The General pivoted to Douglas, ordering him to take over the interview because he was done and going into the water. He stood up and farted loudly, making no gesture to cover up his faux pas.

Shawn was disgusted. He muttered silently under his breath: "This dude must've came out his mama's womb through the wrong hole, I swear."

Douglas did not miss his muttering. "Yes, he is a kind of character. I know you go to school with his cousin Sheila. I hope she told you what to expect. Anyway, let's get to business."

He was taken aback by the reversal Douglas had taken. At one point he was an effective, tireless watchdog of the government's most violent abuses and disregard for public welfare and safety. Now, he was nonchalantly speaking in defense of The General and his father, a known murderous conspirator.

"What I really want to understand," he said, leaning in closer to Douglas, "is how someone as incredibly successful and beloved as Princess Shaki ended up in this situation, waiting impatiently for The General to join her in the pool."

Douglas glanced around cautiously, making sure no one was eavesdropping on their conversation and said in whispers that the background story leading to this moment was far from a romantic tale; it was a detestable account of force, fear, and the constant shadow of threats.

"I can tell you the story, but it has to be off the record, Shawn. You understand, right?"

"Of course, Douglas. I won't breathe a word of it."

With that assurance, Douglas began to recount the chilling narrative that had brought Princess Shaki to this ominous juncture, where even her immense fame and success couldn't shield her from the grim realities of her circumstances.

Princess Shaki had just met The General a month previously when he celebrated his birthday by launching his presidential bid, where she was supposed to perform. She arrived an hour early and was waiting in the parking lot in her car when The General and his security details of about a dozen soldiers showed up. The General knocked on the driver's side indicating that he wanted to get in the car and talk to Shaki. The driver left the car.

The General wasted no time in gushing over his adoration of Shaki, explaining how much he had crushed on her music videos and that it was the highlight of his birthday to meet her. He hoped that the princess would stay overnight after the show, so he would arrange the presidential suite where the two could stay.

"I'm sorry, sir, but I don't fuck married men," Princess Shaki bluntly rebuked. Her tone signaled she would not tolerate any of his nonsense.

The General was obviously pissed. He told the princess he would show her who was in control of the country she called home. He stormed out of the car, leaving the back door open, called one of his security aides and barked out a few short orders. When he returned to the car, his security detail had surrounded it but had their backs facing toward the vehicle.

The princess, normally confident in her outspokenness, was terrified. She heard about his quick temper, which he had inherited from his father and how swift revenge always mattered. She thought at that moment The General might murder her there in a public spot and no one would notice or if they did, they knew enough to stay quiet. But The General had other plans, albeit they were still heinous to a respected celebrity such as Shaki.

He showed the princess his full hand and asked her how many fingers were there.

"Five, sir," she replied, her voice quaking slightly with fear.

He told her each finger was going to have its turn penetrating her vagina and all that she would be able to do would be to count and moan.

The General had his way with her and counted. "Um, one… two… three… four… five." Shaki stayed quiet.

When he finished counting, he exited her car, asked his security detail for a bottle of water, washed his hands in full view of her, and left with his men.

Another security aide, armed with an AK 47 rifle along with several pistols banded around his waist, entered the car and told her to be discreet and not to mention to anyone what had happened. Furthermore, she should never utter The General's name to anyone, even her mother, if she still hoped to live. He ordered her to get ready to go on stage and sing like nothing had happened.

Once The General and his army left and Princess Shaki's driver returned to the car, Shaki, who was still shaking and visibly crying, told her driver, "Take me home."

The driver, sounding confused even though what had just happened was clear, asked, "Are you sure?"

Shaki just nodded her head, making it evident that she would not speak. They left in silence, and she did not perform at the birthday party.

The following day, she recorded a video and uploaded it on Twitter and her other social media channels, telling her fans that she had been sexually assaulted by someone who was celebrating his birthday. She did not mention any names. She didn't need to.

"I'm in my car waiting to perform, and this motherfucker shows up, orders my driver to leave the car and starts assaulting me," she said. Shaki then broke into tears, asking why men with power seem to frequently abuse women, as if they never had mothers, sisters, or daughters.

The video went viral in less than a couple of hours, inundating every social media platform in the country. There was no doubt about whose birthday was just celebrated the day before. Shaki received support but not anything compared to the army of government sycophants, including women, who rushed to defend The General, claiming that such a story was preposterous and exaggerated by a celebrity desperate for more attention.

One troll posted, *The General is not mentioned in the video, and she doesn't even tell us which birthday party. She's lying to gain popularity*. Other trolls feigned some concern but advised the princess that perhaps she should dress more modestly on stage because it can be triggering in enticing men, even among the most powerful in the country.

Finally, at the bottom of the comments, a troll wrote, *You are a Muslim woman. Dress in a black burqa and see if any man will bother you.*

But the trolls were not enough to chastise the singer and defend The General without consequences for the princess. That evening, armed men in civilian and military uniforms surrounded the princess' home in Muyenga, a suburb of Kampala.

"Do you know how we arrived for the operation?" Douglas asked Shawn.

He shook his head.

"We had seven military vehicles and about thirty armed men. It was like a scene out of a war movie. The men ran over the gate to the house's brick fence, and our soldiers were jumping off the vehicles, taking positions. Even though the gate was open, other men just climbed up the fence and fell inside."

"And then what happened?" Shawn asked.

"A young woman in the neighborhood tried to film from her window," Douglas explained, his expression growing somber. "But she was spotted and shot immediately. Our armed men took the phone. It was like a military operation, and all of it was aimed at instilling maximum fear, not just for the singer's family we were approaching but for the whole country. Anyone who hears how we dealt with the errant singer will never dare speak up against The General."

"Oh, poor girl," Shawn said. "She must have been so terrified. She's just a girl. This is beyond brutal, Douglas. It's inhumane."

"You said your name is Shawn, right?"

He nodded in confirmation.

"You don't know how these friends of your country behave down there in Africa. They are really bad. But don't judge me by them. I'm just a low-ranking employee following orders. I'm not even a soldier, and I don't know how to shoot. If I ever refuse any of their orders, they will kill me instantly."

Douglas took a deep breath and resumed telling the story, his voice trembling slightly. "After the chaotic entry, I entered the house with five military men armed with guns and battalions. The soldiers rushed into every bedroom and beat every occupant as we assembled them into the living room."

Douglas identified himself as The General's ambassador, talked on behalf of the gun-wielding cadre, and told the princess, her mother, and two sisters that The General had for the first time been kind in a way he had decided to handle their errant daughter.

Douglas said The General was conceived at gunpoint, so he lives by the gun and will certainly die by the gun.

When telling Shawn the gun story, Douglas said he remembered a story The General told him when he learned that the first lady Jessica Nanjovu was not his biological mother. He had long heard rumors that his real mother was murdered in the civil war by his own father. He surprised his father one evening at gunpoint, when the president exited the shower. The General demanded he confirm or deny the rumor. "Tell me who is my real mother now, or this country is having a double funeral of the president and his son," he said, with fury in his voice.

President Muaji panicked and told his son his mother was dead and confirmed he killed her himself. "After she gave birth to you, she kept telling people in the village you were a son of the rebel leader who raped her," he said, staring down the barrel of his son's gun. "I raided their home one evening, shot her dead, and seized you and brought you to the first lady to adopt you as her son."

"I'm your true father, son, and the gun is your mother," General Muaji told him.

He ordered the village not to bury her remains.

The decision not to bury the guerrilla war victims was born in superstition. When still a rebel, President Katila Muaji's spiritual advisers had told him never to bury the people they shot in a war because once they were buried, their spirits would be reincarnated to haunt them in revenge. If they left them unburied on the ground, the witchcraft lord would monitor their spirits, ensuring that none of the dead could exact revenge on the living. Even when President Muaji seized power in the eighties, large numbers of the dead remained unburied, and their remains were displayed on roads or collected into displays such as genocide museums.

But besides the gun, The General also likes lions, with his favorite named Ichuli, who was in the national park. The General regularly fed political dissidents and disobedient citizens, such as the princess, to Ichuli.

With that introduction by Douglas, the documentary opened with a scene of a lion chasing a herd of zebras before taking down one and mauling it to death. "Did you see how all the zebras kept running from the lion's attack, and not even one turned to rescue the victim?" Douglas said. "That is what will happen to you (pointing to Shaki) once The General starts chasing you. No one on social media can save you."

In another scene, a beautiful young woman was dropped into the country's national park, next to a male lion. The lion chases her as she's being filmed. In just seconds, it jumps on her, pushing its jaws into her neck, and blood starts gushing from her veins. As she succumbed to the lion attack and fell unconscious on the ground, two more lions joined. At a certain point the person filming zoomed in on a lioness, with blood on its mouth. In another shot a male lion was seen pulling off the woman's wig.

Princess Shaki could not even bring herself to imagine what kind of human would be filming another person being eaten by a lion. As the scene ended, Douglas told his shocked audience that the family of the woman eaten by the lion was still waiting for her return. They would never know what happened to her.

"What did she do?" the princess asked.

"It is not important to you. Just know what we are capable of doing to stubborn saboteurs like yourself."

"We are going to see another important scene," Douglas announced. In the next scene, five muscular men in uniform are seen entering a house and arresting a military officer and a woman. They asked for the man, who happened to be a general, to turn over all his guns, as if this is a procedural arrest.

After handing them over, they started beating the detained officer. He tried to defend himself, but he was no match for the five assailants who used batons, hammers, and even furniture to put him down. After this general succumbed to the beating, they checked his pulse and confirmed he was dead. They then ordered the woman to take one of the bloodied batons, announcing that they were sending the police and media to come to her home. They instructed her to tell them that she had discovered that he was unfaithful in their marriage and in her rage, she had beaten him so severely that he died from his wounds. Douglas added that the scene should emphasize to the princess the level of their impunity and zero tolerance for any disagreement or refusal whenever The General asked for something.

Douglas announced that he would show the third and final scene before asking the princess what her decision was: Would she accept The General's advances and renounce the video that had gone viral across the country? Or would she refuse outright to oblige?

In the third scene, an airline hostess was serving a male passenger in business class. After taking a drink, the man started vomiting, and his face and skin turned ashen. Within moments, he was dead. Douglas said that their reach was so long and unstoppable, that even at 35,000 feet in the air, no one was safe if they had refused an order or request from The General or the president.

The film's last scene depicted The General executing the Ichuli lion. As the lion approached the familiar motorcade, anticipating another dinner in the form of a human dissident, it was The General who stepped out. The lion leapt at him, nearly tearing him apart. The guards hurried to shoot and paralyze the lion but not kill it. Once The General regained his composure in the car, he drew his gun and began shooting. The lion was dead after two bullets, but The General continued to empty his entire magazine into its body. "Why is he still shooting at the poor dead lion?" Princes Shaki asked in bewilderment.

"This is to show you that The General has no permanent friends. Also, The General does not need any reasons or explanations to execute his enemies or previous friends. He has already replaced Ichuli with another lion called Banda," said Douglas.

The room went silent as the film ended. The princess and her family members seemed paralyzed in their seats. Douglas broke the silence, "I'm a journalist, and I will tell you whatever The General chooses to do to you and your family, the international community is not interested in your safety. And no journalist in Uganda will publish anything because they know The General kills." The irony of Douglas's words could not have seemed more acute or pained to Shawn.

"Did you see any feminist coming to your defense

when you went public on Twitter?" he asked, adding, "they are condemning you and accusing you of lying because they all understand what is at stake when it comes to attacking The General."

"There is simply no #MeToo movement in Uganda or anywhere else in Africa," Douglas stressed.

Douglas's transformation also had haunted Shawn, an African American, who had believed that Africa was a hopeful location for enlightenment and a productive experiment for democracy and equity for everyone, especially the poorest, most disenfranchised people, including women who had historically been treated as second-class citizens and often much worse.

It also was something that the princess had once believed, although she was skeptical and hardly as naive as many African Americans who had been led to believe falsehoods about her homeland. Douglas reiterated to the princess what she already had long suspected. To the international community, Africa remains a jungle, a realization that is manipulated by the continent's dictators and authoritarian presidents to maximum leverage.

"In the jungle there are no rules, no laws of human rights, no #MeToo movements, no counterpart to the Black Lives Matter movement in the US. The international community understands it can never stop strong African leaders killing weaker Africans the same way human beings have not stopped lions from eating zebras," he said.

"To survive in Africa, one must be both intelligent and obedient to the men with the guns. Because once they start killing, the international media switch off their cameras and microphones only to return after the assault to ask the perpetrators, literally the government authorities, how many died. Here, the killer tells the story and blames the victims for being killed. The killer displays the victims in genocide museums as a sobering reminder to those still living of what could happen to them if they disobey or try to foment dissent."

At this point, Shawn had also begun to comprehend the dangerous juxtapositions at play and their consequences.

Douglas reminded the princess, "I know I'm talking much about what the international community ignores in Africa, but let me tell you what they care about: resources and African markets. A strong man like our president who is willing to secure resources like gold, diamond, and lithium for the international community is called an important strategic ally. Our president is the one that secures Somalia's coastline to ensure international trade is flowing. He secures the uranium, cobalt, gold, and diamond mines in the Congo. He secures petroleum deposits in South Sudan. He is the best proxy for Western interests the international community has in the entire region."

Hearing more about Shaki, Shawn was shocked by Douglas's shamelessness about being so raw, blunt, and crude. Shawn wondered how far one could go in applying Larry's theory of being flexible with morals.

Douglas told Shaki, "Do you think the international community are about to give up on our president, the custodian of their resources in the region, just because his son touched your pussy?" With that word, he turned to Shaki's mother, apologizing for the crudeness of his language, as if it was a gratuitous gesture that he still had at least a shred of ethics and a moral compass left in him.

Douglas continued to explain to Shaki, "If you want to know how the international community operates with men who secure their resources, google a man called Jamal Khashoggi and see. He was killed, and his body was hacked into small pieces, but still, diplomats and officials including the American president shake the hands of the Saudi Arabia Crown Prince whom the media have cited as orchestrating the reporter's execution and mutilation. If today, The General served you as a dinner to the lions, even if the whole world screamed, you would still be dead. If you can't achieve good for everyone, then please don't give up on your own life."

The princess again did not say a word as Douglas continued, "But, let's say a journalist finds out you were fed to the lion and pitches the story to the international media. They will be interested in numbers and not your life or the way you lost your life. For example, they may ask the journalist, 'How many Ugandans has The General fed to the lions?' Even if it's ten or thirty it will be a very small number to make it into their papers. They understand this is Africa, and violence here rules. See how the media ignores natural disasters or accidents in Africa where hundreds or even thousands die? But incidents where a handful of Americans or British nationals are killed, the story takes over the international media stage for days. They can only publish your story if there have been hundreds of Ugandans fed to lions, and even then, it is not a guarantee."

Working with Douglas, Shawn also had learned about the stark truth, something that had been glossed over in school.

After Douglas had finished his presentation to the princess and her family. Her mother, Mama Sanyu was the first to drop to her knees, begging in hopes The General would forgive her daughter and promised that her daughter would do everything The General requested.

"Mum, with all respect, it's the word of your daughter that counts here. We are not here for drama because we shall destroy all of you if she is still stubborn and unapologetic," Douglas said.

The mother then ordered the singer, calling her aloud by her birth name of Shakira Najuma, to drop to her knees and ask The General for forgiveness. The princess obeyed immediately. As the singer knelt, she said, "Tell The General I am sorry, and I will do whatever he wants."

Douglas seemed relieved and told the princess how she should go about rectifying the previous viral video. "This is what you are going to do. You are recording another Twitter post telling your fans that neither The General nor his top aides ever touched you. That the person who abused you has been reported to the police, but you will not be naming him. Ask your fans to leave the matter to the police and sign off. The next step is for you to go to The General in person tomorrow and apologize."

As he exited the home, with the group of armed security detail behind him, he turned back toward the princess, and said, "Please never call The General 'motherfucker' again."

Outside the house, Douglas silently stayed on the doorstep as his men started their car engines. He waited to eavesdrop into the house. Mama Sanyu, the princess's mother, broke down in sobs.

"I'm so ashamed for not being able to protect you, my children."

Princess Shaki hugged her mother, who was still on the floor and told her it was not her fault.

"Shakira, promise me. You will not let that dirty man kill you. Oh God, what kind of parent am I for sending her daughter to a rapist."

"Mum," Princes Shaki said, in a soft voice. "He just wants my body. He will have it, but he will never have my soul."

With that story now fully explained to Shawn, he fully understood why she had accompanied The General to New York and was anxiously waiting for him in the pool.

Douglas returned to business, spending much less time summarizing the military operations that Uganda was conducting in Africa and the Middle East on behalf of the international community. He boasted that Uganda was second only to the US in having its troops in other countries. This was not a point that Shawn enjoyed hearing, but still, he had to listen and take notes because he had to write the story and get paid.

Douglas also told him that besides the military operations, the Ugandan troops were carrying out development work including building roads in the Congo to accommodate the infrastructure for extracting the country's rich troves of natural resources for the international community.

Lastly, he told Shawn they had just discovered what they believed were more than thirty-one-million tons of gold ore deposits in Uganda, worth $12.8 trillion. The international community was to be assured that The General was committed to principles of free trade and that outsiders could join the extraction efforts. This included reassuring the international powers that Uganda would do everything to crush tribal dissidents who opposed having foreign corporations extracting resources in Uganda.

With that, Shawn had everything he needed to write up the promotional pieces. He would make up quotes for The General who had not spoken a single word that afternoon. He was wrapped up in the pool, enjoying the presence of Shaki and several other female models.

Shawn's first interview with The General led to an op-ed he wrote with his byline. It appeared in *The New York Times* with the headline, "The US-Uganda military partnership is the best of our times." He wrote about the armaments Uganda received from the US along with the military training and technology. He wrote about how Uganda had used it to transform the whole East and Central African region. The essay also referenced Uganda sending troops to Somalia, Sudan, Congo, Rwanda, Burundi, and to serve as security guards in Iraq.

Another piece he wrote, published this time with Shawn's byline but quoting The General as the primary source, was focused on Uganda's political dream to achieve capitalism and economic growth. It discussed how Uganda's government had facilitated the efforts of international corporations to extract resources in the region, especially from the Congo. It was as straightforwardly a positive piece as could ever be. Shawn was mastering the art of writing government propaganda.

CHAPTER 21

Lisa

SITTING there in the interrogation room across from Shawn, Lisa was dumbstruck. The story of The General's assault on the Ugandan pop singer Shakira weighed heavily on Lisa's mind. It was a revelation that chilled her to the core, shedding light on the brutal nature of the Ugandan ruling family. She found herself grappling with the unfathomable depths of evil within this African dynasty. It left her questioning why those involved in US foreign policy often engaged with such corrupt dictators.

As she delved deeper into the details of the case, an eerie pattern began to emerge in her mind. Sheila's rape and murder in Acton seemed to mirror the cruelty and brutality exhibited by the Ugandan dictator's family toward women. It was a disturbing parallel that couldn't be ignored. Her investigative instincts went into overdrive, urging her to speak with both Shakira and The General,

Kainewaragi Mlevi, about these unsettling connections.

However, there was a significant obstacle in her path. Taking this murder investigation to Uganda required official authorization, and she couldn't obtain it. The bureaucratic red tape and diplomatic hurdles were seemingly insurmountable. Yet, she couldn't shake the feeling that unraveling this complex web of events required answers from the very heart of the Ugandan regime.

"Did you ever tell this story to Sheila the way you have told it to me?" she asked Shawn.

Shawn's eyes darkened. "Yes," he said. "And she was devastated. She was inconsolable upon hearing the grim accounts of what her cousin was inflicting on the Ugandan people, including the horrifying act of taking women who had rejected him and feeding them to lions."

"So, what did she say?"

"Her commitment to her feminist beliefs and her deep love for her country had stirred something within her. She vowed to do everything in her power to put an end to her cousin's reign of terror even if it meant resorting to drastic measures like shooting The General herself."

"She actually said that?"

"I tried to reason with her, telling her that such a plan was reckless and dangerous. But Sheila's determination was unwavering, and she assured me that she was willing to take the risk. She couldn't reconcile the image of her cousin with the man who would watch humans being torn apart by lions. It was a monstrous revelation that had shaken her to her core, and she was prepared to confront that darkness head-on."

"Did Sheila tell you what she was going to do to The

General?"

Shawn's brows furrowed. He shook his head slowly. "No," he replied, "Sheila never actually said what she had in mind. And that, in some ways, was even more unsettling. I tried to talk some sense into her because I knew just how dangerous The General can be. But how could I reason with her when she wouldn't share the whole story? She simply insisted that she was going to show him, to make him stop his madness."

"Shawn, tell me, what was Sheila's perspective on The General's Project?"

Shawn replied thoughtfully, "Sheila loved her family, but she was always somewhat reserved about The General's Project. She didn't believe that Kainewaragi Mlevi would make a good leader to succeed his uncle, the president."

"Shawn, give it to me straight. Do you think Sheila might have been murdered because of her opposition to her family's General Project? Her family, including her uncle, the president, and his son, The General, are known to be very ruthless."

Shawn nodded solemnly. "I've been wondering. It's certainly a possibility. Sheila's family has a history of eliminating threats to their power. If they believed Sheila posed a threat, well..."

CHAPTER 22

Shawn

LISA'S interrogation continued, and Shawn found himself at the center of more inquiries. She was eager to learn more about a significant project Shawn had undertaken for the lobbyist firm, one that he believed had played a pivotal role in safeguarding the Ugandan government. He couldn't help but feel the weight of Sheila's involvement in most of his work with the Ugandan ruling family, especially considering the tragic circumstances surrounding her death.

As he began to explain the details of this critical project, he could see Lisa's curiosity burning bright.

The project in question had arisen from an urgent call Shawn received from Taylor, a rare occurrence that signaled a true emergency. Taylor had informed him about a crucial situation unfolding in Africa and had insisted that he be in Washington the following day for an emergency response discussion. There was no room for delay or questions, but Shawn had his concerns.

It happened to be the last day of the semester at school, and Shawn had a writing workshop class scheduled for that afternoon. The workshop was led by George Williams, a Black professor known for his strict standards and a penchant for pushing his students, especially those of color, to excel. He pondered how to approach this dilemma, knowing that missing the class without a valid excuse would not sit well with Professor Williams.

In the end, he decided to craft an excuse that he believed would pass muster. He attached his final assignment to an email and added a fabricated note that he had tested positive for COVID-19 and therefore would be unable to attend the final class. It was a ruse, but he felt confident that given the ongoing effects of the pandemic, his professor would accept it without demanding proof. His academic commitments clashed with the urgency of the situation at hand, and he had to make a difficult choice.

He arrived in Washington with just enough time to make it to the crucial meeting. Taylor had summoned the entire team. It was clear that the situation was dire, and Taylor wasted no time in briefing all about the looming international incident in East Africa, one that threatened to disrupt the Ugandan projects the lobbying firm had been handling for decades.

As Taylor spoke, Shawn could sense the urgency in his voice. He informed them that the US Navy expeditionary sea base USS Hershel "Woody" Williams had docked at the Mombasa Port, and its presence had raised suspicions that the United States was signaling support for a regime change in Uganda. A neighboring president to the south-west had been aggressively challenging their client's position as the central contact in the region for the international community.

Shawn could not believe that this rival president had once been a beneficiary of the firm's services. Their colleagues had worked on his image management campaign and lobbying efforts, but he had abruptly severed ties with them, choosing to engage a rival lobbying firm in Washington instead. This rival was now orchestrating a challenge to the company's Ugandan client, leveraging his knowledge of their capacities and connections in Washington and London.

Taylor emphasized the gravity of the situation, emphasizing the potential consequences of this challenge. The recently contested election in Uganda had heightened tensions, with the rival president openly claiming election fraud and disputing their client's legitimacy.

With Taylor's announcement, it was clear that the focus needed to shift immediately—Shawn expected new work, a totally different assignment. The General's Project image campaign was put on hold, and a new initiative called "Operation Wait, Don't Shoot" was launched. Shawn and his colleagues were tasked with projects highlighting the positive contributions of the Katila Muaji government to the international community while also emphasizing the risks associated with its potential overthrow.

Larry, Taylor's associate, quickly divided responsibilities among the staff members. Shawn's assignment was to gather information from countries where Ugandan troops had been deployed alongside the international community, such as Somalia, Sudan, and Congo. He needed to convey the potential consequences for international business if the Katila Muaji government were overthrown.

As soon as that meeting had wrapped up, Shawn's phone buzzed with a call from the university. He was on edge, thinking it might be his Black professor, William Booker, but the voice on the other end was a woman—she introduced herself as someone from the school's COVID-19 team.

"This is Nurse Ashley at the University. Your professor reached out to us, claiming you tested positive for COVID-19 and missed a class. However, we have no record of any positive test results from you. Can you clarify what's going on?" she asked him.

Shawn's heart sank as he realized his fabricated excuse had come back to bite him. He hadn't expected his professor to involve others from the school. Regret washed over him, but he decided not to compound his lie. He apologized and admitted that he hadn't tested positive for COVID-19.

He thought that would be the end of it, but then, as he waited for his flight home, he received an email from his professor. The message was as blunt as it could be: "*According to the COVID-19 team, you did not test positive; you lied. If you don't clarify your missing class today, you FAIL the course.*" The word "FAIL" was in capital letters for emphasis, and it hung over him like a storm cloud.

Shawn decided he didn't need this added stress, especially with everything going on at work. He made the decision to ignore his professor's email and instead focus on how he could contribute to saving the Katila Muaji government, his top priority.

The news of the Expeditionary Sea Base USS Hershel "Woody" Williams (ESB 4) docking at the Mombasa port had triggered panic, particularly among the Ugandan ruling family. Sheila, who he hadn't heard from in a month, reached out with a phone call and asked if he was in Boston.

"I'm in Washington, Sheila, but I'll be back tonight."

"What time does your plane land? I can pick you up at the airport and drive you to your dormitory."

After a month of silence, her voice and urgency filled him with wonder—and hope.

Shawn's United Airlines flight touched down right on schedule at 8 p.m., and as he walked through the bustling airport terminal, he couldn't help but feel a mix of excitement and apprehension. There she was, waiting for him at the arrival terminal, a sight that brought a warm smile to his face.

They exchanged brief greetings. The drive from the airport was mostly quiet, each lost in their thoughts. But as they approached Tremont Street, Shawn had an idea that might let him spend more time with Sheila. He proposed that they make a pit stop at The Tap bar, hoping to ease into the serious conversation ahead. Sheila ordered a neat scotch, and Shawn couldn't help but raise a concern. "You know, if you're planning to have a drink like that, maybe you shouldn't drive. I can always call you an Uber, and you can pick up your car tomorrow."

Sheila waved off his concern with a smile. "Don't worry, I've got it all figured out. I'll Uber back home tonight."

But Shawn persisted, seizing the opportunity to be close to her. "Tell you what, how about I drive you home in your car tonight? I'm just having something milder, a snifter of Hennessy."

Sheila agreed, and they settled in for their drinks. Shawn was nervous with anticipation, but with a sip of his Hennessy, he felt a surge of courage as Sheila steered the conversation toward the crisis.

"How serious is the situation with the navy ship docking at Mombasa? Do you think it's a sign of a push for regime change after the elections?"

"It's still hard to say exactly what's gonna happen, but Taylor put together a crisis team to engage with high-level officials in foreign offices and try to ease tensions."

"But Shawn, how long do you think the Ugandan government could hold out if a strike was launched?"

"It's gonna be 'bout a week 'fore it all comes crashing down, and those leaders end up hiding like fugitives underground—that's if they even make it through the beatdown."

Sheila looked distraught, and who could blame her? The thought of her family in hiding, or worse, had to be weighing on her mind. Images of fallen leaders like Saddam Hussein and Muammar Qaddafi were probably haunting her dreams.

Shawn tried to offer some solace. "Right now, everybody in the media team, myself included, gotta be crankin' out as many articles as we can to back up the government and get 'em out there for everyone to see," he said. "And look—whenever a party receives support from US forces, it emerges victorious. That's a fact."

"Oh yeah? What about Syria, Libya, Iraq, and Afghanistan?"

"Okay, there are setbacks—but this is different. And you shouldn't worry."

Sheila was silent, maybe lost in worry. Then she said, "Maybe China could offer assistance, I know my uncle's got—"

"Sheila, don't be crazy. It would be straight-up dumb for any African government to rely on China if they face an attack from the US. US military has advanced technology like drones and precision-guided systems that China can't match."

Sheila sat there quietly, seeming miserable. To lighten her mood, he told her about how he'd lied to the professor. It worked.

Sheila burst into laughter. "You're a terrible liar! Why lie about something that can easily be debunked like that?"

"I guess I panicked and didn't think it through," he replied.

"You have been studying all semester, doing all the coursework, paying the tuition, and now you're willing to accept a FAIL just because you can't apologize for lying to your professor?"

"Well… hell, I thought he should understand."

"Shawn, you're overdoing it. I know, if you were a white student, he wouldn't have fact-checked you like this. Black professors can be extra tough on Black students sometimes, trying to prove once again that they don't fit in. But be cool and just apologize to let it pass."

"I'm not giving him the satisfaction of making me look dumb and beg for mercy. I'll just retake the course with a different professor next time."

"Shawn, please, just do it for me. Apologize to him,

and you can salvage your grades. Let him give you a weaker grade, but don't let him fail you. Maybe you'd find it easier to apologize to a white professor than to a Black one. That's why I don't want to be part of your Black struggles; you people are too hostile to each other. Always waiting for an opportunity to stab each other in the back. No one forgives a vulnerable throat, not even your comrades."

Shawn sighed, relenting a bit. "Doesn't it seem like the punishment is excessive, though? Missing one class and he's threatening to fail me for the whole course."

Sheila explained, "It's not about missing class, Shawn. It's about the lie. It's personal."

They finished their drinks and headed out of the bar. He asked Sheila for her car keys.

Sheila opened up again to him about her uncle Katila Muaji's concerns regarding her cousin The General's reckless behavior on social media. She mentioned that her cousin had been posting tweets that lacked political caution and were embarrassing the family. Sheila had even reported these tweets to her uncle because he was too old to keep up with social media trends.

In one tweet, The General had boasted about being able to defeat neighboring Kenya's military in just two weeks, a statement that raised tensions and eyebrows. In another, he had attacked the opposition leader, accusing him of not belonging to the same tribe as the ruling government. Sheila wanted him to see the exact wording, so she scrolled through her Twitter account.

"'Marrying a woman from the royal tribe does not qualify you to be the next king,'" she read aloud. "The politician responded, accusing him of being drunk and tweeting in a stupor."

Shawn couldn't help but chuckle at the audacity of these tweets.

"Do you know how he replied?" Sheila asked.

He nodded, intrigued by the unfolding drama.

"That he was 'happy to represent the privileged drunkards with a gun,'" she said.

Sheila continued with her story, explaining that she had contacted her uncle late at night about these tweets. Her uncle, clearly upset, had called The General in the middle of the night and ordered him to delete the tweets. He emphasized the importance of presenting The General as a potential future president to Washington and how these tweets were detrimental to that image.

Sheila paused for a moment and then dropped a bombshell. "Now my uncle wants to find someone to manage his Twitter account—someone who can tweet on his behalf in a professional manner. He asked me if you could do the job and assured me they would pay you more."

Shawn hesitated, not wanting to get any closer to The General after witnessing his behavior in New York and hearing Douglas's horrifying account of how he fed women who rejected him to lions.

"Did I mention that I've already confronted him about this and reported him to my uncle?" Sheila revealed. "I've become his official enemy in the family, and he's threatened to physically harm me. I need to brush up on my taekwondo skills and be ready to defend myself."

"You don't need Taekwondo skills to protect yourself from your cousin; you just need a bulletproof suit. That guy would need a gun to kill a mosquito," Shawn replied with a chuckle.

Shawn wanted to share his observations about the arrogance and recklessness of Uganda's president and his son, who seemed to have no sense of accountability to their people. They appeared to care more about their contacts in Washington and London who propped up their government. However, he refrained from saying anything that might upset Sheila further.

Instead, he suggested, "Let's hold off on this issue until we finish the 'Don't Shoot' project. Then we can address it together, alright?"

Shawn lay on his jail-cell bunk, remembering. Time flew by in a string of memories. A month had passed since the crisis, and the tension that had once engulfed Mombasa had dissipated. The US naval forces had been called back, and President Katili Muaji remained in power. Taylor was overjoyed, and he made sure to personally call every member of the project team to deliver the good news and his signature catchphrase: "It's a happy ending! Our client stays as president." He went on to announce a special bonus for everyone who had worked on the project.

Shawn remembered the scene vividly as Taylor addressed the team in the conference room. Taylor's enthusiasm was palpable, and the room buzzed with energy. They were all eager to hear his insights into the complex political landscape of sub-Saharan Africa. Taylor stood before his assembled team, his eyes flickering with a blend of enthusiasm and shrewd calculation. The conference room buzzed with a charged energy, as if the air itself held the secrets of the intricate political dance that governed the sub-Saharan African landscape.

"Good morning, everyone," Taylor began, his voice resonating with authority. "Today, I want to delve into the complexities that underpin the political dynamics of Africa. We are the architects of perception, and understanding these intricacies is essential for crafting effective strategies."

He gestured toward a large screen that illuminated the room with a vivid map, displaying the territories of Uganda and its neighboring countries. "Our firm has devised a strategy that has transformed President Katila Muaji into more than just a leader. We've turned him into the Policeman of the region, a role that has transformed him into an asset indispensable to the international community."

Taylor's gaze swept across the room, taking in the attentive faces of his staff. "Neighboring countries like Rwanda have taken notice of our blueprint. Just as our client sends his troops as enforcers to neighboring lands, Rwanda is now replicating this approach, sending its own troops to police not just its borders, but those of distant nations as well."

He clicked to reveal a series of headlines, detailing Rwanda's military engagements in various foreign lands. "Our client's strategy of offering troops as peacekeepers and enforcers has been adopted by Rwanda. They're tapping into the same playbook, asserting their influence from Somalia and Congo to Mozambique, Burkina Faso, Guinea, and even Haiti."

A murmur of realization rippled through the room as Taylor's words sank in. "Rwanda's president aims to seize the entirety of the Policeman role, a move that threatens to overshadow our client's position." He paused for emphasis. "Their strategy mirrors ours—leveraging publicity to obscure the brutality of their troops, crafting an image of disciplined saviors in the eyes of the international community."

Taylor's voice grew somber. "In this era, wars are fought not just on battlefields, but on the front of perception as well. Both these leaders have carved a niche where they're seen as sending troops and winning battles without spilling blood. But let's not forget, this strategy was born from our playbook, one we gifted to President Katila Muaji."

He paced across the stage, his words laced with gravitas. "Now, this strategy is the gold standard. Every African president yearns to align themselves closely with the international community, offering troops, enforcing regional interests, and taking in refugees as if it's a currency of power."

Taylor's gaze held a piercing intensity as he looked at his team. "Recently, Kenya's President Kenneth Lutalo joined this league. He sent troops to Congo, Somalia, Ethiopia, and now is sending to Haiti. It begs the question—will we support every aspiring leader who pledges their troops in service to the international community?"

His voice echoed with a touch of skepticism. "Or should there be limits? As more presidents vie for the coveted role of the international community's policeman, a new war is emerging—one not of bullets, but of political maneuvering."

Taylor paused, letting his words resonate in the air. "We've navigated through a standoff, and we've achieved resolution. As the international community's representative, our duty is to ensure harmony between President Katila Muaji and Rwanda's leader. We're sending a beacon of reconciliation, General Mlevi Kainewaragi, the son of President Muaji, to Rwanda. He'll stand as a face of unity, signing a reconciliation agreement that'll bring these two leaders together."

Before he closed the meeting, Taylor told everyone the focus was now going back to The General's Project of promoting the younger Mlevi as the next president of Uganda. The lobbying firm would help him re-establish relations with their antagonistic neighbor in the south, who suddenly had attracted a lot of attention in Washington diplomatic circles.

Meanwhile, The General had indicated his intentions to retire from the army on Twitter in order to be eligible for running for the presidency. The challenge for everybody at the firm returned to getting as many profile features as possible in the American press.

Shawn was astonished by the impact of their work. The articles and ghost-written essays they produced were gaining praise and recognition from some of the most influential foreign policy experts in DC. It struck him that these African politicians were often savvier and more strategic than their American counterparts when it came to manipulating and gaining control of situations, even from thousands of miles away.

He had also neglected Sheila's advice about apologizing to his professor. The F grade had stung, but his stubbornness had prevented him from following her recommendation. However, with his academic status in jeopardy, he finally decided to make amends. He called his professor, apologized for his dishonesty, and promised to prove that he was better than his behavior had suggested.

Professor William, a master of tough love, was satisfied with his apology and changed his grade to a B. It was a relief, knowing that his scholarship and financial aid were safe.

With the academic crisis resolved and work returning to normal, he couldn't help but reflect on the whirlwind of challenges he had faced and overcome. The rewards were equally satisfying. He was no longer academically deficient, and he received a Happy Ending Bonus of $30,000, the most significant sum of money he had ever received in one go.

While others might have chuckled at Taylor's double entendre with the bonus name, he genuinely felt like he had achieved a happy ending. With his windfall, he decided to treat himself to a new Jeep Wrangler, a significant purchase that he couldn't wait to share with Sheila.

CHAPTER 23

Lisa

LISA was engrossed in her lunch, a sandwich half-eaten in front of her. As she took a sip of water, the door creaked open. Bus entered holding a stack of papers. As he walked toward her desk, Lisa noticed the sharply defined outline in his pants, suggesting that his 'cobra' had a mind of its own. Lisa wondered why men of this generation preferred loose boxers that did little to contain their 'cobras,' allowing them to make unwelcome appearances. The thought made her briefly question her own attire. She discreetly tapped her trousers, reassuring herself that she was indeed wearing panties, specifically large black cotton ones, far from the sexy lingerie she'd worn during happier times with her now-estranged husband. Since he had left, the idea of stocking up on alluring underwear had lost its appeal.

He came with news that interrupted her erotic reverie.

"Lisa, I just talked to Chief Flores, and I'm going to re-arrest this guy, Samuel Mugyenyi—the one who found the body. Chief Flores agrees with me that there are just too many coincidences for this guy to be a Ugandan and to find the body of the president's niece in the early morning hours in a car."

She paused mid-bite, her eyes fixed on Bus.

"That's ridiculous. Tell me this is not the CIA again trying to divert us from investigating the family of this Ugandan dictator for murdering *their own* rebellious daughter on our lands!"

"Lisa, this family is still grieving for their daughter. You can't use crazy conspiracy theories to accuse them of murdering her."

"I'm trying to *investigate* them, not accuse them. Get it right, Mr. Detective."

Their voices had grown louder, catching the attention of Chief Flores, who immediately entered their office to mediate.

"What are you two fighting about now?"

Lisa was quick to speak up. "Why does the CIA want to take over the investigation? They have no business in this jurisdiction."

Flores responded, attempting to rationalize, "Listen, Lisa, all they want to do is work with you, not take over. Ugandan intelligence has passed along what apparently is relevant information concerning this man, Mugyenyi, who found the body. Apparently, he is a fugitive on asylum who they believe is a real suspect."

"These Ugandan and Rwandan dictators think they have the CIA in their pockets. What do they think, that the USA is Somalia or the Congo? Tell the CIA this is the United States of America. We do not need any African dictators to intervene in our investigations," Lisa shot back.

Bus said, "Lisa, you're holding this whole investigation hostage for your knowledge of my recent work with the CIA. Every time I try to do something, you respond with 'CIA this' and 'CIA that.' Let's move on and solve this case. You're trying to pin it on the family, and that's wrong. If this case is political, the killer here must be in opposition to the Ugandan government."

Lisa said, "Bullshit. The family of the Ugandan dictator needs to be investigated and you know it. That's the only way we'll uncover the truth. You and I both know that Sheila was rebellious, that she despised the "General Project"—she thought it was a threat to democracy, and she wasn't afraid to speak up about it. So don't tell me she just happened to get murdered by some random person."

Chief Flores said, "Alright, alright, let's calm down here. Tell me your discoveries and stop all the bickering. Who is this 'General'?"

Bus said, "I have no idea, Chief. But Lisa's trying to accuse the victim's family of murdering their own daughter."

"The General, as Bus well knows, is General Mlevi Kainewaragi, the Ugandan president's likely successor. He is a big suspect roaming freely in Uganda, and if you want to actually *solve* this murder, we need to bring him here for questioning. There's no other way."

Chief Flores breathed deep, "Okay, it is not wrong to have two more suspects in a murder case like this. Mugyenyi can be a suspect, and this General can also be a suspect. Let's start by arresting the suspect who is *here* as we navigate the bureaucracy of arresting The General from Uganda as well—believe me, it isn't going to happen overnight. Is that fair enough?"

Lisa nodded, but she wasn't happy.

Bus grimaced. Then he shared the documents related to Mugyenyi that he had secured from the CIA. Lisa picked them up.

> This is a transcription of a hate speech by a Ugandan refugee based in Boston. Ugandan intelligence passed it on to CIA for our investigation. They believe this refugee could be the suspect.
>
> Stephen

The first sheet in the file was a backgrounder about Samuel Mugyenyi, who lived in Acton, just outside of Boston. He hosted a podcast called *Free Africa from Imperialism* and was active on Twitter as well as Facebook Live. His Twitter handle was @M7imperialist. Mugyenyi worked as a Licensed Practicing Nurse (LPN) in Concord, but he also was a blogger from Uganda, and his platform on Twitter hada million followers.

She flipped to a translation of a speech thread that Mugyenyi posted on social media on May 10:

> Fellow Ugandans, we are in this alone. Tonight's show is a sad one because the British foreign secretary has already endorsed President Joel Katila Muaji as the winner of the just concluded brutal elections.
>
> The British, who are also one of the main representatives

of the international community, have not just propped up a dictator but also put a knife in our flesh and turned.

This means even the so-called International Court of Justice in Geneva will not be interested in the case of the fifty-two Ugandans murdered on Kampala streets protesting Muaji's dictatorship.

Fellow Ugandans, the Muaji army raped and the Rwandese army murdered my family in Congo. This fight is not just any fight for me but also a deeply personal one I share with everyone who matters. They have done this to many families not just in Uganda and Congo but also in every country in Africa. Recently, Muaji has even exported some forces to Iraq, and we know so well some will be going to Afghanistan as soon as the US army completes its withdrawal.

We have to take this matter in our hands and do for ourselves whatever little we can. Ladies and gentlemen, today's podcast is to announce a new book. I'm going to write a book in which I will tell stories of all these men and women who were murdered on Kampala streets. Relatives of these people, please reach out to me. I'm only seeking their stories—not fundraising, not money. Let's tell our children that these people once existed, and they lived until Uganda's president decided to murder them.

After murdering them, he continues ruling like nothing happened. And the British congratulated him for hosting a calm and peaceful election while welcoming him back into the international community. And the IMF gave him more loans. Loans that will have to be repaid by the orphans of these murdered people for many generations in the future.

Ladies and gentlemen, I am not here to tell you how poor and desperate we are, that if the international community has chosen our oppressor against us, there's nothing we can do. Instead, I am here to give you hope that even in our weakness, there's something we can still do. To make it clear that these rulers are impostors.

We can start by boycotting everything they own and sell. If you know a business belongs to their family don't do business with it and call out anyone doing business with it. Everywhere they show up, let's go out. Let's ignore them.

Let's not go to their social events, weddings, or even funerals, and if they show up to ours let's abandon the event and walk out in protest. Even when you die and find them in heaven, just protest and move out of heaven because that will be an indication that God as well is corrupt.

And if you are in hell with them, please let other hell dwellers know, there's nothing they could have done worse than the slaughter and corruption that they did.

Lastly, this is very important, and I want everyone to hear it and remember it always as my main point: We don't need to replace Muaji with someone who is going to serve the international community and its corporations but not us the people and citizens. If our presidents are there to serve the international community and not citizens, why do we even have them? This is a dilemma for all of Africa, and therefore we need to start evaluating our independence. And a question for everyone here to ponder about after today, why is the international community so opposed to African leaders like Patrice Lumumba and so supportive of leaders like Katila Muaji?

After reading the full transcript, Lisa passed the pages back to Bus. "Do you, by any chance, know about his immigration status in the US?"

"He filed for asylum, but his case is still pending, for like three years now," Bus said.

"So, you're already on to him—great. Can we also have a copy of his asylum file and see what he puts across."

"I can reach out to Chief Flores on that."

Lisa visited Mugyenyi's Twitter account.

> @M7imperialist: As the US returns its troops home from Afghanistan, Ugandans are asking when their troops from Congo, Somalia, Sudan, Rwanda, Burundi will be returning home. Tune in to my Twitter space tonight.

Samuel's asylum application was on her desk the following morning.

As she flipped through the pages, she noticed that Samuel had first scrawled his story in ink, in a seemingly chaotic penmanship, but he also had taken the effort to type some of his story.

> I was born in the Democratic Republic of Congo. It was around 1990, but I'm not certain of the exact date of my birth, as such details were not kept by my family. My father was also unknown. It was during the turmoil wars that gripped and defined my country after its independence from King Leopold of Belgium.
>
> The only knowledge I had about my father was that he was a rebel from Uganda that had raped my mother. I could understand talks and rumors from relatives and family friends about my poor mother who had been violated and had my first sibling—a sister—and who was violated again in order to have me. The cycle of violence against women was used as a weapon of war in my country, up to this time.
>
> My family memory dates to when I was around five. We were two siblings staying in a hut with my mother and

grandmother. The family had no men and survived on subsistence farming.

One evening, the rumor came that the Ugandan guerrilla rebels were around the village. Whenever such news came, villagers, including my family, would abandon their homes and sleep in the bush, in hiding. The rebels would then be knocking or kicking doors open and stealing whatever they could find in the abandoned homes. Sometimes they would beat up people or even shoot them when they found them in those homes and tried to either fight back or could not give them money.

My mother decided to take us to the bush to hide that night. Our grandmother was sick, so she decided she would stay in the house and explain to the rebels she is sick and poor. When we came back the next morning, she was dead. She had apparently been shot by the rebels who did not take her sick and poor story when all they needed was money.

There was a small funeral, and about five people had been killed in the village that day. The rebels were still in neighborhoods, so we could never have a bigger funeral. But after the burial, our mother was so sad, and she decided to stay in a displaced people's camp to be safe.

Those days, even the camps were not safe. Another day, the rebels came at night to the camp. They were rebels from Uganda. Rebels were often foreigners, either from Uganda or from Rwanda. We could always tell their countries of origin by the languages they spoke. Four men entered our shack.

I was around seven years old then and did understand a lot. When they kicked the door of our shack, they used a torch light to look at our faces. We were sitting in shock on our mattresses on the floor on which we slept. There were no beds. I shared a mattress with my sister, and our mother slept on the other mattress.

My sister was around twelve then, so they ordered her to undress. Another man ordered my mother to undress also. One rebel slept on my sister as the other two rebels watched and cheered. He could not penetrate because my sister was young, and they booed him for not being a man. He then asked for a razor from other rebels and cut her private parts. My sister bled first from the razor and then the rapist rebel's penetration. She then penetrated her as she cried. They then took turns on two other rebels on my sister and then on my mother. After, they left.

A few months later, the rebels came again. This time they were from Rwanda. My mother first hid me when she heard them knocking. She thought they wanted to take young boys to fight. But these rebels wanted women. They were going after pregnant women specifically as they accused them of carrying babies of Hutus who had fled Rwanda because these babies would grow up to fight them.

My sister was six months pregnant from the previous rape. They entered our shack and ordered my mother to spear her daughter's stomach with a panga. She was just crying with it in her hand. They then pulled it away and slaughtered her instead. She kept saying in our language that the rebels didn't understand, "My son, hide, don't come out, I want you to live." Until her last breath.

Then the rebels turned to my sister, and she started reciting the same words my mother had said, in our language: "My brother, please hide, I don't want you to die." They cut out her baby and she died from the bleeding. I came out of hiding when they had left, and I saw two bodies lying there.

I knocked on the door of our neighboring shack, and our neighbor took me in for some days. One day, one of the boys counseled me to go, and we joined the Ugandan side rebels so that we could have food. Employment of child soldiers was common by rebel armies.

In the Ugandan camp, they called me kadoogo, loosely translated as kid, and gave me a gun. I was supposed to carry it, though heavier than my undernourished body. If the gun was so heavy to carry, I knew it was going to be even heavier to fire in case we ran into an ambush.

But I didn't fire my gun at all because I was still traumatized by the murder of my mother and sisterI always thought their unburied bones were in the museums the dictators kept after their victories, to warn future generations not to attempt to overthrow them.

From the horrors of colonialism, when King Leopold massacred ten million people in Congo to pillage for tires for the automobile revolution to the present-day massacres by imperialists agents like Katila Muaji of Uganda to feed the international market of cell phones with tantalum, my country and people have had one of the worst experiences in Africa.

As an adult, I have revisited my hometown inside Congo to see my living relatives. All that used to be our home and compound are now mines where Coltan and Lithium are collected for the global phone and battery market. Once you are there, even the air you breathe in is thick from the pollution of mining.

The main cause of death is cancer from this pollution. But the whole region does not have a single hospital. People just cough themselves to death in their homes.

The local populations are so exhausted, desperate, and tired. Every time they try to push back or demand accountability from these corporations, soldiers are flown in from Uganda and Rwanda to rape and murder them.

Even the international liberal activists who have condemned King Leopold for the genocide and cutting off hands of our ancestors are mute when modern corporations cut off lungs through pollution and foreign soldiers murder our people and rape our women.

The atrocities on my family were committed when the Ugandan army was in retreat and returning home. One Ugandan soldier called Deogratious liked me and was moved by the story of my family's massacre. He asked me to stay with him as we crossed the border, and he took me to his family which became my new family in Uganda.

I started calling him uncle and his wife, Betty, was my aunty. The couple also had two younger biological kids: James and John, who called me elder brother. Uncle Deo also took me to school and paid my school fees from primary to university.

I arrived in the USA in November 2016 on a church choir visa. I had joined the choir at university and stayed with them after graduation. Our visit to the USA was to perform at a Gospel Choir convention. I planned to go back to Uganda, and all my eleven other choir members returned after the convention.

The reason I personally chose to stay here was for my security and safety. When we were performing, I received a text from my aunt Betty that President Katili Muaji's army had attacked our home and the whereabouts of my uncle were yet to be established.

This was not just an attack on the home. The army had attacked the palace of our King Charles Wesley Mumbere in Kasese. My Uncle Deo was one of the King's guards.

Like many people in the palace, Deo was finally killed in the attack. I hurried to the internet and started following the news of the attack and the loss of my second family. I was distraught.

Most worrying was that the army was also looking for the sons of the soldiers, and they wanted to kill all the men who lived and worked in the palace. Aunty Betty told me when I called her that they had raided the home looking for me. They had my name on the lists of young people they were looking for.

Every man they pulled out of the home was executed on the spot and the body carried away. They took the bodies because they didn't want people to count and parade them on social media. She appealed to me to stay in the USA until the situation returned to normal.

Meanwhile, I moved my anger and activism on social media, first by posting news and details of the massacre on Facebook. I wrote small stories about all the people in the palace that had been killed, just to show the wider community that these were real people with families and stories like any other.

Soon, my Facebook gained traction and became one of the leading references of the news of the massacre. I moved the discussion to Twitter and then started an a podcast that I host on both Facebook and Twitter. It is one of the widely circulated blogs on the atrocities of President Katila Muaji not just in Uganda but the whole of Africa.

Lisa's mind was darting in and around contradicting spaces. Was this merely a moment of empathy for a young refugee who had witnessed such horrors firsthand? Or was this a young man whose profound trauma had led him to commit a brutal murder? Without warning, the investigation had changed again.

She still had her hesitations but didn't get in Bus's way to arrest Samuel. As they discussed what they had discovered, they both realized that the likelihood that the detained Shawn was the wrong suspect had changed dramatically. Now, they confronted the possibility that the murder of Sheila was a horrific act of vengeance borne not from a failed relationship but instead by an international political crisis which ended up on a Massachusetts college campus.

She lay back on her couch and stared at the ceiling. Of one thing, Lisa was certain: The investigation was no longer a straight murder case. The diplomatic and political reverberations had seriously complicated their work. In the past, Lisa had believed that more rigorous controls were needed in the immigration and asylum process. She believed that candidates for asylum had to be extensively evaluated for trauma and stress but also their own political views and their emotional need for retribution and vengeance. You don't just let anybody into the country. Too many innocent lives could be lost.

But now, she cautioned herself not to jump to conclusions. If they were wrong about Shawn, they might be wrong about Samuel too.

Either way, she'd have to wait on the arrest warrant.

CHAPTER 24

Bus

AT precisely nine in the morning, Bus walked into the lobby of the Administration Building and pressed the up button on the gold-walled elevator. He was all set to go for the arrest of Samuel Mugyenyi, thinking that Detective Lisa and him were finally on the same page. They had, just the day before, discussed and seemingly agreed that Samuel should be treated as a potential suspect in their ongoing investigation. The ride up was smooth. He was ready for work.

But, oh boy, no sooner did he enter his office that he got hit with a curveball he never saw coming.

Just behind him and seemingly out of nowhere, Lisa entered his office and calmly stated, "You know what, Bus? I've got an interview scheduled with Shawn today, so you can go ahead with that Samuel arrest on your own."

Bus froze in his seat. Hadn't the two agreed on this

course of action just the day before? Was this Lisa's way of getting back at him for not being present during her questioning of Shawn? He couldn't help but mutter under his breath, "Women and their revenge."

Spinning around and walking away, Lisa shouted, "I heard that."

At ten o'clock, the chief came in to tell them they were ready. Bus decided he was going to keep this arrest low-profile, avoiding any unnecessary drama with multiple police vehicles blaring their sirens. So, he decided to stay in civilian clothes and take just one patrol car and brought along one officer as backup, keeping the rest of the team on standby in case things took an unexpected turn.

The destination was a nursing home on state route 2, not too far from their state police Concord offices, just a short two miles away—from where the body was found. This is where Samuel worked as a licensed practical nurse (LPN). When he pulled up to the nursing home in the police patrol car, he went in alone. He approached the receptionist and asked to speak with Samuel Mugyenyi. The receptionist made the call, and Samuel, dressed in his blue uniform nursing attire, soon joined him in the lobby.

They walked out to the designated smoking area, where a couple of Samuel's colleagues were enjoying a break. Bus suggested moving to a quieter, more private space, saying, "Let's go talk in my office. I have a few questions regarding the girl you found dead in the car." Samuel agreed, and they made their way to the state police cruiser, heading toward the police interrogation room, where the intense questioning would continue.

"Have a seat," Bus said, motioning toward one of the hard, uncomfortable chairs. Samuel obliged, and Bus took the opposite seat. "Samuel, we need to ask you a few more questions regarding the incident. I understand you've already cooperated with the police on this matter, but we have some new information we'd like to go over."

"I've already told the police everything I know," Samuel said, his voice trembling slightly.

"I appreciate your prior cooperation, but sometimes fresh information can shed new light on a case. We're just trying to ensure that we have all the facts straight."

Samuel stayed guarded. Then Bus did something he'd been planning on morning. He greeted him in their shared language, Luganda.

"Oli otya?" That meant how are you.

"Eh! Bulungi," Samuel replied with a smile.

Bus introduced himself using the Luganda name Basudde, another layer of their common cultural background.

"You mean your name is like *Basudde Herman Semakula*?" Sam asked, excitement in his voice. Sam then hummed a tune they both knew.

Bus replied with nothing but a warm smile.

"Can we have this investigation in our local language, Luganda, then?" Sam asked.

Bus laughed a little. "Unfortunately, I speak very few Luganda words. My mother is from Uganda, but I was born here to a white American father."

"Still, we are brothers, right?" Sam inquired, as if seeking common ground.

"We're going to be brothers if you answer my questions honestly."

With a nod, Sam indicated he understood the terms.

Bus cut to the chase. "First things first, did you kill this girl?"

"No."

"You found the girl, cold and lifeless, early in the morning, near your home. She's Ugandan, and you are Ugandan. Isn't that too many coincidences?"

"At the time I found her, I didn't even know she was from Uganda. It was just my curiosity that led me to check out the car and find a body there. I called the police."

"You are an anti-government blogger, and she is a niece of the president, is that correct?" Bus asked.

"Yes, that is true. But I swear, I did not know that at the time that I found her—it's horrible. My podcasts… there is no connection."

"The connection is this, Samuel: a few months ago, you did a podcast in which you urged Ugandans to, and I quote, *rise up and kill the ruling family*. Sheila is part of that family."

Sam twisted in his seat, he was sweating now, furrowed brow. "I don't remember urging anyone to kill anyone. Please show me the blog recording."

Bus produced a transcription of the podcast that had been passed on to him from the CIA and handed it to Sam. Sam read hastily, obviously in a panic. "But this is redacted, rewritten. The blog, my blog was to boycott all businesses and functions associated with the ruling family, never to advocate for violence. Please—it's… a mistranslation. If you cross-check with anyone who speaks Luganda fluently, they will confirm this omission."

Bus sighed and nodded. He knew he needed to speak

to an impartial translator fluent in Luganda. "Alright, Sam," he said. "let's conclude—for now. But you better be prepared for more questioning. We'll be keeping you here at the station until we have all the answers to clear you."

"Am I being held or being arrested?" Samuel asked.

"Exactly, you are being arrested. But we need to gather information from you before any charges are pressed."

"Then why haven't you read me my rights? Where is the arrest warrant? Why all this beating around the bush? I wouldn't have talked to you without a lawyer if I knew I was being arrested. You've tricked me, and I find this very unprofessional and unethical."

"You need to calm down, Sam. I give you my word, as soon as we have more information, you'll be out of here."

Bus sent the patrol car back to the station and got in his vehicle. His new destination was his mother's place in Waltham, a suburb of Boston.

When he arrived, he bypassed the elevator and ascended the staircase to the third floor of the building. He then rang the bell to her apartment. Mama Milly Nanyondo welcomed him inside, seated in her small and cozy living room.

Her eyes, still vibrant with traces of the deep brown they once were, looked sternly at Bus as he sat across from her in their living room. The walls were adorned with framed portraits of the King of Buganda, alongside family pictures capturing visits to Uganda. Tables were draped with linens from Uganda, adding a touch of home to their space.

"Mama," he said, "I want you to read this. Tell me if they got it right." Bus pulled out his phone and started the playback.

She listened to the audio recording and read the script of Samuel's blog post. All the while, she shook her head.

"No," she whispered. "Not right. Uh uh. No. That's not it. Ha."

"What," Bus said. "Tell me."

"They change *boycotting* to *killing*."

Bus nodded knowingly.

"Who did this?" Mama asked.

Bus just smiled.

"This is dangerous!" Mama exclaimed.

"I know, Mama. It's manipulation, and it's terrible. I had to bring this to you because it's connected to the murder case we're working on."

Mama Milly sighed heavily. She was proud that her son had been working with the CIA and now State Police, but she had always been worried about the dangerous territory it could lead him into. She knew all about Ugandan dictators and the extent of their ruthlessness. This president was a man who would do anything to keep his grip on the country, anything.

"Basudde my dear," she said, "you have to be careful with this. I've seen too much pain and suffering caused by that regime back home. I can't bear the thought of you getting caught up in their games. You are my son. I want you safe and far away from those monsters."

"I know, Mama."

"No, you don't know. Our people have been beaten into submission by this regime for forty years. Protesters are murdered, and all the Americans care about is how the regime is helping international corporations do business in Africa."

Mama Milly never did back down. When he was younger, she had shown Bus images of gruesome murders the Ugandan government had orchestrated. The violence was bloody: a November massacre which killed fifty-four protesters.

"Bus, you remember the video I showed you. Their military just goes on a rampage of shooting in the streets, killing protesters and poor people going about their normal business. Your allies' puppet government is *filled* with murderers. They have killed more people than HIV/AIDS and all other diseases combined. I understand if the American media don't care about these poor dying souls, but what about you, Bus? What happened to your morality? Do you even remember the conversation about Black Lives Matter this country is having right now? You are better than this. These people are Black like you, your mother; some could even be your cousins—don't let them be murdered to save your job!"

"Mama," he retorted. "Why am I held responsible for whatever issues people in Africa can't manage by themselves? Just because I share part of their race?"

"Son, please don't bring the racist card here. Don't try to explain this away because there is no explanation. This is important, and I would tell it to anyone involved in sustaining President Katila Muaji's dictatorship all this time. If I ever got a chance to meet with the CIA boss, I would go on my knees to beg him to stop propping up this monster. To outgrow his manipulations and look for allies among other decent people, there are so many leaders willing to be an asset to the US while also being less oppressive and dictatorial to their citizens."

"Mama, achieving freedom is no easy path; it's a challenging struggle that demands a lot of effort. People can't just sit idly and expect freedom to come to them effortlessly. They can't be spectators on their own path to liberation."

"Son, you are talking nonsense. Do you realize how powerful the American military machinery and lobbyists supporting this dictator are?"

Mama got up to make some tea. Bus just sat there, simultaneously furious, guilty, and confused. He had recently defended himself with that phrase from Larry's lecture about being flexible with morality. But his mother also was making him question that flexibility as soon as the words slipped from his tongue.

Mama reentered the room with a tray and sat down. "My son, why would you continue preaching morality when you have chosen flexibility instead?"

Bus felt cornered and like a punching bag.

"Mama, I can't think straight right now. Please just… let me be."

He stormed out of her apartment and waited for the elevator, but he needed to leave now, so he ran down the staircase. He worried that she would pursue him out of the building. Before he hit the bottom of the stairs, his phone buzzed. It was his mother, but he refused to answer. Mama Milly always left a voicemail whenever a call went unanswered. After a few blocks, he listened to the voicemail.

"Son, please don't add my voice to the voices of Africans this country hears and ignore. It's a bad feeling when you get ignored while trying to save people's lives. Please don't break my heart. I want to know that you are going to think about all we said. Just think about it. Give your position another thought. It is not unpatriotic to consider other people's lives. It's not unpatriotic to disassociate from the oppression of President Katila Muaji."

As soon as the recorded message ended. He noticed another voicemail from his mother again.

"Son, I know you are upset but... son, if you can listen to me, you can get another job. It is not right you just ignore all these atrocities against other people because of a detective or intelligence job. They are just using you, son."

It was not the first time he had been compelled to consider quitting his detective job and also stop doing CIA gigs in Africa. He just needed to think through his alternatives.

He frowned at the thought of having to hand in his health insurance cards and benefits as a detective and then live without one. He thought she was essentially asking him to sacrifice his own health for the people of Uganda.

He thought this dilemma he was facing right now was the same dilemma the CIA dealt with whenever someone asked to abandon their favorite dictator President Katila Muaji, who policed not just Uganda but the whole East and Central African region on their behalf.

What would happen if the replacements ended up being populists like Patrice Lumumba, who said that to lift up the lives of Africans could be accomplished by starving the international corporation's capacity to exploit the continent's huge reserves of natural resources. That would disrupt international business and trade on a scale too large for the international community to accept without resistance.

He found himself sitting in his car, a tangled web of emotions gnawing at him. It had been a frustrating day to say the least. His investigation into Samuel Mugyenyi had hit a dead end, and his mother's revelations about the manipulated translation had left him deeply embarrassed.

Driving aimlessly, he felt a wave of desperation wash over him. He desperately wanted to close the case, to find the real killer of Sheila and bring them to justice. The weight of that responsibility bore down on him like a crushing burden. He was supposed to be the detective who solved this, but he couldn't even fathom who the real killer might be.

In a moment of despair, he turned his car into a dimly lit street. The neon sign of a bar on Moody Street in Waltham beckoned to him, a flickering oasis of distraction. He parked his car in the lot, feeling an eerie connection to the way General Kainewaragi Mlevi drank, whose dark shadow seemed to loom over his thoughts.

Entering the bar, he felt like a man on the edge, drowning his failures and frustrations in a sea of alcohol. He ordered one drink after another, matching each shot to the beat of his racing heart. He drank until his surroundings blurred, and the voices of other patrons became a distant hum.

Finally, he reached his limit. Struggling to hold his phone steady, he pulled it out of his pocket and dialed Lisa's number. His voice slurred as he spoke, "Lisa, I'm sorry to disturb you, but I'm drunk. I'm here in a bar in Waltham, and I can't even drive my car. I don't know how to get home."

"Bus, what are you doing? Tell me the name of the bar

and stay right there. I'm on my way. Don't move."

He mumbled the name of the bar and dropped his phone back onto the table. He watched the swirling patterns on the wooden surface, his inebriated mind a chaotic storm. And now, he waited, swaying slightly as he sat at the bar, hoping that Lisa would arrive soon to rescue him from this self-inflicted mess.

CHAPTER 25

Lisa

DETECTIVE Lisa had her grip firm on the steering wheel of her police patrol car as she drove to work. Her thoughts were consumed by the events of the previous night, specifically the arrest of Samuel Mugyenyi and the rescuing of Bus from a drinking spree in Waltham.

The incident had left Lisa feeling uneasy. She hadn't had the opportunity to discuss the arrest with Bus—he wasn't sober and rational—there was no way. But now, as she rounded a bend on state route 2 rotary, something unexpected caught her attention—a group of protesters gathering at the rotary just outside the Concord Jail.

Lisa slowed her patrol car and pulled over to the side of the road and quickly assessed the situation. The protesters were a diverse group, all of African descent, their faces filled with determination. They were Ugandans, they had to be. Their colorful clothing and vibrant energy stood out in the early morning light.

As she stepped out of the car, Lisa approached the protesters, her detective's badge gleaming on her hip. She read the signs they held with bold letters that demanded attention:

FREE SAMUEL
WE'RE ALL SAM'S ALIBI
PLEASE REPLACE OUR DICTATOR

Lisa had seen her fair share of demonstrations during her time as a detective, but she couldn't recall any of them leading to concrete change. Even the African American community in the United States couldn't see to achieve their goals through protests. What made these Ugandans think Samuel needed their help by hitting the streets anyway?

A voice from the crowd shouted, "We want justice for Samuel!"

Another protester yelled, "Stop the wrongful arrests!"

With a determined sigh, Lisa accelerated her patrol car and continued her journey to the police department. She needed to speak with Detective Bus, her partner and the one who had arrested Samuel. There were questions that needed answers, and perhaps, just perhaps, together they could figure out what was happening with Samuel Mugyenyi and why these protesters believed they could advocate for his release.

Entering the office, Bus wasn't at his usual seat. That was odd—she was sure she'd spotted his car parked outside. She knew he must be nearby. Where the hell was he?

She couldn't wait to talk protesters. She opened a Ziploc bag of popcorn from her purse and started munching on them while waiting for Bus.

But when Bus finally appeared, he looked too serious, and it threw her. He leaned in close and spoke in hushed tones, even though they were the only two in the office room. "The boss is summoning us," he whispered. "He called me. I just came from his office, and he's really upset that we haven't made an indictment in two months. He told me to wait for you… we're both supposed to see him."

Lisa sighed. "I hate these summons. It feels like we're back in school." She absentmindedly reached for the bag of popcorn.

Bus also reached his hand into the bag and grabbed a handful of popcorn, earning a disapproving look from Lisa.

"Wait," he said with a mischievous grin. "I hope you're not going to throw the rest away just because I touched your food."

"As long as you promise your hands were clean and not dirty from scratching… you know," she trailed off, and Bus completed her sentence.

"I don't scratch it with my hands. If it ever itches, I seek help."

"Enough, Bus," Lisa said, shaking her head. "I'm not having this conversation with you this morning. Let's go and see the boss."

As Lisa walked a few steps ahead of Bus, she turned back to ask him if she had mentioned the protesters outside. However, when she saw Bus's eyes fixated on her behind and his mouth half open, her thoughts spun like a wheel in a fast-moving car. Had he been doing this for a while? Did it mean he found her attractive or had a crush on her? Finally, she blurted out whatever came to her mouth without thinking. "Are you coming?"

Bus snapped out of his daze, his face flushing slightly. "Yes, yes, give me a minute to grab my notepad and a pen," he stammered.

Lisa and Bus settled into their seats, exchanging worried glances as Chief Flores appeared visibly annoyed, not bothering to welcome them into his office. "How long have the two of you been working on this case?" Chief Flores asked as he initiated the meeting.

"Two months, sir," Lisa replied.

"How many suspects have you apprehended so far, and how many are still on the run out there?" Chief Flores asked.

Lisa glanced at Bus, silently seeking confirmation about Samuel, whose arrest had ignited protests outside. "We've apprehended two, Shawn and Samuel, right, Bus?" she said. "*And* we have The General still out there in Uganda."

"Why haven't you made an indictment?" Chief Flores demanded.

Bus spoke up, breaking his silence. "There's not enough evidence to indict any of the suspects we have, sir. They all have alibis that account for their whereabouts when the crimes were committed, and no evidence found at the crime scene links to any of them."

"If the problem is evidence, find it. That's why you two are paid. Do your job. I need an indictment in this case, and I need it now. Seek it through a confession or coercion, I don't care, but there must be one now. This case is supposed to go on trial, and the judge will only be interested in the case's evidence, not how you obtained it. Do you understand me?"

"We understand you, sir," Bus replied. "Unfortunately, the documents of evidence we received about Samuel's activism and blogging were misleading. They had altered the translation of 'boycotting' to 'killing.' He told me this during an interrogation, and I checked with an independent translator from Uganda who confirmed."

"Is he the guy the protesters outside are rallying for?" Chief Flores inquired.

"Yes, sir," Bus confirmed. "He's a popular opposition blogger. With your permission, I will let him go for now."

"So now we have just one suspect, and that's Shawn?" Chief Flores asked, summarizing the situation.

"Yes, sir," Lisa responded.

"And you two think The General could be involved, but his involvement wasn't *physical* because he was in Uganda when the girl died, right?"

"We think The General could have given orders to Shawn to carry out the killing," Lisa explained. "We also believe the victim knew about this plot from sources, possibly within her family, which is why she confronted Shawn on the phone about it."

"Have you talked to the family? On the phone or with any member living in the US?"

"Sir, I've been to the apartment the deceased shared with her brother, Amos," Bus replied. "I spoke to the deceased's father in Uganda using Amos's phone. He was reluctant to talk or let his son speak to me. Instead, he promised that their lawyer would be calling to speak to me. It's been three weeks now, and the lawyer has not called."

"Fine," Chief Flores said. "This is what I want the two of you to do. Corner this Shawn boy, offer him an irresistible deal, let him know *in a manner of speaking* that he really has no options, that he more or less has to confess. And then let him confess *now.* Now get the hell out of here and get to work."

After signing the release papers for Samuel Mugyenyi and witnessing his departure into freedom, Lisa observed him as he merged with the throngs of protesters who had eagerly anticipated his release outside the jail's gates. As soon as he appeared, a group of enthusiastic men rushed toward him, hoisting him up in the air and carrying him triumphantly to a makeshift podium. She and Bus remained at a distance, their eyes trained on Samuel as he was handed a microphone and began addressing the crowd in English.

Ladies and gentlemen,

Thank you, thank you all for gathering here today to witness my return to freedom. But let me tell you, this moment is not just about me. It's about our countries, our nations, breaking free from the chains of imperialism and seizing our autonomy and self-determination.

Our first independence, hard-fought and won from colonial rule, was a significant milestone in our history. Yet, it failed to deliver the true freedom and dignity that we, as autonomous human beings, deserve. It is time for us to embark on a journey toward a second independence—an independence that goes beyond the physical liberation of our lands, an independence that reclaims our sovereignty and self-respect.

This movement for a new independence begins here, in the diaspora, amongst those of us who live as exiles in the shadow of freedom. In this foreign land, we are close to the ears of the imperialists, and it's time we make our voices heard directly in those ears until they ring with the clamor of our protests.

The puppet dictators, like Joel Katila Muaji, are not just agents of imperialism; they are traitors who have bartered away our hard-won independence. The heroes of our first independence, luminaries such as Patrice Lumumba, Kwame Nkrumah, Jamal Abdul Nasser, Sékou Touré, and Edward Muteesa would be appalled by the shame and suffering that have befallen our nations. They would be disheartened to see our brothers and sisters risking their lives on rickety boats to reach Europe or crossing treacherous deserts to make it to the borders of the United States.

These heroes would be heartbroken to witness our troops, once the guardians of our sovereignty, marching into foreign lands to subjugate our brothers and sisters in Congo, Somalia, Rwanda, Burundi, Sudan, and beyond. They would be horrified to see the armies of one African nation after another invading other African nations, all for the benefit of imperialist powers.

The armies of Rwanda marching into Mozambique and Chad, the armies of Kenya advancing into Haiti—these are not acts of sovereignty, they are acts of submission. They are a betrayal of our shared struggle for freedom.

But we are here today to say that enough is enough! It is time for a second independence, a new dawn of self-determination. We must unite, stand together as a united front, and demand the true independence we were promised and that our heroes fought for.

After listening for about ten minutes, Lisa elbowed Bus gently and whispered, "This guy sounds like the ghost of Lumumba." Bus couldn't help but release a sudden burst of laughter.

"Come on, Bus," Lisa said, "We've got work to do."

Without waiting for a response, she turned away from the cheering crowds, and Bus followed her as they made their way back into the jail.

CHAPTER 26

Shawn

SHAWN sat calmly in the interrogation room, his gaze steady as he faced the two detectives, Lisa and Bus. He had grown accustomed to these interrogations over the past three months, his demeanor unshaken despite the intensity of their scrutiny.

Before the interrogation could commence, Shawn posed a question to the detectives. "Are we going to wait for my lawyer?" he inquired.

Lisa responded without hesitation, "We don't have much time, Shawn. Your lawyer was supposed to be here thirty minutes ago, and he has yet to appear."

Bus interjected, his voice echoing Lisa's pragmatism. "Shawn, you have to understand that these pro-bono lawyers don't operate on the same schedule as paid attorneys. Until you secure representation, you'll have to get accustomed to answering questions in their absence."

Shawn nodded, absorbing their words before posing another question. "So, what do you want me to answer today?"

Lisa leaned forward, "We want to know about your sexual relationship with Sheila."

Shawn maintained his composure, "I've stated before that Sheila and I had a strictly professional relationship," he said.

"But that may be hard to believe. Perhaps you could clarify how a 'no-sex relationship' worked for a young couple like you." Bus said.

"We tried a few times to have sex, but she always backed out," Shawn explained. "She told me she was a virgin, waiting for the man who would marry her before sharing that intimacy. She said it was part of her African culture to enter the marital bed untouched. I respected her wishes and didn't push the matter further."

"Did you need her so bad that you killed her?" Lisa asked.

"I did not kill her," Shawne fought back.

"Can you name just one woman who ever said no to you and is still living?" Bus asked. "We will go and talk to her."

Shawn thought about what Bus had said but offered nothing.

The two detectives then turned to talk to each other, seemingly ignoring him. Lisa whispered something to Bus, and Shawn strained his ears to catch their conversation.

"I think we have now found another possible motive for this murder," Lisa whispered to Bus.

"What do you mean?" Bus asked.

"If Shawn murdered Sheila, it could be because she backed out of the possibility of having sex with him. This boy seems like someone who always has problems with women. He wants to give the appearance that he is confident and strong in his masculine identity. Many men get angry when they have been teased only to be left alone abruptly."

"That's not what happened, your imagination is misplaced, Detective Lisa," Shawn interjected, feeling the need to defend himself. But Lisa gave him a brief, dismissive look and turned her attention back to Bus, her tone slightly annoyed.

"Some men process that anger and move on. Others need retribution. Sometimes it becomes violent and so dangerous that someone ends up dying. This boy might seem as if he knows how to control himself. But, considering everything we know up until this point, it is conceivable that he could have released whatever energy and frustration he had held back internally to do such an unthinkable crime."

Bus remained unconvinced, and Shawn could see he had his reservations about Lisa's theory. He probably thought she was too eager to prove herself as someone who could solve such a terrible crime swiftly. He likely believed that she was quick to piece together the puzzle in a homicide investigation and that she always had to be right. However, Bus also seemed to sense that something significant was missing in this case. Something that suggested it was too early to build a solid case against Shawn. Bus, in a measured tone, responded to Lisa, "We'll see, Lisa. We'll see."

Shawn couldn't shake off the heavy weight of suspicion pressing down on him, yet he remained resolute in his determination to assert his innocence.

The detectives redirected their focus toward him, signaling the commencement of another phase in their interrogation. Lisa initiated the line of questioning, delving into Shawn's relationship with Katie and the circumstances surrounding her pregnancy.

"So, tell us about Katie," Lisa said. "How did your relationship with her unfold, and can you shed some light on how your sexual encounters led to her pregnancy? How did you and Katie meet?" Lisa inquired, her pen poised over her notepad.

Shawn leaned back in his chair, collecting his thoughts before responding. "Well, Katie and I both lived in the same dorm, and we actually met through a writing workshop that Sheila had been part of that fall semester," he began.

"After the workshop ended, we happened to bump into each other in the dormitory's elevator," he continued, recalling the chance encounter. "One day she mustered up the courage to ask me about Sheila."

"Are you two still together?" Katie asked.

"Together, like what? We ain't never been together before," he replied.

"Okay, like I didn't see you two sitting together in the Boston Commons Park after every class," Katie retorted.

"And I bet this is the first time you are sharing an elevator alone with a white girl?" she continued.

"I'm friendly to all them white girls, you know," he said with a grin as the elevator doors opened, and we stepped out onto the floor.

"I didn't know you were staying on this floor too, Katie," he remarked.

"I stay here. You are welcome to have a drink and tell me about your girlfriend," Katie offered, opening the door to her dorm room.

As Katie poured a shot of tequila for Shawn, she continued the conversation. "How is your other girlfriend? You said it is not Sheila?"

"Yeah, me and Sheila, we just regular friends, you know. We gave dating a shot, but it ain't work out, so we decided to stay friends instead," he explained, taking a sip of the tequila.

He was trying to avoid the talk about girlfriends, but his responses just happened to make Katie even more curious.

"Were you fighting with her also? The same way you kept fighting me in class."

Katie's attempt to equate the debate in class with whatever argument she assumed he had with Sheila surprised him. He ignored her for a moment as he continued sipping his tequila.

"Tell me what have you been fighting about, please," she said, almost sounding as if she was pleading.

"Sex," he replied, without thinking for a second longer and immediately turned his face away. The embarrassment showed in his face.

"Hmmm, what's it about sex?"

"She ain't 'bout that sex life until she walk down the aisle. It's all 'bout her African culture, you know." he explained in a matter-of-fact tone.

"Wow, and I bet you couldn't wait."

"Yeah, I can't be sexually deprived 'cause of some culture from the middle of Africa. I gotta do me." He said 'Africa' with some disdain about what he imagined was a primitive place with backward and conservative attitudes about sex.

Katie was taken aback for a moment that obviously some Black Americans looked upon Africa with such regret. Katie, however, decided not to pursue the subject further, remembering how cultural critiques in class had triggered sharp debates. Instead, she saw an opportunity and looked to cozy up and learn more about the tall handsome Black man seated on her sofa in her dorm room.

"So, you want to abandon this Brown girl because she's not giving you sex or because she is from Africa?" she asked as she moved closer to him. But she didn't wait for his answer. Instead, she hopped on his lap and surprised him with a kiss.

He was reluctant at first and asked, "You sure 'bout this or is it just the tequila?"

"I'm sober and happy."

The duo was now officially kissing. A simple courtesy visit had immediately upgraded to a date—a first kiss and then more kisses. It was full-on French kissing. He could not tell where this unbelievable, even crazy, surprise would end, but he was ready to explore it to its conclusion.

He helped her strip off her top, and he tossed his clothing into a pile.

This was his first intimate moment with a white woman, and it unraveled all of the raw fantasies he had carried since his boyhood. He noticed she was human, not an alien as he had at some point thought about white people, as if they were from another planet.

Both tightly embraced, so close that he could feel Katie's nipples pressing against his chest. He was starting to sweat as his sexual adrenaline quickly surged. Worried that his sudden excitement might spoil the moment, he slowed the pace slightly. He pulled back from the embrace and looked at her naked breasts and asked like a boy wanting candy, "Can I get a feel?"

"Yes," she said. He caressed her breasts, thighs, and buttocks with a ravenous ecstasy.

"Don't fuck me. Just make love to me," Katie said, breaking what seemed like a long silence.

He had always lusted for her but thought she was so out of reach and based on their classroom debates, he never imagined this moment.

In high school, his friends used to say that if a Black guy hits on a young Black woman and she doesn't like it, she tells him to "eff" off, but a white woman will generally just call the police on the guy.

Now he had her, and she was naked.

"This feels unreal, like I'm dreaming," he said. There was no time for explanations or more words. Their bodies were electrified by their desires. Obviously, both had wanted this moment.

Katie said that she always knew he crushed on her and that she could always tell when a boy crushed on her.

He turned from the sofa without disentangling their hold and helped Katie lay on her back with her legs wrapped around and then slowly entered her. The excitement of penetration almost tore him apart, and he was afraid of climaxing far too soon.

He would never end the sexual game until he was assured his partner had experienced full pleasure, but Katie's body was challenging his capabilities to pull back from the edge—he paced his breathing to stay in the game as long as possible.

Whenever he sensed that he was about to release, he pulled back and waited for a moment or two before penetrating her again. He remembered hearing ever since his boyhood days how embarrassing it would be if any of his Black friends had ruined their orgasms especially before their partner had begun to enjoy the experience.

He thought that this was not just sex but also a racially defined game. He felt like he was representing the whole Black race at this critical moment. He had grown up in a community where Black men were proud of their sexual prowess, experts in sexual gratification. He was determined not to fail the expectations.

He remembered a technique he had learned from others to delay the release. Pull out for a minute at most, inhale and exhale deeply and then resume, with even more force in his thrust. Shawn smiled, proud that this edging technique was working the way he had learned it.

Katie, meanwhile, was just as electrified by the alternating moments of his sexual movement. She responded precisely as he had imagined it.

"It's going deep, deep, deep," Katie said with a moan that sounded more like a grunt.

"Should I stop? Do you want me to pull it out?"

"No, please push it in deeper. I don't care if it ruptures my stomach and chest and comes out in my mouth. Do it. I know you can do it."

And when it came, the first thing Katie did was to examine my cock.

"How come it is still as hard as rock, after coming?" She took my endowment into her hands, with the focus of a scientist measuring a specimen for its weight and width.

"Even its color has changed. Look." She said. He noticed that his cock was covered in a white membranous liquid.

Shawn said nothing. In the awkward silence, Katie asked another question.

"Do I now get to call you the n-word just for myself?"

"No," he tried to respond with a smile, but the question stung. He had recalled the class discussions where he argued that only Black folks had the right to say the n-word with each other.

Katie stood up and went to the bathroom to refresh herself. She sensed his eyes tracking her movement as he admired her nude body from behind.

"Come back over here and take a seat on my lap," he said, pointing to his still-erect cock, which glistened with cum. "This man ain't gonna clean up until it's plugged in again."

"No, I am not feeding it into my ass again. If it keeps on popping its head up like a hungry python, let me tell you what it's getting instead."

"I'm all ears," he said, anticipating something good.

"A good beating that will send it to sleep for the night at least."

Katie flustered him momentarily, reminding him of Sheila. "I'm joining your girlfriend's 'no-sex-club' tonight.

It's up to you to chuck me as well."

"What if your man catches us butt naked in here?" he asked, trying not to let her know how the line had struck him.

"You mean Ryan? Do you remember him?"

He was shocked because he did remember Ryan—perhaps the quietest student in class. He never talked to anyone, not even Sheila.

"Ryan?" he said. "Your boyfriend—for real? That dude was all quiet and reserved."

"There is no way Ryan is going to find us. He never comes here without calling first. Maybe my roommate..."

Katie suddenly realized that the door was not locked while they had sex. Anyone could have walked in on them. She turned around, locked the door, and returned to the sofa.

"So, spill the tea about Ryan. That fine white dude whose girl I just fucked."

"There's not too much about him," she said. "I have been seeing him for about six months now, and it seems like it's not working."

It didn't seem like Katie was herself, willing to give out so much information. She stood up again, picked up all her clothes strewn on the floor, and walked into her bedroom.

She returned with her body wrapped in a pink robe and a white towel in hands. She gave him the towel to wrap himself. And then asked if he wanted to join her in the kitchen to make some dinner.

"I'll just hop in the shower real quick, if you cool with that, and then I'll be outta here. Don't want your roommate walkin' in on us like this."

"Hmmm," she said with a derisive snort. "Some black activist is shy about fucking a white girl."

She showed him to the shower and stood in the doorway as he let the towel slip and stepped into the shower. A few minutes later, he was dressed and kissed her for the night.

He told her she still owed him information about Ryan.

"And you owe me a lot more information about your 'no-sex' girlfriend."

"She's called Sheila," he said, unsure if Katie had heard him. He silently waited for the elevator and disappeared.

CHAPTER 27

Bus

BUS took it all in, tried to see where this white girl could fit. Lisa looked just as stunned. Shawn looked spent. He had told the detectives all of these details. He had an empty look on his face, as if he now realized that he would never see Sheila again.

Lisa broke the silence. "Shawn, your mother kept two men in the house. Are you replicating her by having two girls?"

Bus could see the defiance rising in Shawn's eyes.

"Detectives," Shawn said, "can we keep my mother out of this? You have the right to ask me all your stupid questions, but you don't have a single right to disrespect my mother in my face."

Lisa shot back without hesitation. "You don't tell us what to ask and what not. We do the asking, and you answer."

Shawn stood abruptly, waving to the prison guard as if signaling for his escape.

Bus intervened, raising a hand to stop the guard from approaching. "Hold on a moment," he said, his tone calm and authoritative. "Shawn, please have a seat. I understand this can be frustrating, but we're here to get to the truth. Let's leave your mother out of this discussion for now. I'll be the one asking the questions, and we'll focus on the details of your relationships. Can you tell us if the two girls ever showed signs of jealousy or if there were conflicts between them?"

Shawn hesitated, his anger slowly giving way to resignation. He lowered himself back into the chair, his shoulders slumping. "Look, Detective Bus, Lisa, I didn't consider that the two girls were with me at the same time. I started dating Katie after I was sure my relationship with Sheila had failed and all we had was just a work-related relationship. Still, it wasn't all sunshine and rainbows between us."

Bus exchanged a glance with Lisa, and it was clear that they were both thinking the same thing. The tangled web of relationships and emotions in this case was becoming more intricate by the minute. "Tell us more," he urged gently. "Any details, no matter how small they may seem, could be important."

Shawn nodded, his gaze fixed on the table in front of him.

"Well… I told Sheila that I had started dating Katie, the woman who challenged me in class when we took the writing workshop together and that we already had sex. Sheila was… shocked to say the least. And I tried to explain… it went down real fast, like when she and I first crossed paths by the stairs in the dorm, bam, it happened just like that."

"What did Sheila say?" Bus asked.

"At first, she was cold. She said, 'Okay. I get it. All you ever wanted was sex. I didn't give it to you, and you got it somewhere else.' But that surprised me—tell you the truth, I never expected Sheila to be so concerned about me having or not having a girlfriend. She had always insisted on being just friends and being professional, and it did not appear like she was even remotely interested in me."

Bus could see there was more to the story. "Then what."

"She got madder. Like, 'Why are you even telling me?' So, I apologized. And then she went crazy, saying that I shouldn't be humoring her with my mistakes. She was like, 'Did you sleepwalk and fall into her pussy? There are no mistakes in cheating.' That really caught my attention—how could I be cheating when, well, you know, she had stopped me."

Lisa smirked but Bus nodded, encouraging Shawn to go on.

"Sheila was pissed, really mad. But, you know, I had to be the one to tell her before she could have heard it from someone else. And that was that. She opened the door for me to leave and I left."

"And then?"

"Well, the following day, Sheila called me around noon and asked if I was at Katie's dorm having sex again. She… from then on, she always used this line every time she talked to me. Never said hello. Of course, I denied that I was with Katie, but Sheila kept going, reminding me how she had taken me to meet her family and all that."

Bus froze, clutching his pencil. "What was that like."

"Her family? I met them at their place in New York, Fifth Avenue. It was like a high-rise mansion with seven bedrooms and a large terrace and this insane view of the skyline. I was introduced to everyone living there, including her white stepmother, her brother, her sister, everyone. They all seemed to like me. They had seen my work from the lobby firm, and they commented on how impressive my writing skills were. But… after I slept with Katie… well, nothing was the same."

"Say more."

"She just wouldn't leave it alone. She was like, 'So, are you leaving me because this new girl walks with her legs wide open for any former classmate to enter or just because she's white and I'm colored and not white enough?' She was pissed, she was hurt, and suddenly she's, like, making it all about race. Which was nuts because, before that, Sheila had *consistently* referred to herself as white!"

"Did you defend yourself?"

"I tried. I was like, it ain't what you think! But that just made Sheila even more mad. She was like, 'Ah, see, you're all the same.' And… 'What kind of people just meet in a dormitory lift and end up having sex? Do you know how many of your ancestors were burned alive for just having sex with white girls? Do you even know your history? Do you even care?"

"Okay Shawn," Bus said, "but what about Katie? Tell us how *she* received the news that you and Sheila were still close."

"Katie… Katie told me that she would prefer me to

stop seeing Sheila so often, but there were times we had to spend time together because of the work I was doing for the lobbying firm," Shawn said.

"So, Katie was serious about her relationship with you?"

"Yup. She broke up with Ryan, who she had been dating since they met in class. She wanted me to declare that I was breaking up with Sheila, too, my '*no-sex girlfriend.*'"

"But you didn't."

"I couldn't! Because our relationship was also a major part of my job. I mean, my financial livelihood would be erased if I broke off all communication with Sheila. And..."

"And what?"

"And I didn't want my classmates to judge me for working on behalf of an African dictator, you know? This guy who was known in the press for killing anybody in his circle who betrayed him!"

Lisa said, "Have you ever disclosed to Katie what you were doing for Sheila's family?"

Shawn gave it some thought. "I hadn't shared too much about my work with Katie, partly because I thought she was someone who couldn't keep a secret. She could reveal personal details to a stranger upon their first meeting without a second thought. Katie lived her life without shame or reservation, and she expected me to do the same. I knew Katie wanted immediate reassurance that I was cutting all ties, but I needed time to think it through."

"So, what'd you do?"

"Well, truthfully? Sensing how tense Katie was, I decided that sex might buy me a little time. She always seemed to be in a great mood whenever we had sex. I went by her place and told her I was mad horny. She moved closer, and she slipped her left hand into my pants. She was like, 'You liar, it's not even hard.' We tried but…"

"But what?"

Shawn smiled, a little embarrassed. "Katie was like, 'You never needed any help getting this thing up. What is happening to you? Wake up, wake up,' like she was cradling a sleepy baby. 'God, it's sleeping. It's so peaceful in its sleep. Is it exhausted from entertaining the Brown Ugandan girl, daughter or niece of his excellency, the president? I have never seen it soft. Are you sick, Shawn? Assure me you are fine or am going to take you to the doctor and explain to them how hard it always is."

Shawn scowled at the memory of it. He had tried to concentrate, but all thoughts went back to his relationship with Sheila.

"Keep going Shawn," Bus said. "We need the full story—it might help your case."

"She… she tried to give me a blow job. She kept asking for assurances, that I was gonna give up 'that Ugandan girl in class.' She was like, 'My mouth doesn't take in public property, and moreover, it's unhygienic. No doctor will advise a blow job to a man with multiple girlfriends.' She kept asking if we had an agreement. I kept trying to signal yes, pulling her closer, kissing her, taking off her bra."

Katie marched over to the sofa, and Shawn followed her with his flabby swinging soft dick. "Do we have an agreement?" she asked.

Shawn's nonverbals signaled yes. He pulled closer, kissing her and sliding his hands into her bra, coddling her right breast and stroking her nipple. In seconds, Shawn was fully erect, the cure for both of them to strip off their clothes.

It did not take long for the orgasm. Afterward, Katie asked Shawn if he had ever failed to get it up before.

"Yeah, I remember this one time when I was craving it so bad, but it just wouldn't cooperate. It went completely limp, and no matter how hard I tried, it felt like a car struggling to move with a flat tire."

Katie seemed satisfied and happy, but Shawn felt some lingering embarrassment.

Shawn thought that perhaps she was out of the words on the Sheila question. But, even while the two were cuddling on the sofa, Katie picked up where they left off before the sex.

"Are you still begging that Ugandan girl for sex? For heaven's sake, Shawn, that girl probably has HIV like everyone else in Uganda."

Shawn stared at her with a disapproving look. She tried to explain that it was not prejudice but science which justified her assertion. "I did my research," she said, a phrase that reminded Shawn that Katie always resorted to sweeping generalizations in the writing workshop discussions.

"Did their conflicts ever turn physical? Were there any threats?" Lisa asked.

Shawn shook his head. "No, nothing physical, and they never threatened each other directly. It was more like a battle of words, with me. They never contacted each other."

As Shawn recounted the tumultuous dynamics between Katie and Sheila, Bus couldn't help but wonder if this jealousy and strife had played a role in Sheila's tragic death.

At the end, the interrogation room felt suffocating, with every detail of Shawn's life laid bare before the stern gazes of Detective Lisa and Detective Bus. He had held nothing back, baring his soul, sharing every intimate moment he had shared with his deceased friend, Sheila and his girlfriend Katie. His heart pounded in his chest, desperate for them to believe him, to understand that he couldn't have killed her. His eyes darted between the detectives, searching their faces for any hint of belief.

"Look, I know it's a whole lotta info to process," Shawn said, his voice tinged with anxiety. "But every word I told y'all is the truth. Me and Sheila, we had our ups and downs, like all friends do, but I would never lay a hand on her."

"We appreciate your honesty, Shawn, but we've been doing this job long enough to know that sometimes the truth can be subjective. People can say anything, and it's our job to verify the facts," Lisa said.

Bus agreed. "That's right. We'll cross-check your story with the evidence we have, and if everything checks out, it might help your case."

"I understand," Shawn muttered, trying to hide his disappointment. "But please, y'all gotta believe me. I ain't kill Sheila."

"We're not here to make judgments, Shawn. Our job is to find the truth, no matter how uncomfortable it may be. If you're innocent, we'll find evidence to support that," Lisa said.

"We'll let you know when we've completed our investigations," Detective Bus said, rising from his seat. "In the meantime, you might want to get some rest."

After Shawn's interrogation had revealed these details, Bus and Lisa stopped by the dorm the following day to question Katie. Indeed, they would establish if her recollections corroborated those that Shawn spoke about the previous day. They asked Katie to start from the day they met in the elevator and ended up in her room and had sex, according to what Shawn told them.

"Yes, of course, I still remember," she said. "I jumped on top of him, kissed him, and sat in his lap while we chatted and touched each other. At first, I could feel his heartbeat. He was nervous but he relaxed himself. We kissed again—like two more times.

"Then I could feel his erection pressing against my tights and then ass. I was feeling it—ecstatic that I aroused him so quickly. He was the first man I met that I could arouse that quickly and make him so hard. Shawn knew how to make love, which surprised me because he always seemed a bit shy and was definitely nervous at first. I asked him if I could touch it and he said yes but on one condition.

"I said, 'sure.'

"You allow him to touch your breasts in exchange."

Reconstructing the scene, Katie recalled how she didn't say a word as she removed her top. And there were her exposed breasts pointing directly to his face. He didn't touch them, but he just kissed and then sucked on her nipples.

Katie said, "Detective, that's how it happened. We did it. We had sex. For me to say much more than that would be inappropriate and an invasion of my privacy. It was the most sexually intimate moment I ever had."

Lisa interrupted Katie. "On the contrary, Katie. More details are what we need because what you say will have a major impact for Shawn. They could help acquit him or give us the information we will need to pursue an indictment from a grand jury."

Katie did not respond.

"We want to hear if he pushed you with any sense of aggression or violence. That could indicate a possible behavior about how he treats women. The dead woman was attacked brutally. I remind you that what you have to say will be mightily important. I know this is difficult, but we have other means to compel your cooperation in this investigation. Please go ahead."

"It was consensual, Lisa." Katie said, in a tone that sounded disappointing. "I already made myself clear from the beginning. I don't want you to accuse this poor Black man of something he didn't do. And we had sex many more times after this first encounter."

Lisa launched into an avalanche of questions. "We need to know what kind of consent he received from you and how he sought that consent from you. We need to understand how he behaved when seeking consent to have sex and what he did before he received it. We also need to understand what happened if you change your mind in the middle of it. Did he become violent? Did he become angry and rough? If you didn't want penetration, did he respect this? Is he a sexual predator? Did he bite, slap, pinch, or shove you? Or was he always as intimate as you describe him, gentle, waiting for you to say yes? Any information you can provide could lead us to answering many questions. And that includes knowing if we have the right or wrong suspect."

Katie looked at Bus with eyes that seemed to ask if he was prepared to hear the details of her intimate life with Shawn, knowing that Lisa's questions required revelations that could be uncomfortable for a male detective.

Bus noticed Katie's hesitation and leaned in slightly. "Katie, is there something you're hesitant to share?" he asked gently.

Katie glanced at Lisa, then back at Bus. "It's just… the questions about Shawn and me. They might get… personal."

Lisa, picking up on the tension, tried to reassure her. "We're here to help, Katie. Anything you can share is important."

Bus, sensing the discomfort, decided to step in. "Katie, I've heard a lot in my career. Remember the testimonies of Monica Lewinsky and Stormy Daniels? I've sat through all those details. But today, I think we have enough."

Lisa looked at him, surprised. "You think so?"

"Yeah," Bus nodded. "I think we have everything we need from Katie. We can go."

Lisa turned back to Katie. "If you say so. But Katie, if you remember anything that might help us in this investigation, please don't hesitate to reach out to me or Detective Bus."

Katie nodded, relieved. "Thank you, I will."

With that, Lisa and Bus collected their files and left the room.

CHAPTER 28

Lisa

LISA again reviewed the surveillance camera footage from the campus, and this time a key detail caught her attention: Sheila had left the premises with a young man who wasn't Shawn or Samuel. She was dressed in blue jeans and a white top, the same attire found at the murder scene. With a confirming glance at the timestamp on the camera footage, Lisa grew increasingly convinced that this might have been the last time Sheila was seen alive before her tragic end. Yet, despite these developments, Lisa couldn't jump to conclusions regarding the identity of the young man accompanying Sheila. Nothing about their interaction in the footage seemed overtly suspicious. The young man, clad in a navy-blue shirt with checkered pattern and golf-like trousers, appeared calm, and their body language didn't hint at any danger. Lisa made sure to capture still images from the surveillance and then set out for the campus.

Lisa's first destination was the office of the professor she had previously interviewed for clues in the case. Displaying the images, Lisa inquired if he could identify the young man. The professor promptly recognized him as Ryan. With a cautious tone, he asked, "Do you suspect him?"

Lisa was quiet for a moment. Then she said, "I urge you to keep the information to yourself—no arrest warrant has been issued."

The professor nodded. After a few prior missteps, she was wary of reaching conclusions prematurely. Uncertainty now clouded her suspicions about Shawn's involvement in the murder. But the fact that Sheila had met Ryan on the day before her death didn't provide sufficient grounds to name him a suspect officially.

Lisa decided to take matters into her own hands rather than involving campus police. Ryan might possess crucial information about Sheila's activities or her interactions that day. Lisa harbored hope that talking to Ryan would either strengthen the case against Shawn or lead them to a different trail of evidence.

Approaching the dormitory, Lisa approached the Resident Advisor (RA) stationed at the desk. Her badge said *Emily*.

"How can I help you?" she asked.

Lisa said that she was one of the investigators assigned to the Musinga case. She asked to speak with Ryan privately outside in the common area. RA Emily went to get Ryan. When he appeared, he was visibly apprehensive, in a faded, gray hoodie with the college logo emblazoned on the front, its sleeves pushed up to his elbows revealing a couple of colorful woven bracelets.

Ryan looked miserable. Lisa made it clear that he wasn't under arrest or investigation but rather sought information regarding Sheila's whereabouts on the day preceding the discovery of her body. Ryan initially denied any knowledge. In response, Lisa produced still images from the campus surveillance cameras.

"We were just talking about the class, and we went our separate ways after crossing Tremont Street," Ryan explained, gesturing toward the intersection outside the window. There were exterior surveillance cameras on the building, which Lisa hadn't yet examined. With no further details to confirm, Lisa thanked Ryan for his cooperation.

"But," she said, "did Sheila mention anything about meeting someone or being distressed?"

"No," Ryan replied. Lisa waited for a moment, giving him the opportunity to add more. She then handed him her contact information and asked him to reach out if he remembered any additional details about that day.

Before her meeting with Ryan, Lisa had taken the initiative to research his listed home address. He had omitted mentioning he was from Acton and instead claimed to reside at his grandparents' home in Belmont.

CHAPTER 29

Ryan and Stuart

LISA left, but halfway through the quad, turned around. Ryan was hastily making his way toward the green line train.

As soon as he met up with Stuart, he couldn't help but spill the beans, speaking in hushed tones to avoid prying ears. His nerves were shot, and beads of sweat dotted his forehead. Stuart, observing his anxious state, leaned in, equally concerned and ready to hear whatever news he had to share.

"A cop just came to my dorm," he whispered.

Stuart's eyes widened, "What did they say? Do they know?"

"I'm worried, man. But she didn't say much, just that they reviewed the camera footage and saw that I had left the university building with her on the day she died."

Stuart's face contorted in disbelief and frustration. He

could feel his own heart racing as panic coursed through his veins.

"Ryan, you never told me you met her in the lecture hall and left together. How could you be so damn careless?" Stuart chided, unable to hide his exasperation. "You know there are cameras everywhere. All you had to do was wait for the girl outside and then link up."

Ryan's head hung low, weighed down by the gravity of his thoughtless actions.

This latest revelation hit Stuart like a ton of bricks, dragging him back into the chilling memory of that sinister day and the dreadful events he had a hand in orchestrating, which ultimately led to Sheila's tragic demise.

Ryan and Stuart were buddies since their grade-school days back in Acton. When Shawn started dating Katie while already seeing Sheila, things got messy, and Ryan's anger bubbled. He felt that Shawn's insatiable ego had given both women reasons to quarrel. In his frustration, Ryan confided in Stuart about his desire for extreme revenge: Shawn's death. Stuart was willing to take things to the extreme, suggesting that it wouldn't be too difficult to get away with killing a Black dude.

"How are you planning to do it, though? You can't just put a knee on his neck like a cop," Ryan said.

"No, man," he replied. "We shoot him. I've got an uncle with a gun we can borrow. All we gotta do is tell the judge we were scared of that bastard, and bam, we shot him," Stuart said. "If it's a white judge, they should know how dangerous and scary these Black folks can be. We won't need to be too convincing."

"But what if we end up with a Black judge?" Ryan

questioned.

"A Black judge will distance themselves from these Black fugitives. Black men in white spaces, like the judiciary, police, or even university professors, tend to be harsher on their own kind. They need to prove to white folks that they're 'different,'" Stuart said.

"So, where do we find him and shoot him?" Ryan asked.

"We'll stage a scene," Stuart explained. "You confront him about sleeping with your girl, start a small fight, and I'll come to your rescue and shoot him."

"For a sec there," Ryan said, "I thought you were just cracking some wild joke. But man, your eyes... they are dead serious."

"Yeah," Stuart replied. "I've been thinking this through like it was the plan of my life. But here's the kicker: we thought Massachusetts had a 'stand your ground' law, didn't even bother checking. I was convinced self-defense was our golden ticket, not knowing we were in a 'duty to retreat' state, where self-defense rules were super strict."

"My confidence took a hit when my uncle refused to lend us a gun. Unlike me, he understood the laws well enough not to jeopardize his status as a legal gun owner or be implicated in a rash, dangerous scheme."

However, Stuart wasn't easily discouraged by his uncle's refusal. He suggested an alternative: to beat Shawn up with sticks.

"Okay, Ryan," he proposed. "The two of us can beat that dirty motherfucker to death, right?"

"Stuart, seriously? You think we can take him in a fight? Have you lost it? The guy's a beast; he could take us both down!" Ryan exclaimed, shaking his head in disbelief.

"Ryan, hear me out," Stuart said, "You are hesitant about confronting Shawn head-on, right? Guy's built like a tank. Here is a more serious plan: let's take out Sheila and make it look like Shawn did it. That way, we lock Shawn up for life and get Katie back as your girlfriend."

On that day, Ryan convinced Sheila to meet one of his friends at Boston Commons Park—that was the scene caught on the university building's surveillance camera. Meanwhile, Stuart was waiting there. The plan was for him to pose as an FBI agent, concerned for Sheila's safety due to some inside information he claimed to have received.

Ryan explained to Sheila that he and Stuart had been friends since childhood. Then, he told Sheila about the FBI secretly monitoring the campus for potential troublemakers, and Shawn was on their radar.

Stuart told Sheila that the local FBI office had gotten a tip about a Black acquaintance of hers planning to harm her, and they were convinced it was Shawn. They needed her help to provide information about his whereabouts so they could bring him in for questioning and get an arrest warrant.

Sheila, clearly shocked, asked, "Are you two serious? I thought he was my friend. I never thought he could ever harm me."

Stuart shook his head, "Don't ever trust anyone in this world, especially those Black American dudes. Let's head to our office; you'll be surprised by the evidence we've got. Serious stuff like phone conversations where he's plotting with his friends to harm you."

Sheila, still trying to process everything, asked, "You said we're going to the FBI offices in Acton?"

Stuart nodded, "Yes, that's right. Our offices are inside the State Police building in Acton. You know, the FBI and State Police kind of work together."

"So, is your police car around here or what?"

"No, we're going to use your car. You're driving us. Where did you park?" Stuart asked.

Sheila pointed to a public parking lot on Tremont Street, and they hit the road. She was behind the wheel, navigating with the help of a Waze GPS, while Stuart and Ryan continued to discuss Shawn.

They took the I-93, Mystic Valley Road in Medford, and State Route 2 from Cambridge. Sheila talked incessantly, sharing how Shawn had repeatedly tried to initiate sex but failed every time. She kept repeating her disbelief that he was planning to harm her.

Stuart attempted to calm her nerves, assuring her that everything would be fine soon. When they reached Acton's Great Road, near the state police headquarters, we told her to keep driving for another half mile before turning into the parking lot next to the Acton municipal government building and public library, claiming the FBI office was located there. Sheila began to question this decision, sensing something was amiss for the first time.

She pulled into the parking lot, and Stuart asked her to call Shawn and put him on speaker. Stuart said this would be helpful in expediting the process to find and detain him. Sheila followed their instructions, but her nerves had caught up with her. In front of two men, including one whom she had never seen before and the other a classmate, she was being forced to ask intimate questions that would be embarrassing for anyone. She asked Shawn if he was so angry about her refusing sexual intercourse with him that he would harm her.

"Where did you get such a crazy idea like that?" Shawn said.

"I heard from a very reliable source," she said.

Shawn's voice sounded hoarse and angry. He told Sheila she was delusional and needed to see a psychiatrist.

"Sheila, don't go around making such ridiculous allegations on people without proof."

"I have all of the evidence, Shawn," Sheila said, but before she finished the sentence, Shawn had left the call.

Stuart urged her to call him again and not mention the FBI as her source because that would jeopardize their plan to arrest him. She called again but Shawn's phone went to voicemail. Sheila left the message: "Whatever you are planning to do, please, Shawn, don't do it. I thought we were friends."

Sheila asked Stuart again if this indeed was true. Stuart said yes. Sheila's gut instincts were now stronger than ever that something was wrong. But she also thought that she should try to remain as calm as possible.

Stuart's tone shifted abruptly. He ordered Sheila to drive to another location nearby and to stop on the roadside near a cornfield. Now, Sheila was convinced that this was a setup. *How could I have been so ignorant? Was I going to be robbed?*

As soon as she stopped the car near a cornfield, Stuart pulled what appeared to be a prop pistol and put it against her head. He said that this was part of a plan to take revenge on Shawn because he had taken Katie away from Ryan.

"What the fuck? So, what do you think you're going to do to me?

"Bitch, you're dead. I can't stand the fact that a Black man took a white guy's girl as his own and all because you refused to sleep with him. You see, we're going to kill you and make it look like Shawn killed you—the angry boyfriend. In every case where young bitches like you are murdered, the cops always finger the jilted boyfriend as the first suspect."

"Fuck you. No one would believe such bullshit. You're too stupid to make anyone believe you."

"Well, you did. Perhaps you are not as smart or worldly as you think you are," Stuart said, his voice sounding darker than ever.

Sheila's eyes widened as she stared at Ryan, hoping that he would call off his deranged friend. Ryan said nothing, just shaking his head.

"I'll do anything. You want money? You can have it." She had seven-hundred dollars in cash. "If you want more, we'll go to an ATM. Please, I won't say a word."

Sheila had not yet fully realized that these guys were not thieves as much as they were angry, vengeful racists.

"Bitch, we don't want your money. It's filthy," Stuart said.

"I'll do anything, but don't kill me."

Stuart did not immediately respond. He looked back at Ryan. The two nodded at each other.

"Here's the deal. You're going to have sex with us. That will be the best revenge against Shawn," Stuart said.

"No fucking way. I'm not a whore."

Stuart put his hands over her mouth and held her down. Sheila was so shocked that she could no longer put up any resistance, when Stuart shoved her onto the passenger seat and unfolded it. He unbuttoned his pants and gave the pistol to Ryan and ripped apart the top she was wearing and forced her jeans down. He thrust himself into Sheila, who was paralyzed by what was happening. She tried to scream, but all she could manage was a muffled moan. As soon as he finished, Stuart ordered Ryan to enter her. Stuart held his arms around Sheila's neck as Ryan unzipped his pants and shoved them down past his thighs. He was still thrusting between her legs when Stuart tightened his grip around Sheila's neck and strangled her with immense force. She gurgled and then was dead.

Ryan screamed, "Are you fucking kidding me? Why did you do it?"

"Dude, did you see how she was fighting back? Sooner or later, we had to do it. Better it be a surprise. And, Ryan, man, I could see you being a total pussy and giving in. You were about to weasel out."

"Stu, you fucking dick! I thought the deal was that if we had sex with her, we would be done. Man, we're in deep shit now."

Stuart laughed in the coldest way possible. "That's not sex, boy. It was rape. Face it, if she ever got back to campus, both of us would have been done. You're the one who wanted to get back to Katie. I could care less. But, damn, the chance to give it bad to a Black bitch. It was why I agreed to help you. So shut up and be grateful that we settled this."

"No, no, no. You're an idiot. We're going to get caught. Are you sure that the cops will be convinced that Shawn killed her?"

"Trust me, dude. The cops in this town are too stupid to put two and two together. And, another thing, some cops secretly cheer when something like this happens. White guys gotta look out for each other."

Stuart and Ryan tried to clear the scene of their presence as much as possible. They walked in the chilly air toward Hosmer Road and stopped at a motel and then called for an Uber to take them from Acton back to Boston University where Ryan stayed in Stuart's room.

Now, at this point, with the police aware that Ryan was seen with Sheila on the last day of her life, there was no denying it—Stuart had to get the hell out of Massachusetts.

"We have to leave the country. I know some friends in Canada; we can go there, lie low, and do some crap jobs for about a year until it cools down," he told Ryan.

Ryan, his conscience weighing heavily on him, didn't put up much resistance. He was desperate to escape the mounting troubles, so he barely questioned his escape plan. His only concern was the logistics of their getaway.

"We'll drive as close as we can to the border. Bring your mother's SUV. We need a sturdy four-wheel-drive vehicle. We'll park it at the border and cross over on foot. Don't tell anyone anything, especially your mom," Stuart instructed.

"So, what should I tell her?" Ryan asked.

"Think of any excuse you can, man. Sometimes you have to think on your feet and be a man about it," he replied.

"Okay, Stu," Ryan agreed reluctantly.

"And before you go, give me that card this Lisa cop gave you," he demanded.

"You're not going to hack into a cop's phone, Stu. That's dangerous," Ryan protested.

"When she's home with her husband and kids, she's not a cop."

Ryan reluctantly handed over the card, knowing exactly what his friend was about to do. Stuart had some skills as a hacker. He knew how to phish and break into anyone's phone, and he was willing to do whatever it took to cover their tracks.

Later that night, he sent Lisa a text message.

"BANK ALERT—Did you attempt a purchase of $436.55 today? Reply YES to approve it. Not you? Visit this link immediately to reverse it."

On impulse, Lisa clicked the link.

Stuart was now into her phone. He downloaded all of her messages, phone contacts and any data to his server.

He set up a surveillance audio and video recorder on her phone using a software similar to spyware and attached it to a folder on his hardware. Lisa's phone had become an extension of Stuart's watchful eyes and ears. He could listen in on all of her calls, locate her precisely, access her phone gallery with photos and videos, and check her emails and WhatsApp calls.

He sifted through her email and was able to locate every active device or computer she used for accessing email. He set up audio and video surveillance. With virtually no resistance, Stuart had hacked quickly into Lisa's entire home and work life. The ease laid bare the gigantic holes in cybersecurity that one would have thought impossible with anyone connected to law enforcement. They had firewalls, but it was shocking to see how careless and sloppy the cyber infrastructure was.

He stayed up nearly all night going through Lisa's emails and texts. By the time he fell asleep, he had every detail about the case including every individual tasked with solving the crime. He located their numbers and texted each of them a similar bank phishing scam link.

At the end of the day, Lisa noticed that her phone battery was using power at a faster rate than normal. She had recharged it twice, but still, it ended up going dead by the time she left the office. She figured that her phone battery was no longer usable and assumed that she would have to replace it, but she also did not have a free moment to spare to take care of it.

The following evening, Ryan came over to his place, and he was relieved to see that he had his mother's SUV. "Good work, my boy," he said, patting him on the back.

"You wanna know what I told her?" Ryan asked.

"You don't need to tell me now," he replied. "What's important is you got here with the car. We're taking off at midnight when there's less traffic. For now, just relax and watch some TV in my room. I've got some other stuff to take care of outside."

At midnight, with the roads relatively clear of traffic, they figured it was best if Stuart did the driving to get them to the border quickly. As they hit the road on Commonwealth Ave toward Storrow Drive, Stuart reached into his pocket and pulled out a small bag of gummies. He told Ryan they'd help them stay awake during the long drive.

Little did he know, these weren't your average gummies—they were potent CBD edibles.

Ryan started munching on them like they were candy, and before long, he was out like a light, snoring loudly in the passenger seat.

Stuart changed his route.

He took an exit to East Boston via the Sumner tunnel then passed through Revere before merging onto State Route 107 for about two and a half miles. He stopped for a minute before turning toward Lynn so he could move his bag from the trunk to the floorboard next to him. Back on the road, he turned to Nahant Road and headed to Nahant, the smallest town in Massachusetts. In Nahant, he left the main road and found a sandy path which he traveled for about half a mile. He stopped on the banks of the lake and left the car in drive while Ryan was still asleep. The SUV slowly moved toward the lake, and it quickly submerged in the water.

Stuart ran into the town of Lynn, called an Uber, and returned to his dormitory. He turned on the television, waiting to see any news. He spent the entire night awake, popping out of bed frequently and pacing the floor to figure out another escape plan. He figured Ryan had drowned.

At six a.m., Stuart turned the television on, and there was breaking news with a live crew at the lakeside where he had abandoned the SUV and Ryan. Police had rescued a man whose car plunged into the lake waters.

Stuart screamed, "Fuck!" repeatedly.

He was certain that Ryan would have drowned, even if he had been awakened by the sense that the vehicle had been submerged. Ryan, apparently, had been awakened, and while he was still groggy and hazy, he escaped the car because the door had not been locked.

Stuart suddenly recalled that he did not lock the car doors with the key fob. It was a small slip but enough to upend his escape plan. Ryan actually had slipped out of the car into the water just before the SUV had been fully submerged.

Stuart went as close as possible to the television screen to see if the gurney the EMTs carried showed a dead body. The reporter said that the man had survived but that his injuries were critical.

Stuart screamed in panic. Within a half hour, fresh reports identified the victim as a student at Essex University. At the same time, Stuart was now monitoring video of Lisa's movements. As soon as she arrived at the office, it appeared that she and Bus were arguing.

CHAPTER 30

Bus

WATCHING the late-night news, eating a bowl of spicy Top Ramen, Bus practically fell off his couch—a university kid had been rescued from the sea around Nahant area. Bus shivered with a pang of unease, picked up the line and called Lisa.

"Ryan—you remember someone named Ryan? From Shawn's story."

"Of course I do. He's a classmate of Sheila's. I spoke with him yesterday morning."

"You what?"

"Briefly, at the campus. I identified him from the university building's closed-circuit camera."

"Well, guess what?"

"What?"

"You might want to turn on the news."

While she watched, Bus got serious. "Lisa, I can't believe that you were this messy in your work? You did not tell me any of this beforehand. We were supposed to be investigating *as a team*. What the hell happened? I've been thinking that you wanted to prove that you could outsmart me as a detective and maybe solve the case on your own. That is not how any of this is supposed to work. I don't know what's going on with you but with this case, you have jumped the gun every time and come up short or with the wrong conclusion."

"If you would stop shouting, I can *tell you* what I was thinking," she said.

"Going directly to the school and meeting him! How could you have not figured that this would tip him and his crime team off. And now look, the morning news has this guy being rescued from a vehicle near the lake. Somebody wanted this guy dead to protect themselves. It's not just one suspect. Shit. How could you have fucked up things so bad?"

Lisa said, "So you wanted me to alert you and have you reveal this to your Virginia-man? You think I don't know how you let this investigation get thrown under the bus?"

There was a brief silence as the two seemed to be overwhelmed with the news and thoughts of how to proceed.

Bus broke the silence.

"Look, okay. All of this could have been handled differently. We know that. By now, we probably could have squeezed enough out of him and solved this case. Remember, we have a young man in jail who consistently has told us that he never laid a hand on her. He could have been free by now. What's really going on here, Lisa? I am now certain that we made a huge mistake by fingering Shawn as the killer. And there are going to be a lot of angry voices and protests when the news comes out that the one or more people behind the killing of a Black woman were white."

"Go to hell!" she shouted and hung up on him.

In the morning, when he arrived at the office, Lisa looked no less furious. Her face was red, and one could sense that the blood was pumping faster than ever in her veins. She stood several inches from Bus, staring into his eyes.

Chief Flores entered and asked her calmly to sit and gather her emotions.

"You tell him to calm down, not me. I know what Bus is saying between the lines. Why is it that men always stick up for each other? You guys make a mistake and live for another day. But, if a woman slips up, then all the fire comes toward her."

Chief Flores gestured for Bus and Lisa to both step into his office.

"Come on now, both of you. Let's take a breather. Now's not the time for finger-pointing or blame games. Our priority is solving this case swiftly, before anyone else faces danger or worse. We have to move very fast because if the CIA boys get a whiff of this, they will be nosing their way back into the investigation. Fuck, we don't need another suggestion to check out an angry blogger from Africa. And, Lisa, I know what you want to say. But your political preferences or thinking should never interfere with gathering the real facts of a serious crime investigation."

Lisa, still seething with anger after Bus's confrontation, reluctantly nodded in agreement when Chief Flores spoke.

"Lisa, Bus, I need you both to head over to the hospital. We have to speak with Ryan's mother. She is there already, and she likely knew the people Ryan hung around with, either on campus or in their neighborhood. I'm sure she will be able to tell why Ryan asked to borrow her car. We have no time to waste. We have to act while any lead is still fresh."

"Do we have any reports from the hospital yet?" Bus asked.

"Ryan is currently non-responsive, and the doctors are assessing the extent of his injuries and the effects of his near-drowning. It's a delicate situation, so please handle it with care."

CHAPTER 31

Lisa

DETECTIVE Lisa had a gut feeling stirring within her as she and her colleague, Bus, made their way through the sterile corridors of the Mass General Hospital toward Ryan Newton's room. The air was thick with tension, the weight of unanswered questions pressing down on them with every step.

They found Ryan's room tucked away at the end of a long hallway, guarded by nurses and monitored by beeping machines. Inside, Ryan lay motionless, his young face pale against the stark white of the hospital sheets. Tubes and wires snaked around him, evidence of the battle he was fighting for his life.

The detectives approached the bed, their expressions solemn as they took in the sight before them. Lisa felt a pang of sadness for the young boy who had been thrust into the center of a vicious crime.

"We need to talk to him," Lisa said, turning to one of the nurses. "It's important."

"I'm sorry, Detective," the nurse replied, shaking her head. "Ryan's condition is critical. The doctors have advised against any visitors for now."

Lisa clenched her jaw, frustration bubbling beneath the surface. She knew time was of the essence, every moment wasted was another opportunity for the truth to slip away.

"Then we'll talk to his mother," Bus suggested, his voice steady despite the urgency of their situation.

With a nod, Lisa turned to leave the room, her mind already racing ahead to their next course of action. They found Sarah Newton seated in the waiting area, her eyes red-rimmed from tears shed in the wake of her son's ordeal.

"Mrs. Newton, we need to ask you some questions," Lisa said, her tone gentle yet firm.

Sarah looked up, her gaze meeting Lisa's with a mixture of fear and determination. She nodded, steeling herself for whatever revelations lay ahead.

"Tell us what happened," Bus prompted, his voice a steady anchor in the storm of emotions swirling around them.

Sarah took a deep breath, her hands trembling slightly as she began to recount the events that had led to her son's brush with death.

"It was Stuart," she said, her voice wavering with emotion. "He was Ryan's friend, or so we thought. They grew up together, went to the same schools… I never would have imagined he'd try to hurt Ryan."

Lisa and Bus exchanged a glance, the pieces of the puzzle beginning to fall into place. Stuart's connection to Ryan ran deeper than they had initially suspected, a bond forged in childhood innocence now tainted by betrayal and violence.

"What happened?" Lisa pressed, her eyes narrowing with determination.

Sarah took a shaky breath, her hands twisting in her lap as she spoke.

"Stuart asked to borrow my car," she said, her voice barely above a whisper. "He said he needed it for something important, and Ryan, being the trusting soul that he is, agreed to help him."

Lisa's jaw clenched at the mention of Stuart's manipulation, a cold anger burning within her chest.

"Go on," she urged.

Sarah swallowed hard, her gaze fixed on some distant point beyond the confines of the hospital walls.

"They went out together, just like old times," she said, her voice trembling with sorrow. "And then… Stuart drove them into the lake."

"We'll find him, Mrs. Newton," Lisa vowed, her voice steady despite the storm raging within her. "We'll find Stuart, and we'll make sure he pays for what he's done."

Sarah nodded, her eyes brimming with tears as she reached out to grasp Lisa's hand in gratitude.

"Thank you," she whispered.

Back in the office, around 4 p.m., Lisa's phone suddenly rang. Having already briefed her boss and colleagues about her interview with Ryan's mother, the team was now hard at work gathering information about Stuart, who, according to the mother, had gone camping with her son.

Lisa ignored the calls, but finally Bus said, "Your phone apparently won't stop ringing, so you'd better answer it because someone definitely needs to talk to you urgently."

Lisa pulled the phone from her bag and clicked on to answer it.

"Is this Lisa?" a caller said on the phone.

"Yes."

"Okay, a girl called Amy is here with me. She says she is your daughter. Is it true?"

"*What the fuck. Where are you? You'd better put her on the phone now. You don't know who you're messing with!*"

"Bitch, stop shouting. Put the phone in front of you and click on the camera. I want to talk where I can see your face."

"Who are you? How can I be sure that you have my daughter?"

"Less questions and more cooperation, bitch. This is not a shouting match." The caller put his phone camera to show her seven-year-old daughter asleep in the car.

"You have just two hours to save your daughter. Then, anything can happen. Do not try anything funny. Or something awful could happen to her."

Lisa trembled, flushed with nausea. She put her phone on speaker so that everyone could hear. She glanced at Bus.

Bus talked loudly enough so that the caller could hear. "Ask him what he wants,"

"I need half a million from you. That imbecile Bus with a needle-length dick should help you mobilize. You show me the money here on camera, and I tell you where to deliver it. Then fifteen minutes after my boy collects the money, I will tell you where to find your daughter. Are we good? Let's get to business now. You stay on camera where I can see your facial expressions all the time."

Lisa was shaking now, drawing every will in her body to keep her composure. Emotional responses and acts never worked in these scenarios.

"If you ever want to see your daughter again, this is your chance to cooperate."

Lisa and Bus exchanged a knowing glance. By now, Lisa was sure this was Stuart.

"The only department you can talk to is finance to arrange my money, and I'll be strict about your daughter's safety," Stuart said so loud that everyone in the office could hear.

Bus said, "You are loud and clear, sir. Hope you don't have any more surprises for us."

Bus went over to Lisa, trying to comfort her. He hugged Lisa tightly, whispering into her ears that it was okay and that everyone would do everything to make sure her daughter was returned safely.

As the situation unfolded, Chief Flores retreated into his office, tasked with raising the kidnapper's ransom funds while simultaneously alerting the I.T. team about the phone call. The team immediately seized upon this one slip-up, which inadvertently revealed Stuart's location before he could plan his next move.

A text message popped up on Chief Flores phone: *We've got the location*,

Flores replied: *tread carefully*.

Lisa beat her brow over what had happened. Her children were alone at home because her marriage crumbled after she hired a nanny, an immigrant from El Salvador, who eventually fell in love with her husband, Liam. At the time, the nanny was an undocumented immigrant, and she had thoughts about marrying Lisa's husband. But Lisa was infuriated, refusing to grant her husband's request for a formal divorce.

Lisa left her seven-year-old daughter in the care of her teenage son at home. Now, if she survived this abduction, Lisa knew she would also have to answer several questions from social workers.

Chief Flores discreetly gave the orders to dispatch police cruisers, accompanied by unmarked FBI vehicles that had been informed about the kidnapping. They were headed to Newton, an apartment complex close to the playground area for residents' children.

"The units are on the way, and the FBI's in the loop. We're heading to Newton," an officer heading the operation texted Chief Flores, who switched on his computer screen to watch the action unfold.

Meanwhile, two civilian cars and four officers in plain clothes stealthily closed in around Stuart's vehicle. He remained engrossed in his phone conversation with Lisa and only realized something was amiss when he looked up, finding himself encircled by SWAT officers.

"He's focused on the phone. Get ready," the head officer instructed.

Stuart, realizing the peril he was in, hastily grabbed the sleeping girl from the back seat, intending to use her as a human shield.

"If you shoot, the girl is dying with me!"

As more police cruisers with sirens wailing arrived at the scene, an officer's voice boomed over a loudspeaker, urging nearby residents to stay indoors. Officer on loudspeaker also had instructions for the kidnapper.

"Step out of the vehicle, place the child down, and lie on the ground with your legs spread and hands behind you!"

Overwhelmed by the swarm of law enforcement, Stuart's facade of a fearless white supremacism quickly crumbled inside the car. He pushed the girl to the side and exited the vehicle, no longer a threat. Tears streamed down his face as he knelt and placed his hands behind his back.

"He's giving up. Secure him and check on the girl," the head officer instructed.

The tense standoff had come to an end, and the priority now was ensuring the safety of the young girl, who had been caught up in this harrowing ordeal.

CHAPTER 32

Shawn

THE sun began its descent, casting a warm golden hue over the vast expanse of Concord, Massachusetts. The towering walls of the historic Concord Prison stood stoically, guarding the stories of the lives it held within. Today, those walls would release Shawn, a man who had been unjustly confined.

He could see the two detectives, Bus and Lisa, waiting alongside Katie, his white girlfriend, at the entrance. Katie held her pregnant belly with trembling hands. Her heart pounded in her chest, a mixture of joy, relief, and nervousness coursing through her veins. She adjusted her hair, ensuring every strand was in place.

The clock ticked closer to the appointed time, and Shawn's mind wandered back to the agonizing months leading up to this moment. He had been arrested for a crime he did not commit, accused of a murder he had no part in. The detective battle had been grueling, but finally, justice prevailed, and he was declared innocent after the real perpetrator, Stuart, was found.

When the prison gates opened, Katie's eyes widened, taking in the sight before her. The sprawling complex, surrounded by tall stone walls and barbed wire, seemed like a world unto itself. The architecture, a blend of historical charm and institutional severity, created an atmosphere both imposing and somber. A surge of emotions overwhelmed her. She held her breath, straining her eyes to catch a glimpse of Shawn among the newly freed inmates. And there he was, stepping into the sunlight, his gaze searching the crowd until it found her. Their eyes locked, and time seemed to stand still. Detectives Bus and Lisa watched on as the two lovebirds were reunited.

Katie rushed forward, her heart pounding with anticipation. As she neared him, she noticed the look of disbelief etched across his face. Shawn's eyes darted to her rounded belly and then back to her face. It had grown bigger than the last time she had visited him, and though she had revealed to him while in prison that she was pregnant, the idea of being a father still awed him.

"Katie," he stammered, his voice barely audible.

A tender smile graced her lips as she reached out and took his hand, guiding it gently to her abdomen.

"Shawn, meet our baby," she whispered, tears of joy pooling in her eyes.

Shawn's disbelief transformed into sheer wonder as he felt a faint kick against his palm. His eyes widened, and a joyous laughter erupted from his chest, intertwining with the rhythm of his racing heartbeat.

"Our baby?" he repeated.

"Yes, Shawn," Katie affirmed, laughing. "Our baby, a testament to the times you lied to me that you released outside."

The recollection of his confident claim about withdrawal skills brought a knowing smile to his face, their connection strengthened by their ability to find humor even in the face of challenging circumstances.

"You always be keeping me on my toes, Katie," he said, "I never saw my messed-up withdrawal game coming into play like this."

"And here we are, facing the most beautiful surprise of all. Our love has created life, defying the odds and expectations placed upon us," Katie said.

"Do you like the baby or nah?" Shawn asked.

"Yes, of course," she replied.

"I love you, Katie," he said. "Thank you for giving me the biggest blessing, even when the world be sleeping on us."

Now, Detective Bus cleared his throat, letting Katie and Shawn know that he and Lisa were also here. "We're here to give you a lift, Shawn," he said. "No more questions, I promise. We're just taking you back home because your girlfriend couldn't drive."

Lisa chimed in, "And we're also trying to make right what went wrong, like I promised you when I arrested you. I'm really sorry you had to go through all this, Shawn."

Shawn walked away from the prison gates, hand in hand with Katie, as the detectives guided them toward the waiting state patrol car. They settled into the back seats, and the two detectives sat in the front, Lisa driving, the engine humming softly, as they left the prison grounds behind. The air felt different outside those walls, carrying the sweet scent of freedom and the promise of a brighter future.

As they drove away on State Route 2, the landscape transformed before their eyes. The dense prison walls gave way to picturesque countryside, adorned with lush green fields and vibrant wildflowers. The vibrant colors of the Massachusetts sunset painted the sky, reflecting the dawn of a new beginning for Shawn, Katie, and their unborn child. Their journey was far from over, but with their hearts entwined and the strength they had discovered within themselves, they knew they could overcome anything that lay ahead.

The drive from Concord to Dorchester was long. In the car, Shawn was silent for a while. His mind buzzed with a cacophony of worries and doubts. The truth had come to light, revealing his innocence in the heinous crimes he had been accused of. But the scars left behind by the system's failure would forever mar his reputation, casting an unwarranted shadow over his future.

The cool breeze brushed against his skin, whispering secrets of freedom and possibility. Yet, fear still lingered within his heart like a stubborn stain. How would he reintegrate into a society that had so harshly judged him, his dreams trampled upon by the very system meant to protect him?

But as Shawn's thoughts wandered, a cruel reality set in. Returning to college, the dream he had once nurtured, now felt out of reach. The halls of academia seemed closed off, guarded by an invisible barrier that barred his reentry. The stigma of his unjust imprisonment would forever taint his educational aspirations, leaving him adrift in a sea of shattered dreams.

He knew that seeking employment would prove equally challenging. Each job application demanded a background check, a probing into his past that would inevitably uncover the trauma he had endured. The lingering question of his innocence would cast a doubt upon his character, overshadowing his qualifications and accomplishments.

His gaze settled on the swelling curve of his girlfriend's belly, a tender reminder of the life they had created together. He would find a way to provide for their child, to build a future that defied the constraints imposed upon him.

Shawn's fingers clenched into tight fists, his knuckles turning white under the strain. The weight of responsibility pressed upon him, threatening to suffocate his spirit. How could he provide for his growing family? How could he ensure their well-being in a world that seemed determined to keep him at arm's length?

The patrol finally pulled into the driveway of his family's two-bedroom home. As the detectives stopped the engine, Shawn suddenly snapped out of his sea of thoughts. The drive had been mostly silent and reflective. After they arrived home, Bus asked,

"Mind if we come in for a bit?"

Shawn turned to Katie, as if she held all the answers, and asked, "Should we invite them in?"

"Yes, of course," Katie replied.

Shawn's footsteps slowed as he approached the front

door of the house he once called home. The memories flooded back, intertwining with a sense of guilt that clawed at his conscience. His mother's death had been a devastating blow, a loss that cut deep into his very being. And as much as he tried to shield himself from the truth, a part of him blamed the system, blamed his own arrest, for her untimely demise.

During his unjust incarceration, his mother had been his pillar of strength, her unwavering belief in his innocence the fuel that sustained him. But the fight for justice had taken its toll on her frail health. Hypertension, diabetes, and the overwhelming stress had ravaged her body, leaving her vulnerable and broken. The strain of her son's arrest had cost her more than they could have ever imagined.

He stepped into the empty house, the silence echoing through the rooms that still held traces of his mother's presence. Shawn's eyes welled with tears, his heart aching for the conversations left unsaid, the moments stolen by the cruel hands of fate. He walked into his mother's room, the place where she had spent her final moments. The walls seemed to whisper her name, their faded photographs capturing the essence of her love and sacrifice. He sank to his knees, his trembling hands tracing the familiar contours of her belongings. The weight of his emotions threatened to suffocate him, as grief mingled with regret in a tumultuous dance.

If only they had found the true perpetrator sooner. If only the arrest had never happened. Maybe, just maybe, his mother would still be alive, her health intact, and her spirit unburdened by the pain of his absence. The weight of that guilt settled upon Shawn's shoulders, seeming insurmountable.

He returned to the living room where his girlfriend chatted with the two detectives. They had also switched on the television, and there was a news anchor standing outside of the jail, reporting on his release for ABC television. Shawn switched the channel to CNN, but it seemed all news channels were covering his release. Here, he caught the image of the Ugandan president Katila Muaji who apparently had just spoken about the murder case.

Shawn was shocked at the president's words. Standing with his brother in Washington, DC, the Ugandan president announced that while Stuart was paying for his crime now that he had confessed what happened, the Government of Uganda would forgive him as a good gesture for healing in the face of racial hatred. The CNN report also showed the statement the US president gave to the media following the Ugandan leader's stunning announcement. It read,

> The president of Uganda is a friend of the international community. He has demonstrated an exceptional act of grace and forgiveness today. He is a staunch capitalist who opened up the markets and resources of Africa to international organizations. A globalist—not only in Uganda, but in the neighboring countries as well, especially the resource-rich Congo. International organizations are more prosperous because of him. If all African leaders can work like him, the international community will stand with them.
>
> When the whole world turned away refugees, he made his country the main host of refugees. It's personal for him,

as his parents were also once refugees in Uganda from Rwanda.

When Islamic terrorism gripped the world and America announced a new war on terrorism, Mr. Katila Muaji offered himself to lead the war in Africa, as a bulwark against Islamic fundamentalism, hitting Islamists on the head in Somalia and Sudan as well as his own country of Uganda. Today, he has troops in more African and Middle Eastern countries than any other nation, except the US. Despite Americans who have demanded the US withdraw troops from Afghanistan, Ugandans are not demanding their president to withdraw Ugandan troops from any country.

As Americans continue to grapple with race problems in their cities and in their neighborhoods, the president of Uganda is here in Washington to give this great country his wise counsel and offer meaningful insights. On the matter of race, his message to Americans today is that through forgiveness, we can all move forward in peace and prosperity. There is healing in forgiveness.

Shawn felt disgusted and quickly turned off the TV. He thought for a moment about Sheila and how her life and violent death could be swept under and hidden now that a Ugandan president had forgiven a man who murdered his niece and whose views were known to affiliate with white supremacists.

He felt exhausted and bored. Inside, he was angry and frustrated that his innocence had been denied for so long. The travesty of justice had taken a toll on his psyche and his will, but he also had to start thinking about his life going forward, not just for his professional career but also for the fact that he was about to become a father. Politics, which had excited and motivated him ever since he was old enough to watch the news, now seemed like something too distant or uninteresting to continue pursuing. The tragic disappointment fell way short of a meaningful return on the investment he had made in his education and work.

Katie and the two detectives noticed Shawn's frustration and anxiety, and they started talking him into calmness and therapy.

"We are here for you, Shawn," Lisa said. "Anything that can make you feel better and get back on your feet, we shall do it for you."

"And I'm here for you too, darling," Katie said, inviting him with wide arms into a hug.

The two lovebirds hugged and kissed. For a moment, he was lost in Katie's hands and lips. He closed his eyes, savoring the intimate embrace he had missed for so long from his girlfriend.

When he opened his eyes, they fell on the two detectives, also embraced in each other's arms. The detectives were sharing a kiss. He immediately made Katie turn around to see what he was seeing. The couple then started clapping for the detectives.

"Oh my god, this is so overwhelming and embarrassing to do in your home, Shawn. We are so sorry," Lisa quickly said.

"Oh, you don't have to be sorry. I've always seen love flowing between you, even as you questioned me," Shawn said.

"There's nothing to be ashamed of, Lisa. Love is beautiful," Katie added.

"Oh, we have to go now, right Lisa?" Bus asked.

"Yes, we are going now, and please give us a call if you need anything," Lisa said.

"Please make twins and name them Katie and Shawn," Shawn shouted over their shoulders as they left.

As the detectives left, Shawn prepared for a hot bath after eating a decent meal prepared by Katie, it suddenly dawned on him that for the first time, Shawn felt that this was what it meant to be a full adult. He decided that it was best to wait until morning to figure out what he was going to do next. For the moment, he decided to sleep in the bed that his mother used. At least for one final night, he could feel close to her.

THE MISSING CORPSE
The General's Project Series 2 of 3

When CIA intelligence catches wind of a shocking revelation—a general and son of an African president suspected of murdering his father and concealing the body until he seizes power—they send in their top agent, Shawn Wayles, to gather crucial intelligence. Teaming up with an LGBTQ couple, Shawn embarks on a daring mission to retrieve the president's body from the clutches of the GENERAL'S security team. As the general scrambles to recover the missing corpse, a high-stakes game ensues, where possession of the body equates to ultimate power.

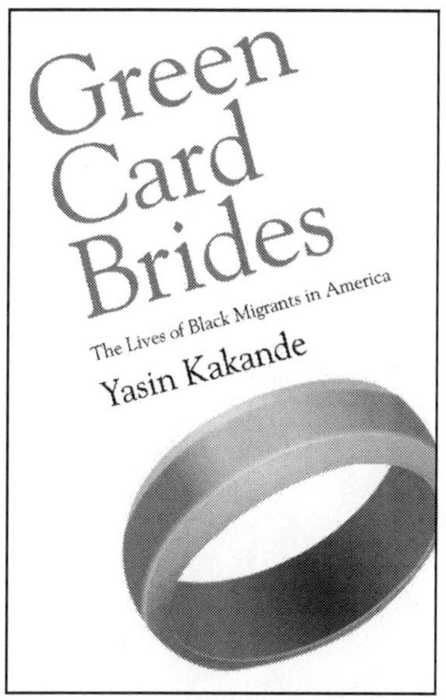

GREEN CARD BRIDES
The Lives of Black Migrants in America

A personal exploration of the American Dream's elusiveness, this book follows the author's struggle to make ends meet while working long shifts as a caregiver and Uber driver, all while applying for legal status in hopes of bringing his wife and children to join him. It's a clarifying backdrop for the global migrant crisis and a rallying cry for change for those who must take 3D jobs to survive (dirty, dangerous, and demeaning). The author's harrowing journey as a Black African essential worker highlights the need for a shift away from corporate greed and exploitation, advocating for a different political conversation about why so many migrants look westward for better lives.

Made in the USA
Middletown, DE
25 October 2024